JAN 18 1995

STORAGE

ZO

9-2-98

Hunters & Gatherers

By the same author
THE FOOD CHAIN

Hunters & Gatherers

Geoff Nicholson

THE OVERLOOK PRESS
WOODSTOCK • NEW YORK

3 1336 03597 8858

First published in 1994 by
The Overlook Press
Lewis Hollow Road
Woodstock, New York 12498

Copyright © 1991 Geoff Nicholson

All Rights Reserved. No part of this publication may be reproduced or transmitted
in any form or by any means, electronic or mechanical, including photocopy,
recording, or any information storage and retrieval system now known or to be
invented without permission in writing from the publisher, except by a reviewer
who wishes to quote brief passages in connection with a review written for
inclusion in a magazine, newspaper, or broadcast.

Library of Congress Cataloging-in-Publication Data

Nicholson, Geoff, 1953–
Hunters and Gatherers / Geoff Nicholson
p. cm.
1. Collectors and collecting–Fiction. 2. Authorship–Fiction.
3. Authors–Fiction. I. Title.
PR6064.I225H86 1994
823'.914–dc20
94-3356
CIP
Manufactured in The United States of America on Acid Free paper
ISBN: 0-87951-559-7
First American Edition

ONE

The accumulation

'. . . *in all collections, Sir, the desire of augmenting it grows stronger in proportion to the advance in acquisition; as motion is accelerated by the continuance of the* impetus.'

Samuel Johnson, quoted in
Boswell's *Life of Johnson*
Tuesday, May 8th, 1781.

Dust collects. It falls on old moquette, on walnut veneer, on corduroy and melamine. It settles on picture rails, in the curves of porcelain shepherdesses, in the corners of junk-rooms; ground-in dirt unmoved by dusters and vacuum cleaners; an amalgam of carbon, dead skin, industrial waste; fall out. It passes through doors and windows, lodges in our clothes and hair, collects in every crevice.

We call in the dustmen, the refuse collectors. They take away what we no longer need. Our waste is smashed, burned, compacted, taken to tips and dumps where mountains of waste grow, decay and collapse.

We throw away what no longer suits us, what we no longer want to have near; the left-overs and the peelings and things out of fashion, and old love letters; things we once thought part of ourselves.

Men scavenge the dumps. They, and flocks of seagulls, live on what is thrown away. It is a salvage operation and a re-cycling. The men select. They have an eye for what is still usable and repairable, what can be sold, what still has value.

In bedrooms and attics and garages, or displayed on shelves, and in cases and cabinets, on mantelpieces, in drawers and boxes and albums, people keep their collections. Anything and everything. The small, delicate and personal, the vast and public; snapshots, Roman coins, architectural masonry, steam engines, biplanes. Things to be treasured. Collectors' items. Antiques and curios.

There is a mental junk-room. It contains decades-old conversations, childhood games, class registers, amazing facts, lines from songs, bad jokes, strange but true stories, dates of battles, anecdotes. It does not seem a very complete collection. It is not the full set, yet we seem to need it all. We don't like to throw anything away, even though much gets lost. It is a gathering, a build-up, a load of rubbish, like the hoard of gold and the stockpile of weapons. It is more than the sum of its parts.

We need our accumulations and conglomerations, our massing and amassing. There is safety in numbers. There is miserliness and acquisitiveness. The coffers are never full enough.

Money sits in banks. It works. Interest accrues and compounds. Taxes become due, are assessed and collected. Money attracts money. Litter collects in the gutter, dirt under the fingernails. People collect their wages, their dole, their carriage clocks, their pensions. At the bookmakers one or two collect their winnings.

In our rooms, after the furore, we collect ourselves, collect our thoughts. We wish to appear cool, calm and collected. Clothes are collected from the dry cleaners, children are collected from school. Fares on the buses, tickets on the train. The postbox gives the time of the next collection.

These groupings, these special interest collections, souvenirs, forms of tourism, these archives and museums and reference libraries of the self, these fine words and fine stories to be found in the collected works, this treasury, this high point in the anthologist's art, this miscellany . . .

There is nothing random here. There is a significant clustering, deeper structures, a raking-in and rounding-up, localised stacks of meaning. Groups of things: flocks, schools, prides, exultations. Collective nouns. An accumulation of detail.

Charms against dissolution, protection against loss and dispersal, against the unconnectedness of things.

It begins with a visit from a woman claiming to be a market researcher.

On the outskirts of Sheffield, Jim is lying on the bed in his mobile home. He is thinking about the nature of obsession; about fame, about washing cars, about people who commmit murders in order to become famous. He has a couple of pints of extra-strong lager inside him. There is a knock on the door. He opens it, and the young woman standing there says, 'Hello, I'm conducting a survey into educational resources. I wonder if you'd mind answering a few questions.' He is a bit drunk so he says, 'Well, come on in.'

She isn't the type of woman who normally comes knocking

4

at Jim's door, and she's not the type who would normally step inside if invited. Above all else she looks business-like. She is wearing a severe, navy blue business suit, with just a hint of shoulder-pad. Her hair is very short. She carries a heavy brief-case. Her face is young, pleasant, and not nearly as business-like as her clothes.

'Want a beer?' Jim asks.

'I shouldn't.'

'Go on.'

'Usually I wouldn't, but it's been a long day, a very long day. You're very sweet. Thank you.'

'I'll try to find a glass.'

'You're wonderfully kind.'

'You know, just before you knocked on the door, I was thinking how easy life must be for some people. They know what they want and they can see a way of getting it, and they just pursue it. Or they have an all-consuming interest in something, and personally I don't think it matters all that much what it is, whether it's model railways or ballet or poker, but, for people like that, life's easy.'

'I can see you're an intelligent man,' she says.

He pours her a beer.

'But I'm not like that,' Jim continues. 'I'm not obsessed. I think I could be if I found the right thing, but so far I haven't. I'm just ordinary. I watch television. I go for a walk. I go to the pub . . .'

'This survey is a very simple one,' she says. 'It's designed by experts at a well known American university. We're trying to find out people's attitudes on a range of educational issues.'

Jim isn't much interested in educational issues. He considers the weight of his beer can. It is light, nearly empty. He thinks he'd better have another one lined up before she begins her questions. He shambles into the kitchenette. She is not thrown.

'Would you say that education is a good thing?' she calls after him.

He agrees as he takes the beer from the fridge.

'And do you agree that education should be accessible to all?'

He returns with his beer and agrees to that too.

'And do you think that the amount of money a person has should or shouldn't be a determining factor in the quality of that education?'

5

'I think it shouldn't,' he says earnestly. 'You see, I was thinking about people who get fame for the stupidest reasons. Like all those people in *The Guinness Book of Records* who are only famous for knocking down dominoes, or regurgitating goldfish. I suppose it's like an obsession for them. And, like I said, I don't have any obsessions. I'm interested in things in general but not anything in particular. You know?'

'I do. Yes. You're obviously a thinking person. That's good. So would you say that knowledge is power?'

'I've never thought about that one, but I suppose it could be. It depends on what you know, probably.'

'Excuse me,' her voice changes and is no longer briskly professional, 'would you mind if I took off my shoes? They're killing me. It's been a bad day, a really, really bad day. Sorry. Let me get back to the survey. If there was a simple, easy, cost-effective, infallible way of increasing knowledge, then wouldn't you agree that all reasonable people would be interested in it?'

'I suppose.'

'So, in other words, *you* are interested in finding a simple, easy, cost-effective way of increasing your knowledge.'

'Oh no. Is this where you try to sell me a set of encyclopedias?'

The muscles in her face dance. She tries to smile but her mouth can't be forced into the necessary adjustments, and tears are about to ooze from her eyes.

'Shit,' she says. 'That's what everybody says.'

'It seems a bit obvious.'

'I know it's obvious. That's the whole problem. It's really stupid. This is my first week doing this job. There's a script you have to follow. There are all these things I have to say, and they're all really stupid. I don't see why anybody would ever fall for it. I don't see how I'm ever going to sell any encyclopedias.'

She makes a noise that in other circumstances might be mistaken for a yelp of hysterical laughter, but Jim recognises it as a howl of misery.

'I really don't think I want any encyclopedias,' he says.

'Of course you don't. Nobody does. People just want to wallow in their own ignorance. They think it's bliss.'

Jim wonders if he's entitled to feel insulted, but she doesn't seem to be trying to insult him, at least not him personally. She is looking girlish and petulant now. She throws her brief-case, which

6

she's been holding on her knee until now, on to the floor. It is unfastened. Its contents slew across the floor; sample pages of text, maps, line-drawings and photographs fan out like a deck of cards. They are undeniably eye-catching. Jim's eye is caught. He sees a map of Africa in purple and lurid orange, a photograph of Marilyn Monroe in *Some Like It Hot*, a diagram showing the reproductive organs of different animals (not to scale), a cut-away drawing of a steam train, an artist's impression of Mercury, and several pages of large, easy-to-read text with sub-headings such as Plato, Hoagy Carmichael, War, the Spitfire, Sex.

'Don't worry about it,' Jim says. 'Drink your beer.'

'I feel such a fool.'

'Don't worry.'

'You probably didn't want me in your lovely home in the first place, and you didn't want to do my stupid survey, and naturally you don't want any encyclopedias, and I'm absolutely certain you don't want some silly woman sobbing all over the place.'

That isn't true. Jim is, in fact, extremely pleased to have her there, to have anyone there, but especially a female someone, sobbing or not. Jim is lonely.

'I'm going', she says, 'before I make things any worse.'

'No. Don't.'

But he is too late. She runs out and runs away. When he realises he has no hope of catching her, he picks up the loose pages from the floor. She's gone without her brief-case. He hopes she might come back for it.

I want to tell a story. Telling stories is one of the less harmful activities I indulge in, and this is perhaps not so much a story as an anecdote. You've probably heard it before, but don't stop me.

According to this story a large, official dinner was being given to mark the retirement of Charles de Gaulle. A great fuss was made of the General and his wife. They were well fed and watered and treated with the utmost reverence. Towards the end of the evening someone asked Madame de Gaulle what she was most looking forward to now that her husband was retiring, and she immediately replied, 'A penis.' A shocked, embarrassed silence fell on the table. Nobody knew how to react to her reply. Was it some saucy French joke? Then her husband leaned over and said wryly, 'No, my dear, I think you mean "happiness".'

You may find this a good story. You may find it funny and revealing. I'm sure lots of people must agree with you because the story gets repeated quite often, but personally I don't find it a good story, and I don't find it funny and revealing because I don't believe a word of it.

For a start I don't believe that anybody would actually say they were looking forward to 'happiness'. They might say they were looking forward to having a nice long rest, or a quiet life or a chance to take things easy, but would anybody really say they were looking forward to happiness? I don't think you *can* look forward to happiness; you can, at best, hope that you'll find happiness in the future.

Of course, you might get round this by saying that Madame de Gaulle was French, her grasp of the English language was slight and therefore she might well say the sort of thing that nobody would normally say. But that only brings me on to my other objection. However French you are, however rocky your English may be, I don't think you'd mispronounce 'happiness' so that it came out sounding like 'a penis'. That isn't how the French speak.

So, if you don't believe the premise and you don't believe the punchline, you may well start doubting whether there was ever really such a dinner to mark the retirement. Was Charles de Gaulle the sort of man ever really to retire? Was his wife really there with him? Would he have been sitting near enough to hear his wife's conversation and correct her?

I suppose the only answer you can really give to any of this is 'maybe', but I still don't believe the story.

Now, I realise a couple of things about this. First, the fact that it seems entirely unlikely doesn't mean that it didn't happen. Second, the fact of whether or not I believe it isn't a matter of much significance in the greater scheme of things.

On the other hand, I do think this example is typical of certain kinds of anecdote that get told and re-told, and I do wonder why so many of these 'good stories', that are well known, that get endlessly repeated, and are supposed to contain some nugget of humour or wisdom or truth, don't seem to stand up to a bit of close scrutiny.

Why is that? Surely a 'good story' that won't stand up isn't a good story? How come the people who repeat these anecdotes don't realise that they have holes in them? Or perhaps they *do* realise but keep on telling them anyway. And why do people tell anecdotes anyway? What sort of person tells them? What is a 'good story' supposed to do? Is there a difference between a story, an anecdote and a joke?

Don't ask me. I only work here.

It is a good day for washing cars. It is dry, warm and bright, but without any direct sunshine. It might almost be a pleasure to be on the forecourt of Killer Kars, bucket, sponge and chamois leather in hand, enjoying the fine weather and bringing a row of secondhand cars back to clean, polished brilliance. Not that Jim has any choice in the matter. The cars have to be washed whether it's a good day for washing them or not. In the winter there is snow to be swept off them. If it rains he has to keep on working regardless.

Over the last few years Jim has become intimately familiar with the lines and contours of a dazzling selection of used vehicles sold through Killer Kars. He has brought a sheen to tired, dull paint jobs. He has de-greased engines, made chrome proud of itself again. Tyres have been returned to their original, serious blackness. He has learned the mysteries of T-cutting, Gunk and Autosol, of oil-removers, hide foods, silicon-based sprays, of vacuum cleaners, hoses, brushes, lint-free cloths and lamb's-wool mittens. His hands have travelled many, many miles, over thousands of styling features, over light clusters, along wings, across grilles, spoilers, louvres, gutterings, even fins.

For Killer Kars is no ordinary used-car lot. You won't find any family saloons here, no shopping cars, no runabouts, no aunty's cars, not even many hot hatchbacks. No, these are *flash* cars: Yanks, Italian semi-exotics, sportscars, English classics. He has cleaned Mustangs, Ford Pops, Zodiacs, Chevvies, Fiat Dinos, Metropolitans. They are cars with a certain amount of class and character, but they are old cars that also need a certain amount of work. This they don't usually get. They don't have expensive mechanical skills lavished upon them, only Jim's. The cars come in looking careworn, past it. Jim gives them an hour or two of his attention, and they look like different cars.

Mike Gombrich has never seen anything like it. Neither has anyone else for that matter, but Mike Gombrich is the one who counts. He owns Killer Kars. He, as they say, *is* Killer Kars.

Mike has a past he will never talk about, and this gives rise to all sorts of speculation. Most think he was some sort of villain, or at least reprobate, who at some crucial moment redeemed himself by the discovery that he could live most fully and intensely by selling flash cars to flash buggers.

Mike Gombrich is a young forty, with salt and pepper hair, still more pepper than salt, a rough face and a smooth manner. He looks slim and fit, but as though he's worked at it. He has a taste for soft-leather jackets and light-coloured shoes. His voice is mellow, strong and well spoken. He is all charm. No doubt he's a lady's man, though Jim doesn't see much of that except in so far as he once found a pair of lady's leopardskin briefs under the front seat of Mike's car. Mostly what Jim sees is Mike's charm, ease and careful manners directed very forcefully in the direction of selling cars.

Mike Gombrich is delighted with Jim's work, so delighted that he sometimes feels like promoting him. He already pays him enough to make him the best-paid car cleaner in the north of England. Probably there is someone in London who earns more, but Mike knows that London is an insane and dangerous place, and what goes on there doesn't bear any thinking about, and not only in the matter of rates of pay. Yes, he'd like to improve Jim's lot and advance his career, but Jim doesn't seem to want to do anything else, doesn't seem to be good at anything else and, if Jim gets promoted, who will clean the cars?

In fact, Mike is so overwhelmingly happy with Jim's skills that he even lets him clean his own (Mike's) car, hence the discovery of the briefs. This is an honour indeed. Few people are allowed even to touch Mike's Corvette. He wouldn't touch it himself if he didn't have to in order to drive it. Jim cleans it with all the gentleness and immaculate care that a Holy Mother might apply to her own overgrown, fibreglass, but nevertheless heavenly offspring.

It is not your average Corvette, even if there were such a thing as an average Corvette. It began life as a '69 model, then Mike had one or two little modifications wreaked upon it. It is now decked out with non-original front and rear spoilers, side skirts and wheel-arch flares, square Monza headlights and chromed Hooker pipes. It is painted black, as rich, thick and smooth as enamel. It is a bastard to keep clean so it's just as well that Jim's on hand to

10

do the job. Mechanical changes included heavy-duty suspension, a hi-rise manifold and a Holley double pumper. Mike will tell you all about this, and more, if you're not careful.

When Jim has finished cleaning the row of cars for sale – a Jensen Interceptor, a Thunderbird convertible, a Cobra replica, a TR7 and an MGA roadster – he will give Mike's car one of its regular cosmetic treatments. The car gets polished more often than it gets driven but that makes no difference to Jim.

Before he starts a cleaning job, Jim likes to walk round his subject to get an overview of the project. The Corvette is parked by the workshop, looking low, dark and wicked. Jim circles it. It already looks as spotless and flawless as most cars will ever look, but he's sure there must be some little thing he can do to gild the lily. He surveys it from the back, from the passenger's side, from the front. Then he goes to the driver's side.

He immediately experiences nausea, faintness and palpitations. The entire side of the car has been mutilated by scratches; deep, crude, deliberate gouges that penetrate through layers of lacquer, paint and primer down into the fibreglass. Then, as he looks more closely, even though he hardly has the stomach to look at all, he sees that the scratches aren't random scars, as he'd at first supposed. In fact they spell out words, a message that reads, 'You're a cunt Gombrich.'

Jim has a vision of the effect this will have on Mike. It isn't a pretty sight. He can see apoplexy, fury, threats of murderous revenge, an urge for immediate violence, an urge to destroy the office furniture, or lash out at some handy, unsuspecting employee, the messenger who brought the news, the bloke who washed the car. He sees uncontained, impotent, self-destructive rage.

Jim has to sit down.

Mike Gombrich is some miles away from the scene of the crime and of his impending over-reaction. He is out letting a lady customer have a test drive in an Alfa Romeo Spider.

'Is this a good car?' she asks. 'I don't know a thing about cars.'

She is young, plummy-voiced, sleepy-eyed. She appears completely self-possessed, yet vague and preoccupied. Her body is lean in that skinny, elongated, almost adolescent sort of way, but she is no

11

adolescent. She carries herself with an alert, contemptuous sophisti-
cation. She is dressed all in black; soft, expensive fabrics hanging
loosely but purposefully over her long limbs, and emphasising her
long pale hands and curved neck. Dark eyes and lips and a bundle of
black hair, scooped up and tied on top of her head, set off the wide,
white face, a face that expresses many things but chiefly ambiguity.
She drives the car as if she already owns it.

'I only sell good cars,' Mike Gombrich says.

'Good.'

'I'm not trying to say that it's a supercar. It isn't a Ferrari or a
Lambo.'

'What is it again?'

'An Alfa Romeo. Like Dustin Hoffman drove in *The Gradu-
ate*.'

'It seems quite fast.'

Mike Gombrich braces himself against the dashboard with one
hand as she takes a tight bend with great, inexpert enthusiasm.

'It's a real driver's car,' he says.

'Do they rust?'

'I'm afraid all cars rust.'

'Is it reliable?'

He pauses for effect, then goes into one of his set-pieces of
salesmanship.

'If you want my opinion, far too much importance is attached to
reliability these days. It's over-rated. With modern technology it's
relatively easy to buy a so-called reliable car. All you have to do is
go out and buy a bog-standard, mass-produced Ford or Vauxhall.
They sell enough of them that they can't be all bad. They'll run all
right. Six thousand miles between services, parts are cheap, every
mechanic on every street corner knows how to work on them.
They're reasonably economical. They're not bad to insure, but
so what? You get in it and drive it and is there any excitement,
any thrill? Does the blood start racing? Of course not. It's all a
big nothing.

'Whereas, you take something with a bit of character, and all
right, it might be a bugger to service, it might need re-tuning
every 500 miles, you might have to wait a few weeks for parts,
but once you've got it sorted and it's up and running, you get in
that car and it's special. It's an experience!'

'I like experience,' she says.

'Of course you do.'

He remains silent for a few moments so that the import of his speech can sink in.

'You're a very elegant woman,' he says.

'Thank you.'

'Elegant, stylish, with a lot of personality. You want a car that's like you.'

'Do I?'

'What sort of driving do you do?'

'Hardly any.'

He hadn't had her down as a time-waster until now.

'My husband does most of the driving.'

'Right.'

'I'm buying this for him. It's a present.'

'Right. Okay. What kind of car does he have at the moment?'

'He's got lots of cars. I forget all their names. All different types. Bugatti? Is that the name of a car?'

'I'd say so.'

'I think he's got one of those. But he doesn't drive his cars all that much.'

'Is he a collector?'

'That's it.'

'He's a very lucky man.'

'I suppose he is. He's got a lot of nice cars, anyway. He's a bookmaker. He's got lots of money to throw around.'

'I'd like to meet your husband.'

'Well, that's an option.'

'Maybe I could do some business.'

'Probably. He likes doing business. I thought I'd buy him a little something for his birthday.'

'A classic car's a very good idea. An appreciating asset.'

'Yes, but I want something he hasn't already got. I was wondering about a bubble car, or a three-wheeler, something like that.'

'That's not really my line of country, but if you're serious, I've got contacts.'

She brings the car to a halt in a bleak lay-by. She parks next to a mobile shop that is selling tea and snax.

'The cockpit's quite small, isn't it?' she says.

'That's one of my favourite things about this car,' Mike counters, brightly. 'You don't so much get in it as strap it round yourself.'

'Not much room for any hanky-panky.'

He smiles in what he takes to be a roguish manner. 'A lot of wives

13

might think it was a good idea to give their husband a car that didn't have any room for hanky-panky.'

She laughs. 'I'm not like that.'

'Would you like a coffee?'

It isn't the most romantic offer he's ever made but this lay-by doesn't suggest many other delights.

'Thank you,' she says.

He climbs out of the car and goes over to the van, and returns with two polystyrene cups of coffee that have no discernible flavour yet still manage to leave an unpleasant aftertaste.

'You could kiss me if you wanted to,' she says.

He continues to taste his coffee.

'Here?' he asks, looking round the lay-by.

'Anywhere you'd like.'

He doesn't kiss her, but he reaches out his hand and strokes her bare arm with practised gentleness.

Mike Gombrich is not as surprised by this proposition as many men would be. He knows his worth. He knows he's attractive to women, and even prides himself on being occasionally irresistible. He is well aware of the sexual imagery and the persuasive power of taking women for fast test drives in exotic cars. Nevertheless, he's a man who likes to take the initiative, and the initiative here has been firmly wrested from him.

'We could go to my house,' she says.

'What about your husband?'

It isn't a serious question. He doesn't care much about husbands. He only asks to give himself a moment or two to get to grips with the situation.

'He'll be there, of course,' she replies, 'and, of course, he'll want to join in.'

Mike Gombrich doesn't say a word. The situation seems to be spinning away from him.

'Would that be a problem?' she asks.

'I think it might.'

'Don't worry. He's not strange or anything. He wouldn't touch you or anything disgusting like that. The three of us would be naked in bed together but there'd be nothing queer going on. The two of you would simply give me all the attention you could.'

Mike Gombrich stares into his polystyrene coffee.

'Couldn't we just go to a hotel?' he suggests. 'Or a wood, or a beach, or back to my place and do it the ordinary way?'

14

'No,' she says. 'I wouldn't enjoy that.'

He is smart enough not to ask why, though that question looms very large in his mind.

'You see,' she explains, 'I've slept with a used-car salesman before, but I've never slept with a used-car salesman *and* my husband at the same time. It would be something different.'

This he can't deny, and yet his brain is sent reeling with all sorts of humanistic naïveties. Is he only a used-car salesman? Does she not want him for himself? Does she not even only want him for his body?

'Sleeping with *me* would be different,' he says.

'Not *very* different.'

He wonders if he ought to show a bit of anger.

'You're a bit of a wet blanket, actually, aren't you?' she says.

'No. No, I'm not.'

He would never let it be said that he was a wet blanket. In fact, if anything, he prides himself on being the life and soul of any occasion. He is famous for his parties. He strums his fingers on the dashboard, quite unnaturally hard. He is lost for words. He isn't one to look a gift horse in the mouth, he enjoys a good sexual adventure, but this horse seems to come with unwanted strings, and he likes his adventures, even if adventurous, to be simple.

'I don't know,' he says. 'I don't think group sex is really me.'

'Three isn't a group.'

'No, three's a crowd. I don't like crowds much, either. But look, I'm not saying a definite no. All I'm saying is I don't think so.'

The conversation stops. There is an uncomfortable silence. Something has come to an end.

'Perhaps you'd better drive us back,' he says.

When they arrive at Killer Kars, having driven back without saying a word, she skids the Alfa to a halt beside the row of newly washed cars.

'All right,' she says. 'I'll take it.'

'What?'

'The car. Remember the car?'

He does, vaguely.

'Good. Congratulations,' he says at last.

He can feel himself slipping back to the security of his role as salesman.

'Can I give you a cheque?' she asks.

'We'll have to wait for it to clear.'

15

'That's all right. You can deliver the car to my house when you're sure I'm bona fide. Perhaps you'll have thought things through by then.'

He gives her his professional smile. She gives him a cheque (he sees her name is Victoria Havergal) and the impressive address of her Derbyshire country house.

Let me tell you about this book I was trying to write. It was going to be called *The Collectors* by Steve Geddes (my real name). I thought it had a ring to it. It was going to be a serious but good-humoured, off-beat, non-fiction work about people who collect things. It was going to look at who they are, what they collect and why. It was going to investigate the whole notion of collecting; what it means, whether it springs from a certain kind of personality or a certain class, whether it's tied to materialism, acquisitiveness, capitalism, and so forth. I planned to look at the psychological, sociological and philosophical aspects. The possibilities were endless.

I wasn't particularly interested in serious collections of fine art or important antiquities, rather I planned to find a series of dubious but entertaining eccentrics who had unlikely, bizarre, or exceptionally useless collections. I was looking for the oddball and the kitsch. I wanted to interview the collectors, ask a few gentle, ironic questions, let them talk, and hope they made endearing fools of themselves.

I thought I was absolutely the right person to be writing this book. I felt I had the right combination of scepticism and distance, which is to say that I couldn't even begin to understand why anyone would want to collect anything.

All my life I'd been trying, more or less successfully, to avoid clutter. Not only did I not collect in the sense of not collecting stamps or cigarette cards, or blues records; I didn't keep anything for a moment longer than I needed to. After I'd read a book I almost always gave it or threw it away. I didn't have any souvenirs. I didn't keep old love letters. I didn't have a photograph album. I didn't even try to save money. I'd even managed to lose my wife. I was genuinely baffled about why people had the urge to collect things.

At bottom I was somehow opposed to the activity. I thought it was a 'bad thing'. I thought the collecting instinct was a form of grasping covetousness. People owned collections in order to experience the

16

dubious pleasures of ownership. What were these pleasures? What pleasure came from owning, say, ten Fabergé eggs, as opposed to only owning five? Only the pleasure of partially satisfied greed, and it is in the nature of greed that it can never be *wholly* satisfied.

Then there were all those collections that somehow missed the point. People collected toys that couldn't be played with, plates that couldn't be eaten from, jewellery that couldn't be worn. That was insane. And then there were the collections of things peripheral to the activity that caused them to exist. I could see why people might want to go to the theatre or to football matches, but not why they wanted to collect theatre and football programmes. I could see why people might go wild about Elvis Presley's music, but not why they wanted to collect Elvis memorabilia.

I was also struck by the inherently uncreative nature of collecting. Painting a picture is a creative act. It means that you have some skill, however limited, some urge to make something and that you do it. Collecting pictures, however, just means that you have some money, go to the right galleries or auctions and take part in a financial transaction.

What was collecting, anyway? You took one thing and you took another thing, you put them next to each other and somehow their proximity was supposed to create a meaning. You put certain artefacts together, drew an artificial boundary around them, and there you were with a collection. So what?

As for the people themselves, I suspected that collectors were deeply inadequate human beings, compensating for a lack of personality, intelligence or love. I pictured them as a bunch of unsocial dullards: shy, oafish, unhip.

These were all the opinions I had before I started the project. It sounds, I know, as though I'd reached my conclusions before I'd done any research. This was true, and I always knew that this wasn't the best journalistic or scientific practice; but having a few firm ideas of what the hell I was doing before I started seemed necessary, and it had no doubt been essential for convincing my commissioning editor that he had a potential winner on his hands.

This was the best part of it all. I'd been given an advance to write this book. Some months earlier, as the split with my wife was in full, horrific swing, I went out boozing with Alastair, who was a book editor and was my only friend in publishing. We talked about the wickedness of the media, the vanity of authors, and I talked at length about the combined wickedness and vanity of my wife; and at the end of this increasingly heavy night I told him about this book I was burning to write. I began to speak eloquently about collecting, in the terms I've just described. At least it seemed eloquent to me at the time, and it couldn't have been entirely slurred and incoherent because (and even though I knew it was partly the house white talking) Alastair said he thought it was a bloody fine idea, and he offered to advance me a sum of money to write the book, a sum for which I would have sold my soul, though my soul went very cheap in those days.

Next morning I sobered up. I assumed that Alastair would have too, and would no doubt wish to withdraw his rash, drunken generosity. But he didn't. He phoned me up to say how thrilled he still was with the idea. The contract came through, followed at some distance by a cheque; and thus I became a professional author.

The idea was that I'd trot round the country, visiting public and private collections, talking to the curators and the individual collectors, or rather letting *them* talk while I dutifully and meticulously noted down what they had to say about this activity that I found incomprehensible.

I never at any time pretended that this book was going to address the key issues of the day, or was trying to make a contribution to literature. But I seriously believed that so long as I could track down the right people I had the makings of a quirky, entertaining, readable book. I could see it selling moderately well, especially if it had one or two relevant photographs and was marketed smartly. I saw myself being interviewed by the more light-minded magazines and radio programmes, and establishing a small but enviable reputation for myself somewhere between James Boswell and Studs Terkel.

Such are the dreams of the naïve and the recently separated.

Mike Gombrich walks into his office. Jim is already standing in the centre of the room attempting to look as though he belongs there. He's tried to get one of the salesmen or mechanics to be with him when he breaks the news, but there are understandably no offers. He has to face this alone.

'All right Jim?' says Mike. 'What have you got there?'

Jim has almost forgotten that he has in his hands the sample encyclopedia pages that the girl left behind a few nights ago. He

18

thought that if he pretended to be reading something his presence might look more natural and casual.

'Nothing,' he says, folding them up and hiding them in an overall pocket.

'What can I do for you, Jim?'

'It's your car.'

'What about it?'

'There's a bit of a problem with it. You'd better see for yourself.'

They walk from the office to the car. Jim follows at a safe distance, to be out of reach should Mike see the damage and hit out at the nearest available object. Mike looks at the message scratched on the side of the Corvette. He squats, looks closely, runs his fingers over the gouges.

'Somebody very sick did this,' he says calmly.

'It wasn't me,' Jim says, just in case.

'I'm aware of that, Jim. There are some strange people in the world, aren't there?'

'Definitely,' Jim says.

Jim looks into Mike's face. It is eerily calm. There is sorrow where there ought to be anger. Jim doesn't understand. Perhaps Mike has something else on his mind.

'Can I ask you a question?' Mike says.

'Of course.'

He can ask all the questions he likes so long as he doesn't hit him.

'Supposing you met a girl you found attractive.'

'Yes,' says Jim.

'And let's say you decide to pursue her.'

'Knowing me I probably wouldn't.'

'But supposing you did and then you discovered that she'd got a husband.'

'Yes.'

'But the husband didn't mind.'

'Oh.'

'So long as he could join in.'

'Blimey.'

'What would you do?'

Jim mulls the problem. He is flattered to be asked his opinion. Not many people come to him for advice on affairs of the heart. It is not his area of greatest expertise, but expertise isn't everything.

19

He thinks about it for a long while. Then he says, 'I'd run a mile.'

Mike Gombrich considers Jim's answer for at least as long as Jim considered it.

'I think you're probably dead right,' he says finally.

He slaps Jim gently on the shoulder. Jim flinches in anticipation of something far worse. Mike Gombrich enters his office and locks the door. For the next ten minutes there is the sound of an office being demolished, glass being broken and furniture smashed against the walls. Outside on the forecourt Jim allows himself a smile that is at least partly of relief. For a moment there he'd been worried about Mike.

There is a story, told by Simon Raven, about Maurice Bowra, that I also find very hard to believe. Perhaps it isn't so much a story as a fact, though certainly a 'useless fact'. Raven claims that Bowra, in his bed, in the dark, as a preliminary to buggering some lad, reached into his bedside cabinet for a tin of vaseline, found it, coated the relevant parts, performed the act, and only then discovered, as the tides of passion receded, that he hadn't found a tin of vaseline at all, but a tin of boot polish.

Now come on! Surely it couldn't have been as dark as all that! Surely the texture of the boot polish didn't feel right, and therefore surely it didn't do the job required of it. Surely the smell was all wrong! And who keeps boot polish next to vaseline in their bedside cabinet? The whole story doesn't work at all.

So why does Raven tell the story? Surely he's enough of a story-teller to realise it doesn't work, but he doesn't seem to care. Does he think his readers won't notice? Does he just want to shock them? Does he just want to abuse Maurice Bowra?

In fact the whole episode is in some danger of pitching into that area of stories which are so unlikely they might well be true. But that still doesn't cut much ice as far as I'm concerned. When did being true have anything to do with anything? A good story can be untrue but convincing, but a true story that doesn't convince is a complete dead loss. Maybe Simon Raven would disagree.

There is a much better story about a young Yorkshire lad travelling on a tram with his father. Across the aisle from them is a mother with a baby. The baby starts to cry so the mother unhitches her clothing and hauls out a large, white, floppy breast and gives it to the baby who sucks gratefully.

The little lad has never seen anything like this, so he says to his Dad, 'Eh up Dad, what's that baby doing?' Dad replies, 'He's having his tea.'

The lad's even more puzzled than he was before. He thinks about it for a while, then says, 'He's never going to eat all that lot w'out any bread and butter, is he?'

Personally I find this a really good story, by which I mean that I find it funny, and not merely in that 'kids say the darnedest things' sort of way. I think it actually does say something about the way children think, about breasts and babies, and about Yorkshire eating habits.

The story sounds plausible. I think it's probably made up, and yet it sounds authentic. It rings true. It certainly rings truer than the story of Madame de Gaulle and her penis, or Maurice Bowra and his tin of boot polish. And I don't happen to think that it's a great slur on motherhood or the female body, though I can see that there are those who might.

It also demonstrates the way that some anecdotes will only work if they're about famous people, whereas others still work even if they're about a lad on a bus.

It was a Tuesday evening and I was meeting Jim for a drink. I went to the mobile home site to pick him up. I think it was quite a good site as they go, though I hadn't seen many others. It was neat and orderly, calor gas canisters hidden behind potted shrubs, even some stretches of white picket fence.

Jim was one of the least mobile people I'd ever met. He didn't even have his own transport. You'd have thought it would have been easy enough for him to get a good bargain, if not a good car, through Killer Kars. I sometimes wondered if he was making a statement.

I suppose I found Jim 'interesting' even then. He seemed too bright to spend the rest of his life, or even very much of his life, cleaning cars by day and sitting in his mobile home getting drunk by night. Every now and then I suggested that he 'bettered himself', by which

I suppose I meant get a better job and start leading a more respectable and middle-class life. I sometimes pointed out possible jobs in the local paper, or told him he should take evening classes, but I knew these were lame suggestions and I knew that he wouldn't take any notice of me.

I don't want it to sound as though Jim and I were ever great pals. We weren't boisterous, back-slapping, Hemingwayesque buddies. We weren't even exactly friends. I found him a 'character', and I'm fully aware of the condescension that term implies. Nevertheless, he wasn't bad company.

I'd be tempted to say we talked about everything under the sun, but when I really think about it I realise our topics of conversation were limited. We talked a lot about women, but it was always very general and never smutty. I can't pretend we ever came up with any great insights into the subject. Jim seemed incapable of getting or keeping a girlfriend. My separation from my wife had dissolved whatever certainties I'd ever had about what women were like or 'what they wanted'.

We talked about books sometimes, though I was keener than Jim, and we talked about God, though Jim was keener than me. We talked about the nature of obsession, fame, washing cars, famous murders. And obviously we talked about politics, money and sport, because, after all, that's what men talk about. I'm sure we must have exchanged a few anecdotes. I can't remember that we ever told each other jokes.

'Let's go somewhere different for a change,' Jim said as he settled in the car. He named a country pub a little way out of town. I'd never heard of it but he gave me directions and I set off driving.

I'm not sure that Jim was much of a philosopher but he did have an annoyingly philosophical 'streak'. I mean that he thought about things in a detached way. He looked for clues. He found connections and came up with theories.

'Everybody's looking for something,' he said.

'I suppose.'

'But most of them don't know what they're looking for. You see married people, couples, they're not happy, there's something missing and they don't really know what it is. So what do they do? They have children. They think maybe that's what's missing. I'm not saying they're bad parents or that they don't love their kids, but they discover that the thing that was missing wasn't children at all, it was something else. But they still don't know what else, only now they're saddled with kids and it's a bit inconvenient to start looking for the something else.'

'What are *you* looking for?' I asked.

'What?'

'If everybody's looking for something, then you must be looking for something too.'

'It's funny you should say that. I think for a long time I was just looking for something to look for. I wanted an interest, a real obsession.'

'Are you sure?' I said. 'People with obsessions can be a bit dull.'

I felt I could speak with some authority on this, having already interviewed a few people who were obsessed with collecting things.

'People with obsessive interests,' I said, 'tend to be highly undeveloped in other areas of their personality.'

'Not necessarily,' Jim said. 'And, anyway, it makes no difference. I've always wanted an obsession and now I've found one: general knowledge.'

I sniggered. I wondered if he was joking. Jim wasn't known for his dry sense of humour but I couldn't believe he was serious.

'How does an obsession with general knowledge manifest itself?' I asked.

'It'll manifest itself by my knowing everything. You'll only have to mention Julius Caesar or Oliver Cromwell or Milton, and I'll be able to tell you all about them. I'll know the dates of battles. I'll know capital cities. I'll know who invented things, and who wrote which books, and painted which pictures and composed which symphonies. I'll know the kings and queens of England, the definitions of technical and scientific terms. I'll know who said what, the names of architectural features, which plants belong to which families, and all about wildlife. All that and more.'

'Sounds great,' I said dubiously. 'And how are you going to come by all this general knowledge?'

'I'm going to buy a set of encyclopedias.'

'Oh no.'

'What do you mean "Oh no"? I'm all signed up. This is going to change my life. This is the best thing I've ever done.'

He told me the story about the arrival of the encyclopedia saleswoman, whose name I discovered was Elaine, and how she departed in tears leaving her brief-case behind. She duly returned for the brief-case, but in the meantime he'd looked at the sample pages and been incredibly impressed. When she arrived he said he wanted to sign up. She'd even tried to talk him out of it, but he was adamant. She said it was the first sale she'd ever made. She was so pleased and grateful she'd almost accepted when he asked her out for a drink. He liked her. He hoped to be seeing more of her.

I don't exactly know why I thought Jim was crazy to buy a set of encyclopedias. I have the same prejudice against encyclopedias and their salespeople as everyone else does. Why is that? I thought, for one thing, that Jim would never use them, that they'd sit in a corner of his mobile home, a thick coat of dust wearing its way into the fake gold and leather bindings. Which is to say that I didn't take his sudden quest for knowledge very seriously. When he told me the price he'd agreed to pay for them I was even more horrified.

'Money well spent,' he said. 'Just from reading the sample pages I've learned that Saint Augustine went to school in Carthage and was a master of rhetoric. I've memorised the first ten kings of England and I've learned Bernoulli's principle.'

'Are you sure about this?' I said. 'Maybe it's not too late to change your mind. You might still be legally entitled to a refund.'

'I don't want to change my mind. I don't want a refund.'

'Okay,' I said.

It was his life and his money. It was nothing to do with me.

'But even if you do start suddenly absorbing pages of information, aren't you a bit worried about filling your head with useless knowledge?'

'Useless? How can knowledge be useless? Knowledge is power.'

'Okay,' I said, 'and what are you going to do with all this knowledge when you've got it? How are you going to use this power?'

'Responsibly, of course. I'm going to start appearing on quiz shows; in pubs at first, then local radio, then national radio, then television. Nothing frivolous, only serious stuff. And obviously it's going to take time before I'm up to the required standard, but once I'm fully trained and fit I expect to win. I won't be doing this just for fun. I'll be doing it for glory. I expect to win and win well. I expect to become a bit of a celebrity – opening supermarkets, making guest appearances, after-dinner speeches, doing ads for educational products, giving lectures.'

'What would you lecture on?'

'General knowledge.'

'Of course.'

I peered through the windscreen. We seemed to be lost. There

24

was not a pub in sight and we were driving down a gravel road full of pot-holes. I must have been driving too fast and my mind was more on general knowledge than on the road. The front off-side wheel smashed into a deep crater and we had a puncture. Neither of us knew how to operate the jack.

I've always admired stand-up comedians. The work they do is brave, lonely, difficult and absurd. There seems to be something significant and important about a man standing alone on stage without a musical instrument or song or any conspicuous virtuoso talent like plate-spinning or tap-dancing; just his speaking voice and his wits, and *talking* to an audience. This seems to me to be very close to what great art is about.

As for absurd, I don't think there's anything absurd about entertaining people and trying to make them laugh, but there's something absurd about *only* trying to make people laugh. If you tell a story that happens to be funny, then all well and good; the story has some life and some point independent of the laughter. But most comedians seem only to be trying to provoke laughter and that is absurd. Laughter for laughter's sake is as barren as art for art's sake.

It's obviously a pointless and thankless task to do any sort of theorising about comedy, but I couldn't avoid thinking about one or two of the larger issues as I went to interview a stand-up called Ted Langley. He was the latest of the collectors I'd so far contacted.

Ted had a reputation as a comedian's comedian (whatever that meant). He was a name. He'd made television appearances and was never out of work, but he'd never got the success a lot of people thought he ought to have. He apparently worked the clubs with devastating effect. He did long, long sessions of quick-fire jokes and one-liners. He went through floods of material in the course of his act, and perhaps that was why he didn't appear on the box very often. Television simply uses up too much material.

Being the poor researcher that I am, I hadn't seen his live club act, but I had seen him once on a TV variety show. I was unimpressed. Worse than that, I hadn't found him funny. The jokes came thick and fast but they were tired and old. However, that didn't matter much in the present context. I wasn't going to interview him because I thought he was a comic master. I was going to see him because I

25

had it on good authority that he kept the largest collection of jokes in Britain; written on file cards, stored in cabinets, occupying two rooms of his house.

I rang the doorbell. The house was a large semi in a pleasant but unluxurious area of Manchester. There was a newish estate car in the drive. The gardens were neat: a monkey puzzle tree and some well pruned roses. I noticed there were venetian blinds at all the windows.

Ted Langley opened the front door. He was wearing suit trousers, a dress shirt and trainers. He was ugly in an interesting, unthreatening way. He had a comedian's face with big mobile eyes and mouth and jowls. He held a piece of chocolate cake in one hand, and a cigarette in the other. His mouth was too full for him to say hello, but he gave me a welcoming nod. When I'd seen him on television he'd looked younger, thinner and more sprightly. Such is the nature of television.

We shook hands as best we could. He transferred cake crumbs from his hand to mine. He seemed welcoming and glad to see me. He showed me into his living-room. It was comfortable, plain, very red, smelling of cigarette smoke, and the only thing that was at all showbiz was a table littered with framed photographs of Ted Langley standing with other, more famous, performers.

We sat. I set up my tape-recorder to record our conversation. His wife, altogether younger, shyer and more delicate than him, brought us coffee and a plateful of biscuits before slipping silently away.

'What paper do you write for?' he asked.

'Different ones at different times,' I said. 'But right now I want to interview you for a book I'm doing.'

'You're writing a book about me?'

'I'm afraid not.'

'About comedians in general?'

'It's more about people who collect things.'

'Like stamps?'

'That sort of thing.'

'All publicity's good publicity, I suppose,' he said. 'And obviously I'm the man when it comes to collecting jokes.'

'That's what they tell me. I understand you have the world's greatest collection.'

He was flattered. I could see him warming to me.

'I don't know about the world. There's probably somebody in America who's got more. You know what Americans are like.'

I said that I did.

'You'd better come upstairs and have a look.'

We went up to the two spare bedrooms. He threw open both doors proudly. The rooms were fitted with custom-made wooden filing cabinets that ran floor to ceiling around the walls, leaving only gaps for windows and door. They were designed to hold postcard-size file cards. The cabinets were beautifully finished and lovingly polished, and each drawer had a label, hand-written in copperplate with various inscrutable abbreviations such as Moth-I-L, Wom-Dr, H & H. 'Mothers-in-law, women drivers, heaven and hell,' he explained. 'One of these days, I can see it coming, I'm going to have to put this little lot on computer. That's going to be a job and a half.'

'Do you know roughly how many jokes there are here?' I asked.

'Not roughly. Exactly. 527,345! They're all arranged by subject, then each one's graded by quality according to how good a laugh they get.'

'And you wrote all these yourself?' I asked disingenuously.

He looked at me as if I had said something incredibly stupid.

'I don't write them,' he said. 'I just tell them.'

'Then how do you come by them? Do you have a team of writers?'

'Jokes aren't like that,' he said, irritably. 'Jokes don't get written. They just exist. People tell them to each other in pubs, at work, in the school playground. They have a life of their own. I just keep my ears open, listen, then write them down, file them away, then they're ready to use in my act.'

'So they're all jokes you've heard other people tell?'

'Look son, there's nothing new in this world, certainly not when it comes to comedy. There's no such thing as a new joke. There are only so many basic comedy situations, and only so many things that make people laugh. It's the same now as it was in Plato's day.'

'I can see that.'

'You get these so-called new comedians, bright young lads with their so-called new material. I've been on the same bill as some of them. Every "new" joke they tell I've got filed away in here. Most of them I told on stage fifteen years ago.'

'What about people who don't do jokes?'

He was puzzled. 'You mean like jugglers or something?'

'No. People who just do monologues and observations, like Lenny Bruce.'

'Never heard of him, so he can't be much cop, can he? If you don't do jokes then you're not a comedian. It's as simple as that.'

'Right,' I said.

'Go on, try me out. Give me a topic, any topic, and I'll lay my hands on a gag straight away.'

'How about quiz shows?'

He went into the other bedroom and opened a lower drawer. He riffled through some file cards and plucked one out triumphantly.

'This bloke goes on a quiz show. The question-master asks him, "What's a Hebrew?" The bloke says, "A male teabag."'

I feigned amusement. I was tempted to ask how that one was graded in the laughter stakes but I didn't want to offend Ted in his own home.

'Of course the beauty of a joke like that', he said, 'is that you can adapt it. You can make the bloke Irish, in which case you've got yourself an Irish joke.'

'I see,' I said, attempting a complex facial expression that I hoped implied that I was amazed at the cleverness of his system, and that I was grateful and delighted to be initiated into these arcane technical mysteries.

He insisted I try him on other topics. I offered secondhand cars, pubs, and door-to-door salesmen. He had no difficulty coming up with jokes, but I'd heard them all before and I had some difficulty not keeping a straight face.

'Try me again,' he said.

'Charles de Gaulle,' I said.

'Good. I like a challenge.'

He opened another drawer and after some consideration extracted a card.

'The best thing about this one is it's a true story. Right. Now Charles de Gaulle and his wife were having dinner at this posh hotel in London . . .'

He proceeded, with a few variations, to tell me the 'happiness' story. I had to admit that he told it quite well. I smiled at the punchline.

'Of course,' he said, 'you don't get the full effect of these jokes with you standing there and me standing here telling them. You need a bit of atmosphere, an audience, the lights, a few drinks inside you. Have you ever seen me work?'

'Only on TV.'

'Not the same. You should come along to the show. You've got to see me in my natural environment. I'll get you some comps.'

'Thanks.'

He put away his cards about quiz shows, secondhand cars, pubs, door-to-door salesmen and Charles de Gaulle.

'So let's say I'm doing a show next week. Let's say it's in Huddersfield. Preparation's everything in this game, so before I do the show I have a session with my files. I'll see if I've got anything under Huddersfield. Not very likely, so I'll probably have to adapt something. Now, for a start, I know they've got a football team in Huddersfield, so I'll see how they're doing in the league and I'll come up with some tailor-made gags for the football fans of Huddersfield. And let's say the nightclub's called Napoleon's, then I'll dig out some Napoleon jokes. And I may have heard there's a party of hairdressers going to be in the audience, in which case . . .'

'Yes, yes, I think I see.'

We grinned at each other, acting the part of people who understood each other.

'Can I ask a silly question?' I said.

'Why not?'

'Do you have a bad memory?'

He laughed at me in a warmly contemptuous way.

'You think I ought to be able to remember over half a million jokes, is that it?'

'No.'

'Of course not. Don't be daft.'

'What about ad libs? Do you ever do those?'

He pointed at a couple of drawers at floor level.

'I've got over a thousand ad libs right here. And put-downs, attention-grabbers, heckler-stoppers. I've got the lot.'

'You certainly have. I'm impressed.'

'I knew you would be. People like a good joke, you know. People need to laugh.'

I didn't doubt that they did. I was reminded of an old joke about the man who joins a group of people in a bar. Every now and then one of them gets up and says a number, 'thirty-two' for instance. Everybody falls about laughing. Somebody else gets up, says, 'forty-nine', and they fall about again. The new arrival asks what's going on. Somebody explains, 'We all know each other's jokes, so to save time and effort we've given each joke a number and when we want to tell a joke we just say the number.' I'm sure you've heard it so I won't bother with the punchline.

I thought Ted Langley was probably right in saying there was no such thing as a new joke. Nevertheless I still held on to some notions of originality, or at least of freshness. I couldn't see much joy or satisfaction in getting on stage and reciting your file cards. It was comedy by numbers all right. I thought it was another 'bad thing', but I also thought it might make a very telling chapter for my book.

It is a clear June day as Jim drives to the big house, but it isn't as warm as a June day might be expected to be, and the air that whips over and around the windscreen and into the cockpit of the Alfa Romeo Spider cuts sharply through his thin clothes. He has never driven an open car before, and he can't say that he's enjoying it much. It makes him feel conspicuous. People look at him as though they think he is some terrible poseur. Someone even tosses an empty Fanta can into the car when he stops at a traffic light. He's glad to reach his destination.

He doesn't understand why he's been asked to deliver the car to its new owner. It isn't a thing he's ever been asked to do before. Mike said he was too busy to do it himself, but he didn't look all that busy. Jim wonders if he is being groomed for promotion. He hopes not, though he could do with a pay rise to offset the cost of the payments on his encyclopedias. He has begun reading the first volume; Aalto (whom Jim discovers is a Finnish architect and furniture designer) to Azurite (a blue mineral).

Jim has already expressed some concern about how he will get back to Killer Kars after making the delivery, since the house is some fifteen miles out of town. Mike blithely assures him that the lady buyer will give him a lift back, because she'll be so grateful and she'll want to give the car a run; and if he wears his usual hangdog expression it will be the least she can do.

Mike Gombrich is a hard man to argue with, and Jim knows he's a fair judge of character, so probably he's right and she will give him a lift. At the worst he can hitch slowly back. If nothing else, it will have been an afternoon in the country.

He arrives at the house. It is big, elegant and perfectly proportioned; full of angles, steep roofs, eighteenth-century red brick weathered into endless shades between terracotta and rose pink. Greenery threatens to overwhelm one face of the house, while a line of yew trees off to one side tries, but fails, to hide a new, blue, metallic, hangar-like construction that has been built separately from, yet uncomfortably close to, the house.

Jim pulls up outside what he takes to be the front door. Then he thinks better of it and drives round to the side in search of a tradesmen's entrance. He sees a door that looks likely, gets out of the car and rings the bell. Nobody comes. He peers through the glass in the door, into a large, white-tiled kitchen with polished copper pans hanging from every wall; but there is no sign of life. Ringing at the front door produces no response either so he crosses a trim though lived-in lawn to see if he can locate anyone in the 'hangar'.

It is a building that would not look out of place on an industrial estate. It is lofty, corrugated, windowless. Tall, sliding doors, large enough to drive a juggernaut through, give access from one end. These are closed, but an adjacent, human-sized door is open. Jim approaches and enters.

Once inside he is struck by the brightness of the artificial light, showering down from spots and tubes on to a score or so of fine cars. They are older and more thoroughbred than he's used to seeing at Killer Kars. He recognises the slab-like radiator of a Bugatti, a Morgan three-wheeler, a Model T. He notices that, despite being kept under cover, they all look as though they could do with a good clean. He might mention this to someone if there was someone there, but the building is uninhabited. He thinks it's a good job he's not a thief.

He leaves the hangar to explore further. Moving behind the house he goes down six stone steps to a broad, flat area, lined with bushes, in the centre of which is a small, neat swimming-pool. He would have thought it was far too cold a day for anyone to be swimming, but a girl in a black bikini is doing vigorous backstroke along its short length. He just about recognizes her as the one Mike Gombrich took for a test drive the day his car was vandalised, the details of that afternoon being rather firmly etched in Jim's memory. She gives him a wave.

'I haven't got my contact lenses in,' she shouts, 'so I can't see who you are. I'll be out in a minute.'

She completes another three lengths before getting out of the pool. Her skin is untanned, roughened by goose-pimples, her nipples

31

prominent through the black triangles of the bikini top. But all this is only briefly visible. At the poolside she pulls on a man's black towelling dressing-gown, comically too big for her and obviously belonging to a giant of a man. She ties the cord round her waist, and pulls a pair of horn-rims from a pocket, and puts them on to look at Jim. She obviously has no idea who he is.

'I've brought the car,' he says.

'Oh, you're the delivery boy.'

He is only mildly insulted. He smiles, hoping it may be a joke. She smiles back. She sets off for the front of the house leaving wet footprints that soon fade out along the paving slabs by the pool. It is on his mind that she doesn't look like the sort who'd feel any obligation to give him a lift.

She discovers the car. She stops smiling. She doesn't look especially pleased.

'It isn't quite as red as I remember it.'

Still, she slides into the driver's seat, plants her hands on the big steel and wood wheel, and her bare feet on the pedals. She looks like someone playing at driving. The keys are in the ignition but she makes no attempt to start the engine.

'If you'll just sign here,' Jim says.

He offers a receipt for her signature. She signs, then he gives her a copy, the registration document, the handbook, an MOT certificate, a spare set of keys, and a leaflet extolling the virtues of Killer Kars for all her motoring needs.

'You've got very clean hands,' she says.

Jim is taken aback.

'I thought all you mechanics or grease monkeys or whatever you call yourselves always had dirty hands and oil under the fingernails. I find it quite attractive.'

Jim explains that he isn't a mechanic, just the bloke who washes the cars.

'And delivers them.'

'Well, yes.'

'So they must trust you. You must be a very good and careful driver.'

'Yes,' he says, seeing no reason to rebuff her compliment.

'Why didn't Mike bring it himself?'

'That's what I'd like to know.'

'I suppose the boss has more important things to do than make deliveries. I suppose he's the salesman. Once his glib tongue has turned a girl's head and made her part with her money he thinks his job's over.'

'We do try to give a good after-sales service.'

'Was he scared I was going to drag him into the swimming-pool and have his jockey-shorts off?'

'I wouldn't like to say.'

'Or was it my husband he was scared of?'

Jim suddenly realises that he may have been obtuse in not connecting Mike's remarks about troilism with the test driver of the Spider. But he hadn't. He now understands why he was asked to make the delivery, and he thinks that Mike might at least have had the decency to explain.

'I wouldn't really have dragged him into the pool,' she says, 'but there's always the greenhouse.'

Jim imagines that would be preferable. He can think of few things less erotic than being dragged into the icy water of a swimming-pool on a sunless June day. He smiles again, for want of a more appropriate response.

'I don't care what I say,' she says. 'And I don't much care what I do. Are you interested?'

'In?' he asks, thinking he must have missed some vital turn in the conversation.

'What do you think in? You are a chump.'

'You mean threesomes?'

'So your Mr Gombrich's been talking, has he?'

'Well . . .'

'It's no skin off my nose.'

'He did mention something.'

'So are you interested? I've never done it with a professional washer of cars.'

'It's a kind offer, but no thanks.'

'You aren't one of those people who just likes to be friends?'

Jim has a feeling that being a friend of this girl might be every bit as arduous as being her lover, but fortunately he has a good excuse.

'I'm already spoken for,' he says.

'Oh, do tell.'

'She sells encyclopedias . . .'

He tells her he has lost his heart to a door-to-door saleswoman, a saleswoman who doesn't even know he exists, or at least exists only as a client, a sales figure, a slice of commission. He says he has certain schemes in mind with which to win her heart, but he'd rather not divulge them yet. The new owner of the Spider thinks it all sounds very romantic and terrific fun. She says she can give him all sorts of tips on how to win a girl's heart, but Jim suspects her advice might be a little idiosyncratic. She then says she'd love to stay here chatting all day, but her husband will be home soon and she wants to have the car wrapped in ribbon and tissue paper before then. Jim nods as though he understands. He asks about public transport and soon realises he will be hitch-hiking home.

'There is one thing before I go,' he says. 'I've got a friend who's writing a book about people who collect things. I bet he'd really like to meet your husband.'

'What's his name?'

'Steve Geddes.'

'That's a nice name. Tell him to come along. The more the merrier.'

It was about this time that I discovered an author called Thornton McCain; not him, of course, just his writing. I realised this was a bit late in the day. He was over seventy years old and a lot of people must have discovered him before me; but not all that many, and he was still sufficiently obscure to remain a cult author. I often wonder exactly what that phrase means. I suspect it means that the whole world ignores you, but there are a couple of thirteen-year-olds in Nebraska who think you're the bee's knees. I suppose McCain must have had a bigger readership than that, but it was good to come across a comparatively unknown author over whom I could enthuse, and in some way appropriate. I think, in fact, it's precisely this sense of appropriation that makes a cult author, the sense that he's 'yours' and doesn't belong to the world at large. There were other things that added to his cult status; the lack of biographical detail on his dust-jackets, the fact that I'd never seen a picture of him, the fact that his books were out of print.

Inevitably you discover most cult authors when you're an adolescent, when you're in rebellion against your school, your parents, and the cosmos in general. You feel that nobody in the whole universe can comprehend what you're thinking and feeling, except possibly Bret Easton Ellis and Kurt Vonnegut. You think if only you could hitch over to wherever Bret or Kurt are hanging out these days, you'd have somebody to talk to who'd understand you perfectly, and then *everything would be all right.*

At my age, pushing thirty, I was obviously a bit old to be appropriating novelists, and I had at least learned enough to know that whatever problems I had weren't likely to be solved by sitting at the feet of some literary father figure, but I did feel that in Thornton McCain I had found a writer who, at least as he appeared in his writings, was as strange, fragmented and confused as I was. However foolish the premise, I felt that Thornton McCain was mine.

I said to Jim the next time I met him for a drink, 'You really ought to read *The Bottle Blonde.* I've never come across anything like it.'

'I'd like to,' said Jim. 'I'd like to read everything that's ever been written, but I don't have the time. I'm so busy reading *The Books of Power.*'

'Huh?'

He explained that *The Books of Power* was the name of the encyclopedia he'd bought. It sounded worse and worse. The title seemed to contain echoes both of fascism and barmy mysticism. I didn't much want to talk about encyclopedias. I wanted to sing the praises of Thornton McCain, but Jim only wanted to sing the praises of *The Books of Power*, so we found some common ground by discussing whether or not we liked women who shaved their armpits.

A few days later I was in the Sheffield Central Library, surrounded by earnest sixth formers and day-release students, trying more or less unsuccessfully to track down some information on the Burrell Collection. Having failed, and having nothing better to do, I decided to look up Thornton McCain in a dictionary of twentieth-century novelists. I found him easily enough. The entry read:

MCCAIN Thornton
Born Seattle 1919. American father. British mother. Educated at Brown University, Providence, Rhode Island, and Jesus College, Cambridge, England. Served in United States Infantry 1944–46.

Married (1) Alice Westbrook, 1941 (divorced 1947), two sons (2) Chantal Porchet, 1953 (divorced 1963), one son (3) Zita Jollife, 1966 (deceased 1980), one daughter.

Assistant editor, the *Philistine Review* 1947–50. Editor, *Inner Spaces* 1966–70.

Worked variously as a janitor, chef, cuttings librarian, antique dealer, book-keeper, barman, and latterly teacher of creative writing at Berkeley and the Richmond Institute. Recipient of Xavier Clinton Harley Honorarium 1977.

Now lives in Scotland.

Fiction: *The Foxhole, 1947*
           The Profane Comedy, 1951
           The Bottle Blonde, 1957
           Burn Little Sheba, 1969
           The Stiletto and I, 1972
           The World Seen Through Plexiglass, 1978
Play: *Nirvana: an Episode*, 1971.

It is all too easy to under-estimate the significance McCain has had for a whole generation of English and American writers, both as an inspiration and as an innovator. The present neglect of his work is an injustice that should shame us.

Initially poor and ill-educated, he embarked on an heroic programme of self-improvement, supporting himself by any means possible, not least as a cocktail waiter, as described in *The Stiletto and I*. Later, not without the help of a wealthy patron or two, he overcame ill health and a devastatingly unhappy personal life to write a handful of indisputable masterpieces.

The Foxhole paints a profound and disturbing picture of a debauched cuttings librarian at the end of his tether, while *The Bottle Blonde* presents a chilling vision of apocalypse, set in a Palm Springs manicure parlour.

But his greatest work is undoubtedly *The World Seen Through Plexiglass*. Written in the late 'seventies, it juggles artfully, if often bafflingly, with many crucial modern themes; among them materialism, sexual perversion, espionage, the Seven Years' War, and writer's block.

Patchy, erotic, obscene, lush yet disciplined, occasionally demented, he is a man for our times and for all times. We neglect him at our peril.

I was delighted to find McCain included in the dictionary, and especially pleased to find him praised. I wasn't sure that praise from a dictionary of twentieth-century novelists to be found in the Sheffield Central Library was worth much, but it showed that he had some vague toe-hold on posterity.

I tried to imagine Thornton McCain, where he was now and what he was likely to be doing. I pictured a wild, barren spot, bitter winds blowing in off the Highlands, disturbing the bracken and heather, rattling at the windows of an old granite croft. Inside would be McCain, as craggy and as bleak as the landscape, swathed in coarse tweed, tossing another block of peat on the fire, pouring himself a wee dram. The room would be beautifully spartan. So far as I knew he'd written nothing for a decade, so I envisaged no hint of the literary life, no journals or little magazines, no proofs to be corrected, no typewriter. I saw an old man in a desolate place, keeping a solemn and dignified silence, little suspecting that here in Sheffield, if nowhere else, there was someone who still loved his writing.

I also took some consolation from knowing he'd once been a barman. It was a job I'd often done myself. Perhaps there was still hope for me.

When I say I'd discovered McCain's work, that is only to say that at that time I'd read *The Bottle Blonde* and *The World Seen Through Plexiglass*, both books bought secondhand in hardback at a hip, chaotic bookshop near the university where they played Eric Dolphy as background music.

Both books were first editions, but I suspected there had never been second editions, and, as far as I knew, they'd never made it into paperback. I thought, briefly, about making a determined effort to track down his other books, but I was loath to become a Thornton McCain collector. He was a good writer and I liked his work a lot, but I had no intention of getting obsessed with him.

Today, of course, I own his complete works, and I know them all inside out, but I still remember the excitement I felt on first discovering his writing. Like the man says, it's patchy, but often it's wonderful. It isn't a good read. It isn't a real page-turner. It's loose, disconnected, messy, arbitrary, easy to get lost. Sometimes you don't know what he's on about or why. It sometimes appears to be merely a stream of inconsequentialities, non sequiturs, irrelevancies; just (at the risk of sounding like a complete imbecile) like life.

Let me tell you about my marriage. At least let me try. I don't know how, or if, it differed very much from other marriages. Other people's married lives always seem inscrutable. You see them form, continue and break up. You watch the behaviour. People you know well drop hints and clues for you to pick up. Once in a while one or other partner will unburden themselves to you, and their unburdenings may sometimes have a certain familiarity about them, a certain distant ring of truth; but ultimately they're completely alien. You read accounts in books and on the problem pages, but you suspect these are different forms of lying. To an outsider any marriage must look mysterious and incomprehensible. Sometimes it looks that way to the insiders too.

So, in that sense, my marriage was perhaps much like any other, by which I mean it was a complex and curious series of small triumphs, small hurts, love and sex, sharing and exclusion, joy, irritation and anger. Many other things too. You have some good times. You get some support, some understanding, affection and companionship, and these are well worth having; but you store up the irritation and the anger and the small hurts, the real or imagined betrayals, and one day, when your store is full, when you've collected the full set, you unleash them. They overwhelm everything else, and suddenly you don't have a marriage any more.

It seems to me that I remained unchanged throughout our marriage, and that was precisely the problem. Rachel, yes, that was her name, meanwhile changed completely. Nobody would say she changed for the worse. Not even me. But she changed from being moderately successful to being overwhelmingly successful, while I continued to be a moderate failure.

When I met Rachel I was working long hours as a barman in the evenings, and by day I was trying to be a writer. Rachel found that appealing. She was working for an advertising agency and she seemed to believe that I, the unsuccessful but apparently fulfilled artist, had access to some vision of integrity that would help her keep her sense of proportion and be good for her soul. People have got married for worse reasons.

For a time Rachel and I made each other very happy, and I believe that we were very much in love; but try as I might, I can't remember what being in love was like. There are all sorts of literary and poetic models to help me. There are enough movies and pop songs that ought to work as powerful mnemonics; and yes I suppose that's what it must have felt like. But I find now that I can't recall, much less describe, what being in love with Rachel was like. This is probably no bad thing. Descriptions of being in love are very tedious for the reader.

38

I never knew what went on in the Slater, Skeat and Goodenough advertising agency where Rachel worked, and I preferred it that way. I was always happy to rail against the evils of advertising, and the purity of my antagonism would only have been tainted if I'd actually known anything about it.

Of course, through Rachel I picked up a lot of gossip; more than that I picked up the language, the baffling references to sectors, tie-ups, briefs, product concepts and positioning. Some of it sounded exciting. The language described a planet that was infinitely more vivid and alive than the one I lived on; a planet of flagships, watersheds and cutting edges. And everything, but everything, was creative.

However, whatever it was that Slater, Skeat and Goodenough did, and whatever it was they wanted their employees to be able to do, Rachel obviously did it supremely well. When we got married she was an account executive. A year later she was a director. Being a director, in itself, didn't seem to mean much. Most people in advertising appeared to be directors of one sort or another; sales directors, art directors, account directors, and, of course, creative directors. But, however nebulous and bogus the titles, Rachel's success and the money she earned were undoubtedly authentic. Her salary had always looked like serious wealth from where I was standing, but now it became ridiculous. There were new cars on the firm, a new flat, weekends in New York, a lot of meals out and a lot of champagne. Her earnings swamped mine so completely that after a while it seemed perverse for me to carry on working behind a bar. I felt no great threat to my masculinity at becoming a kept man. I became a full-time writer. It was an ambition fulfilled. It felt very much like being unemployed.

The hours Rachel had to put in were ridiculous too, that was why the holidays in New York were only for weekends. For her there were late, late nights, business socialising, working breakfasts, working weekends. We simply didn't see much of each other. I had a lot of time alone, a lot of time to write, and a lot of time to feel resentful. I would brood on the injuries I considered had been done to me. I would amplify and re-manufacture them. Before long I was feeling hurt all the time. But Rachel wasn't. She didn't have time to notice such trivia. Her career filled every moment of her waking day. Soon she didn't have time for me. She didn't have time for anything but her work, and I didn't see how she could possibly find the time for an affair, but somehow she managed that.

Even so, I couldn't pretend that it came as any great surprise when she told me. It just seemed very obvious. The last straw. I don't doubt we could have 'got over' the affair if we'd wanted to, but by then neither of us really did. And even if we had I think we wouldn't have allowed ourselves to show it. The affair was a convenient excuse to end things.

We remained civilised and amicable. I said I would leave. There was no other option. We agreed to a separation, to be neatly followed two years later by a divorce.

There was no way I could afford to buy a place in London, not even a small jerry-built conversion in some undesirable, outlying area. So I moved north to Sheffield, where I'd been to university. The housing was cheap, the unemployment was high, the council was socialist, and I was able to rent a little red-brick terraced house.

It was a two-up two-down with flowered wallpaper and carpets, an old teak-finished gas fire, a kitchen full of unmatching units. It suited me very well.

When I arrived I knew nobody in Sheffield. The people I'd been to university with were long gone, and after six months the only person I ever saw regularly was Jim. I sat in my house most days trying to write my book, still being a moderate failure.

I realise that all this doesn't really tell you much about my marriage. At bottom I suppose I'd really rather not talk about it.

Early one morning I was enjoying the sleep of the just (and of those who had taken a beer or two the previous night) when the phone started ringing. I padded slowly downstairs, thinking it was bound to stop before I got there, but it didn't. I swooped on the receiver and it was Rachel, 'my wife'. When we were married I never used that expression. Now that we were separated I couldn't think how else to describe her. Her voice was bright and cheerful, a voice that was trying hard to imply that this was just a social call.

She had taken to phoning me from time to time, not very often, perhaps every two or three weeks. She liked to pretend it was done out of enduring affection, but I suspected she wanted to be sure I hadn't killed myself in a fit of northern despair. As long as I was alive and able to answer the phone she had nothing to feel guilty about.

'How are you?' she asked.

'Not so bad.'

'Are you writing?'

'Trying.'

'And is it going well?'

'Not so bad.'

'How's Sheffield?'

'Okay. Quiet. At least the bits of it I see are quiet. I'm sure there are parts of Sheffield that make Rio look tame.'

'Really?'

'No. Not really.'

'You're joking.'

'That's it.'

We hadn't seen each other for a while, but even so I didn't think she'd have forgotten so soon that I made the occasional joke. I remembered a time when she even appreciated them.

'Are you seeing anybody?' she asked.

That threw me. It seemed an impertinent question for an estranged wife to be asking her husband.

'You mean women?' I asked.

'No. Well, I meant anyone. Have you met many people up there? Made many friends?'

'You know me better than that.'

'Yes.'

All she said was 'yes', but I could feel sympathy oozing down the line for her poor, friendless, socially inadequate husband.

'So how are things with you?' I asked.

'Oh, you know, busy.'

'Of course.'

'Work's as hectic as ever.'

'And the flat?'

'No different,' she said, 'and that's the real reason I'm ringing. I came across a box of your things, things you left behind.'

'Yeah?'

'I don't know if it's important or not. It's got some old tax documents, some letters, a few old photographs. There are some of your parents. I thought you might want them.'

'They don't sound very vital.'

'And I didn't want to put them in the post in case they got lost.'

'You know I've never been a great one for old photographs and letters.'

41

'I thought you might collect them in person if you were coming down to London.'

'I don't have any plans to come to London.'

'To see your publisher or something.'

'Possibly.'

'I thought, if you wanted lunch.'

'With you?'

'Who else?'

'I don't think so. I'm not trying to be difficult. I just don't like the idea.'

'I was trying to be friendly.'

'I know.'

'I thought you needed all the friends you could get.'

'Look, what are you trying to sell?'

'What?'

'I know you. You're in advertising. You know all about images and wording, and right now the words and image belong to some poor little helpless girl who wants her husband to be nice to her. It's quite persuasive and not unconvincing, but I suspect that at the end of this there's some product that's going to be given a very hard sell.'

She put the phone down on me. Who wouldn't? I didn't really understand the exact nature of the pleasure I got from insulting Rachel, but it was a very real one. Of course, insulting her was also a form of self-laceration. In truth I wouldn't have minded being nice to her. I did feel sorry for her alone in her big, new, empty flat with only her work for company (although no more sorry than I felt for myself), and yes, it would have been very nice to go down to London for the day and have lunch with her. We'd probably get a bit drunk and affectionate and there might be some sort of reconciliation, and yes, in lots of ways that was very desirable and it might even make us both happy; and that was precisely why I didn't want it. In order to make Rachel unhappy I was prepared to make myself unhappier still.

It was a bad start to the day. It took me a long time to get to my desk, a couple of hours of footling around and 'getting ready', and when I got there I couldn't work. In that respect it wasn't so very different from a lot of other days, but at least today I had an excuse.

★

'Are you all right?'

I'd agreed to meet another of my collectors in a pub in Coventry. He wasn't convinced he wanted to show me his collection, so we had to meet first on neutral territory, so that we could talk, so he could look me over and decide whether my motives were pure. Or perhaps he wanted to make sure I wasn't planning to rob him. I had his home address but he'd made it clear that his collection was kept off-premises at a secret location. This struck me as a bit excessive.

I asked him if he was all right because when he'd finally arrived at the pub, three-quarters of an hour late, he looked anything but all right. He looked terribly, perhaps terminally, ill. He was thinner than anyone I'd ever met before. The skin hung loose on his face, his cheeks apparently fleshless, and his body an arrangement of large, sharp bones that pushed his suit out at awkward angles. The complete absence of fat made his head, hands and feet seem to be built on a larger scale than the frame to which they were attached. His nails, eyes, teeth and hair had a ghastly yellow stain to them, clashing alarmingly with the awful greyness of the rest of him.

'I'm fine,' he said defensively.

'Then let me get you a drink.'

'A double tomato juice, no Worcester sauce.'

I went to the bar and got him a drink.

'I thought you'd have ordered a can of beer,' I said.

He didn't smile. A lot of people must have said that kind of thing to him.

'I gave up beer several years ago,' he said.

I wondered if he was sending me up. The man before me was Edwin Rivers, reputed to be England's foremost collector of and expert on beer cans.

'The fact is,' he continued, 'I was never really all that keen on beer in the first place. For years I used to pretend to enjoy it. I thought I had to. I had an image to keep up. I thought people would laugh at a beer can collector who didn't drink beer. I don't care any more. Let them laugh. These days I buy the can of beer, throw away the beer, add the can to my collection.'

'Exactly how big is your collection now?' I asked journalistically.

'Thirteen thousand cans, but quantity isn't everything.'

'Sounds like a lot of dusting.'

I knew I sounded like an imbecile. My theory was that if I appeared absurd this would relax my interviewees and make them less inhibited about showing their own absurdities.

'Dusting them is actually one of my joys,' he said. 'I used to let my wife and my good-for-nothing son help with the dusting, but I found they simply didn't dust to the standard I require.'

'So would you say beer can collecting is a hobby in which the whole family can become involved?'

'Not if they're like *my* family. My son's been a great disappointment to me, and my wife, well . . . She made me take my collection out of the house. She said I cared more about the collection than I did about her. Perhaps she understands me better than I think she does. As you know, I now keep it at a secret location.'

'I'd really like to see it,' I said.

'So would a lot of people. But let's not walk before we can run, eh? Ask me some more questions and I'll see if you're the sort of person I want to show my collection to.'

I did my best to be winning.

'Which are your favourite cans in the collection?'

'One loves them all, of course. One is reluctant to have favourites because that means that one has to like some others less, but naturally some stand out from the crowd.

'One relishes age, I suppose. The canning of beer is a comparatively recent phenomenon. It began in the 1930s, and I have some fine examples from the very early days; British cone tops such as Barclay's Export, Britannia Lager, Felinfoel, Simonds Coronation Brew, this latter being particularly choice. From the United States I have a Krueger's Cream Ale of 1935, Champagne Velvet, a Goetz Country Club.

'Then there are the rarities like the Gretz Fleet Car series, the so-called "Porno" cans from Denmark, the King Snedley series from Lucky Brewing of San Francisco.

'There are some fine commemorative cans, issued to celebrate all manner of events, the United States bicentenary, World and Trade Fairs, horse races, the completion of New Zealand hydro-electric projects.

'Then there are the oddities, cans made of plastic, cans containing half a yard of ale, cans shaped like barrels, cans with handles, cans in unusual sizes, all manner of curiosities. All human life is there.'

His words were enthusiastic enough, yet he seemed too bloodless a character and his voice was too dry and papery to convey or express real enthusiasm. For my part, I pretended that this non-existent enthusiasm was contagious and that I had caught it and that I was exactly the type of chap to whom he ought to show his collection.

'My wife doesn't comprehend any of this,' he said.

'Wives never do,' I replied.

I don't know why I let that slip out. I'm not given to making generalisations about wives, and certainly not to complete strangers in pubs in Coventry.

'Problem with your wife too?' he asked.

'Not any more. We're separated.'

'You're lucky. Mine won't go.'

I found myself talking about my marriage, how cut up I was, how lonely and empty I felt, how I didn't know what I'd done wrong, etc., etc. After I'd indulged myself for a while I could see him warming to me, and before long he was suggesting that I accompany him to the hide-away where he kept his cans.

Some men rent a retreat in order to have somewhere to take their mistresses in the afternoons. Edwin Rivers rented a bedsit in order to have somewhere to be alone with his beer cans. It was on the third floor of a big Victorian terraced house, paint peeling from the stucco frontage, heaps of split bin sacks lolling outside the front door. We walked up the bare, unswept stairs, past the doors to other bedsits. I could hear TV sets, a country and western record, two people arguing, someone practising Spanish guitar. We came to Edwin's room. He put the key in the lock and opened the door. He reached in and turned on the light.

I could see there were shelves along the walls of the room, made to accommodate the different sizes of beer can. In the centre of the room, at right angles to the walls, were several room-dividers, also with shelves of beer can height. However, there wasn't a beer can to be seen. The shelves were all completely bare and empty.

I turned to Edwin to ask the obvious question, but he was no longer in a position to give me an answer. He had fallen to his knees and there was thick white saliva dribbling from the corners of his mouth.

'They did this,' he said. 'That wife of mine and her good-for-nothing son.'

Slowly he told me his story. When he'd last visited this room, only a couple of days ago, it had been full to bursting with beer cans, every surface packed with cheerful, multi-coloured metal. Someone, apparently someone with a key, since the door hadn't been forced, had come to the room in the last two days and stripped it bare.

Edwin was unable to do anything except remain on his knees on the threshold of the room. I didn't know what to do. I tried to help by knocking on doors and asking the other inhabitants of the house if they knew anything about the collection's disappearance. Naturally they thought I was mad. They found it hard to believe that anyone would keep their prized possessions in a rented room in a place like this. They certainly wouldn't admit to having heard or seen anything suspicious. I didn't call them liars to their faces, but it seemed a little unlikely to me that a person or persons unknown could have moved 13,000 beer cans down three flights of stairs without somebody noticing something.

Edwin, speaking with difficulty, told me he was convinced that his wife and son were behind it. They knew he had a secret hide-away, but he'd never told them where it was. One of them could have followed him to discover its whereabouts, then they could have found a way to make a copy of the key, then hired a van, come to the bedsit and emptied it while Edwin was out of harm's way.

'They'd have to be very vindictive people to want to do that,' I said.

'You haven't met them.'

'I don't think you should jump to conclusions, Edwin. What about the other people in the house?'

'They wouldn't have keys.'

'What about the landlord?'

'What would he want with 13,000 beer cans?'

What would anyone want with 13,000 beer cans, I asked myself, but I suggested to Edwin, 'Maybe he's a rival collector.'

'Beer can collectors are an honest and honourable group of men!' he insisted.

No doubt they were. I helped Edwin to his feet. I asked if he wanted me to call the police. He didn't. He knew they wouldn't want to interfere in a domestic dispute, and if they did they'd only make things worse. In that case I asked if he wanted a drink to steady his nerves, something stronger than tomato juice. He shook his head.

'It would choke me,' he said.

'Why don't we get this sorted out?' I said. 'Why don't I give you a lift home? Why not confront your wife and son, ask them straight out if they're responsible?'

'If I so much as set eyes on either of them I'd try to kill them.'

I didn't think he looked very likely to succeed. He didn't have the build to be a wife and son murderer. Even so, it was probably better if he stayed out of their way for a while. There didn't seem much else for me to do. When I left Edwin he was squatting on the floor of the empty room. He was looking round the bare shelves, his eyes glazed and unfocused, perhaps staring at some ghostly after-image of his precious cans.

I thanked him for at least trying to show me his collection. I told him to look on the bright side. His cans would probably turn up. 13,000 cans couldn't just disappear. I found it hard to stop sounding absurd. I told him he wasn't to hesitate to phone me if he needed someone to talk to.

On the drive home I came to the conclusion that this episode probably wouldn't work as a chapter of my book. I had at first envisaged a photograph of Edwin Rivers, tragically lean and spare, surrounded by a superfluity of beer cans. A picture of Edwin in the middle of that desolate room would be too tragic by half. I didn't want to depress my readers.

In the dressing-room of a Bradford nightclub, Ted Langley prepares himself for the night's performance. He settles down with three buttered slices of date-and-walnut cake and listens over the Tannoy to the audience as it reacts quietly, but favourably, to a charmless girl singer who is making a stab at 'Among My Souvenirs'.

Ted prides himself on being able to read an audience. He's had them all: the good, the bad, the murderous. He's had them all eating out of his hand. He knows how to work them, to get them on his side; but it *is* work. It's always a struggle, even though it's a struggle he wins. He can never go out there and be instantly loved. He wishes he was one of those performers who steps on to a stage and immediately receives waves of love and good will from the audience. Tommy Cooper, Eric Morecombe, Tony Hancock, they received that kind of love. Great performers; all dead, of course. He finds it easy to be generous to dead comedians. It's the live ones he feels less charitable towards.

The dressing-room is a bare, white-walled cube, On the floor, carpet tiles are stained with the traces of previous acts, ground-in make-up, cigarette burns, spilled beer and coffee. It smells of old fried chicken.

There's a knock on the dressing-room door, and before he can shout either 'Come in' or 'Sod off', the door has opened and a young woman in a smart business suit and carrying a brief-case, has walked purposefully into the room. It is Elaine. He knows he isn't lucky enough for her to be a groupy. Maybe she wants an autograph for her crippled mother, daughter or aunt. Maybe, stranger things have happened, she's from a television company. But she soon disabuses him of any such hopes.

'Hello, Mr Langley,' she says, 'I'm conducting a survey into educational resources. I wonder if you'd mind answering a few questions?'

He looks at his watch. There's a good forty minutes before he has to go on. Why not answer her questions? He's nothing better to do. It'll kill some nerves. He agrees. She asks him whether he thinks education is a good thing, and whether it should be accessible to all, and whether the amount of money a person has ought or ought not to be a determining factor in the quality of the education a person gets. He offers her a piece of date-and-walnut cake and a cigarette. She says she wouldn't normally but it's been a long day, a very long day, and he's very sweet and yes she will.

Ted Langley is no fool and soon realises that she's going to try to sell him something. That word 'education' is the giveaway. She may be trying to unload some educational videos, or possibly trying to get him to enrol in a correspondence course; but encyclopedias are the favourite.

'You're flogging a dead horse here,' he says.

She feigns puzzlement.

'Nobody cares about education,' he says. 'It's the wrong approach. Whatever it is you're trying to sell you should be using a different selling point: sex or foreign holidays, or anything except education.'

'Later I say that knowledge is power.'

'That's better,' he says. 'People like a bit of power. But I don't think that's enough.'

'So you don't want a set of encyclopedias?'

'Of course not.'

'Nobody ever does.'

'They wouldn't. People don't care about education or knowledge. All they care about is money, drink, power, like you said, and maybe sex.'

'Do you think I could try selling encyclopedias on the basis that education would help you make more money or have more sex?'

'They wouldn't believe you.'

48

'Some people are a lot cleverer than some other people think they are.'

'Some.'

'I'm really making a mess of this job,' she says, starting to get tearful. 'I got so fed up going from door to door that I decided to try different tactics, approach famous people, people like you. But that's not working either. I only get commission, no wage. I don't know how I'm going to get by.'

Elaine cries. Ted Langley lights a cigarette, cuts himself another slice of date-and-walnut cake. He coats it thickly with butter, getting thick curls of the stuff on his fingers, then licking them off. He makes no response to the girl's tears, neither embarrassment nor sympathy.

'Is crying part of the script too?' he asks.

'It is, actually,' she says, her tears turning off like a tap.

'I bet it works sometimes.'

'Once in a while. Only with the very gullible.'

'Now if you were selling personal computers . . .'

'How's that?'

'I don't know if you're familiar with my act.'

'Oh yes, Mr Langley. I'm a great admirer.'

'All right. All right. Then you realise that I'm known for being a walking encyclopedia of gags. But the gags don't walk with me. They sit in dirty great filing cabinets at home, and every time I need a joke it's like digging for coal. The system works but it's slow, old-fashioned and cumbersome. Now if I could get them all on floppy disc . . .'

'It's funny you should say that, Mr Langley, because as well as encyclopedias I can also sell you a personal computer.'

He can't believe it. An ambush. He should be too smart for this sort of con; but she shows him some leaflets that look very impressive and she tells him, clearly and concisely, what kind of system he'd need in order to do what he wants to do, and it all sounds very, very attractive. She explains the easy low-cost credit system, and within half an hour she has sold him several grands' worth of computer; a comprehensive package that includes keyboard, screen, printer, software, discs, manuals and service plan. He barely has time to sign the forms before he has to go on stage.

He is stunned. He can't help admiring the little bitch, and no doubt the package may turn out to be as state of the art and as user-friendly as she says, but even so, the smoothness and the ruthlessness of the

49

sell has left him breathless and queasy, though that could be because of the financial commitment as well.

He goes on stage.

'A funny thing happened to me in the dressing-room just now,' he says, as his introductory fanfare recedes. 'Somebody just sold me a computer.'

There are a few souls in the audience who actually find this funny, and titter in anticipation of a cracking punchline, but not many, and when, after a minute or two, as he tells the full story of his encounter with the saleswoman, and that punchline is not forthcoming, the audience grows restless, little pools of conversation and hostility break out in parts of the club. Somebody shouts, 'Get on with it, Langley!'

Ted looks offended.

'Truth is stranger than fiction, you know,' he says.

'Yeah, but is it funnier?' shouts the heckler.

The audience laughs. Ted is the only one around here who's allowed to get laughs. This is dangerous territory. Something needs to be done.

'Hey,' Ted says to the heckler, 'if I'd known I was going to do a double act I'd have asked for double the fee.'

It isn't a great heckler stopper but it does the job. Ted snaps back into his professional manner. In less than a minute he is in control again. The walking encyclopedia of comedy soon has the audience in his power.

My initial research into collecting consisted of amassing a vast array of books and magazines on the subject. These tended to be staggeringly general or staggeringly arcane. I put myself on the mailing lists of a lot of booksellers and bought anything that sounded relevant and wasn't too expensive. There was a whole range of books with titles like *What Shall I Collect?* or *Collecting for Fun and Profit on a Budget*, which were designed for people who had it in their heads that they were going to collect something or other but they couldn't decide what. These books were full of helpful suggestions about what you might choose: Valentine cards, railway signs, tin soldiers. They told you how to make a start, advised you about scope and variety, and about investment potential. They contained anecdotes of how people had found priceless items in attics, junk shops and jumble sales. (These stories had something of the urban myth about them.)

There were many suggestions about what the next collecting growth area might be, yet it seemed that by the time anyone had identified a potential growth area it was already too late, prices were already rising and the vultures had gathered. Actually, it was hard to believe there was anything so worthless that somebody somewhere wasn't already collecting it. You name it and somebody had already formed a collection, written a book, become a world authority and cornered the market.

Markets were all-important. There had to be supply and demand before a form of collecting became respectable. There had to be somebody who shared your estimation of whatever it was you were collecting, and agreed it had some worth, otherwise you missed the full joys of the activity.

These joys, the books assured me, consisted of trading, swapping, pooling information, attending auctions, conventions and swapmeets, and savouring all the delights of a shared enthusiasm. Collecting was able to provide a social life, travel, and a chance to wheel and deal, to realise your true self, and to make a pile of money.

Many of the books gave stern advice to be selective. A hoard is not a collection, they warned. Whatever you collected there were notions of high and low quality. Even if it looked like junk there was still a distinction to be drawn between high-quality junk and low-quality junk.

The specialist magazines were bulletins from distant fronts, detailed guides to unknown worlds. The language they used and the shared knowledge and values they assumed were bafflingly alien. It didn't much matter what the magazine was ostensibly about, the attitudes and the feel were the same. They were devastatingly hard on heretics, mockingly dismissive of sceptics. They were full of solemn, hair-splitting articles, endlessly subdividing their subjects until the writer of each article had identified a minute area in which he could be expert and priest.

Then at the back of each magazine were thousands of ads, secret messages from one devotee to another, or trade ads that would help the collector become a pure and true believer.

People might collect anything. Naturally I'd come across model-railway enthusiasts, brass rubbers, collectors of first-day covers, cigarette cards and matchboxes. I knew of people with collections of thimbles, turnip watches, cricket scorecards, pot lids, paperback editions of Agatha Christie in all languages. But these were too tame by half. I preferred the individuals who went for sunglasses, padlocks, slogan tee-shirts, religious bric-à-brac, barbed wire, primitive percussion instruments, ballpoint pens and condoms.

Of course, I knew of the Opie Collection of wrappers and packaging, the now defunct Bakelite Museum in Greenwich. I had learned of a museum of erotic postcards in Herefordshire, a collection of dog collars (for dogs, not the clergy) at Leeds Castle, the National Collection of Marjoram at a herb farm in Staplehurst, and a man in Ontario who had three thousand toy figurines of Mickey Mouse.

My budget, not to say my sanity, wouldn't run to travelling round the world to meet all these people and see all these collections, but I regarded it all as good background. The foreground, however, still seemed evasive and out of focus.

As ever, fame reared its head and would put a premium on any item. A satin jacket from an early Beatles' tour would be worth a few hundred pounds, but if you had some way of proving it had been worn by one of the band its price went up tenfold.

There's a story that John Lennon, when on tour with the Beatles in the early 'sixties, had the habit of disappearing into the toilet for an hour at a time, because that was the only way he could get any privacy and do any writing. After one such occasion he emerged with an envelope and two brown paper bags. On the backs of them he'd written what was to become the first story for *A Spaniard in the Works*. He copied the text into an exercise book and gave the envelope and paper bags to a journalist called Don Short, saying, 'Here Don, they're yours. Flog 'em if you ever go broke.'

I was well aware of the trade in literary autographs and manuscripts. I knew that first drafts of major literary works were valuable and I could see that there was some intrinsic worth in a manuscript that the author had actually owned and worked on.

I had even, as a precious adolescent, kept early drafts of all the feverish poems I'd written, believing they showed fascinating insights into the poet's mind and method. But I stopped doing that about the time I started needing to shave every day. Other authors, infinitely better authors than me, obviously hadn't stopped. There was a fine trade in notebooks, letters and laundry lists.

I didn't approve of it, naturally, but I could sort of understand it. Ezra Pound's laundry list, though not exactly a crucial text of modernism, was at least unique to him, written in his own hand, and a helluva lot more personal than a satin tour jacket would have been to one of the Beatles, even if he'd worn it.

I would even have been prepared to admit that I would have quite liked to have something in Thornton McCain's handwriting, preferably something better than a laundry list, something that related to his work. Maybe I was slipping. Maybe I did have some collecting instinct after all.

One of the areas of collecting I found particularly objectionable, and I knew I had strange, personal, psychotic reasons for feeling that way about it, was advertising ephemera. This mania took many forms. There were all sorts of things you could collect: posters, coasters, mugs, ashtrays, leaflets, enamel signs, seven-foot-high Guinness bottles, anything.

There were, I was given to understand, people who were assembling vast and all-embracing collections of TV commercials. They sat by their sets, their video-recorders primed, ignoring the programmes, waiting for another piece of TV advertising to appear, then be recorded, catalogued and stored away.

I didn't like advertising at the best of times. I didn't like it for all those liberal anti-manipulation reasons why I'm sure you don't like it either. It told lies. It didn't do anything except sell stuff. It wasn't 'creative' in itself yet it chewed up a lot of people's creativity. I was a bit repelled that anybody should be stockpiling these messages, these commands to buy and consume.

I also found it oddly disturbing to think that Rachel and her creative department might even now, fuelled by spritzers and cocaine, be writing scripts, devising campaigns, looking at story boards, that would be unleashed on a public, at least some of whom would cherish and collect the stuff. Call me small-minded, but I didn't like the idea of Rachel having a place in posterity.

Even on the phone, Victoria Havergal's husband sounded like a big man. His voice was deep and expansive, perhaps with a touch of Irish raconteur, warm, confident, moneyed. He was unsurprised that I wanted to interview him about his car collection. I could come any time I liked, but actually fixing a date proved difficult. He was a man with a lot of pressing business. Eventually we set a date for my visit, a weekday afternoon when both he and his wife would be at home.

At that time I'd heard nothing about the various sexual high jinx that had been offered to Mike Gombrich and to Jim. I don't know if I'd have been deterred or not. Since my split from Rachel it seemed to me that sex was something that happened to other people. However rich the sexual buffet, I couldn't see anyone handing me a plate and telling me to help myself.

I'm sure that people give out a signal, perhaps like radio or perhaps like semaphore, that conveys all sorts of information about the present state of their libido and sex life. It tells whether they're active, fulfilled, inhibited, celibate, or whatever. I suspected that I was sending out a strong, clear signal that said there was nothing doing. So even if I'd been told about the offers likely to be made at the big house, I would still have thought I was immune.

I arrived in mid-afternoon. I had my notebooks and tape-recorder, and a list of questions, at least one of which I thought was a real winner. 'Mr Havergal, it is a cliché to say that a man's personality changes when he gets behind a steering wheel, yet the personality that he adopts is obviously determined by the nature of the car. You have a range of cars, each one different. Do you undergo profound personality changes as you move from one car to another? Doesn't that lead to a multiple-personality disorder?'

I also had a load of mundane questions about when he first started collecting, how much he thought the collection was worth, what his wife thought about it, and so on.

I pulled up outside the house. I couldn't get an answer from either front or back doors. I went down to the swimming-pool but that was smooth and empty, so I tried the hangar where Jim had told me the cars lived. The big sliding doors were open a foot or so but the lights inside were turned off. Enough daylight spilled in for me to see there were some interesting cars in there (if you were interested by cars), but the far corners of the space were dark and impenetrable. I squeezed inside.

'Anybody there?' I called.

'I'm here,' a woman's young, plummy voice said quietly from the darkness.

'I'm here to do an interview with Mr Havergal.'

'My husband had to pop out.'

'I could come back later.'

'He won't be long.'

54

'I'll wait then.'

Standing quietly in the darkness, speaking to an invisible woman, made me feel very uncomfortable. I thought talking might help.

'He's got a very nice collection of cars, what I can see of them.'

'He likes them, anyway.'

'Meaning that you don't.'

'Did I say that?'

As we talked I moved deeper into the building, following the direction of the voice. Our words rattled around the metal of the walls and roof, and bounced up from the concrete floor. Eventually I was standing quite close to the voice, and as my eyes got used to the darkness I could just see that the woman I was talking to was seated sideways across the front seats of an open sportscar, her bare legs hooked over the passenger's door, her head resting on the driver's.

She said, 'It's very peaceful in here.'

'I suppose it is.'

'Watch this.'

She apparently had one of those automatic garage-door controls in her hand. She pressed it, and behind me the metal doors slid shut. If I'd thought it was dark before I now knew what real darkness was like. I couldn't see anything of the walls, the cars or the woman.

'Isn't that peaceful?' she said.

'It's dark, anyway.'

I heard her giggle. It was a giggle that managed simultaneously to sound girlish, cantankerous and seductive, not that I knew anything about being seduced by cantankerous girls.

'Do you like this any better?'

She switched on the headlights of the sportscar. They hit me full on, blinding me and illuminating me.

'You look like a startled rabbit.'

'Isn't this what everybody looks like when they're caught in headlights?'

'Maybe. Look behind you.'

I turned and saw a shadow version of myself cast on the corrugations of the far metal wall. She flicked the lights back and forth between dipped and full beam so that my shadow did a jerky dance.

'My husband hates me wasting his battery.'

She switched off the lights. We were drenched in gloom again, but now my eyes were full of yellow and white fireworks, after-images from the glare.

'So you're writing a book about people who collect things.'

'That's right.'

'I collect things.'

'Yes?'

'I collect people.'

I'd heard other people say that. I thought it was an absurd expression. I was planning to make a few barbed remarks about it in my book.

'Well, lovers really,' she said.

'Sounds more interesting than paperback editions of Agatha Christie in all languages.'

'Yes.'

Then she giggled again. I could hear her rustling around in the car seat. There was another sudden blare of light, but smaller and less vicious than the headlights. I saw that she was holding an inspection lamp now. She held it at arm's length and moved it in an arc so that the shadows kept sweeping in new directions. She drew her legs into the car and sat up in the driver's seat. I couldn't be sure, given the unreliability of the lighting conditions, but I got the distinct impression she was naked.

She clipped the inspection lamp to the top of the windscreen and said, 'Would you come over here and give me a hand?'

I moved gingerly towards her, becoming certain on the way that she was indeed naked.

'What do you need a hand with?' I asked.

She didn't say anything, but she took my hand and pressed it against her bare left breast. I was feeling a little giddy by now. Men of my age, class and background generally don't come across naked women in sportscars who want to have their breasts felt. My life experience hadn't prepared me for this kind of thing.

I took the breast gratefully and kneaded it with what I took to be reasonable skill. Certainly I felt the nipple hardening, so I wasn't being completely inept. She then unfastened my trousers. She took my penis in her hands, tweaked it a little, then took it to her face, rubbing it over her cheeks, chin and neck as though it was some kind of fleshy electric razor. It did, however, lack the steeliness and essential usability of an electric razor, in fact it stayed as limp and as useless as a soft watch, though not so surreal.

I tried to busy myself around her body – not easy given that

56

she was in the car and I wasn't – thinking my limpness might disappear if I thought about something else, but as with dalmations so with limpness and, busy though I certainly was, the erection wouldn't come. I was about to give it one more try before calling it a day, when all our enterprise was brought to a very abrupt halt as the overhead lights came on. I felt not so much like a startled rabbit as like one of those dreamers who suddenly finds himself making love in public, on stage, in front of an audience. This stage was not too public, and the audience was limited to one spectator, and this wasn't a dream, and the spectator didn't seem very pleased with what he'd seen. It was, of course, Victoria Havergal's husband, every bit as big as he'd sounded on the phone; huge, tanned, cropped grey hair, a heavy cube for a body, a smaller but equally weighty cube for a head. And he was furious.

'This is no bloody good,' he yelled.

The voice was angry and booming, yet that seemed a comparatively mild declaration for a husband who had caught his wife naked with another man. I fastened up my trousers, my haste making my fingers thick and useless. I was prepared to run, but I was also prepared to take the beating I might have coming to me.

'If you can't shit, then get off the pot!' he bawled.

It was then that it occurred to me that since no door to the building had been suddenly opened, he must have been in there from the beginning, watching proceedings by the light of the inspection lamp. I felt suddenly rather glad that I hadn't been able to perform, but it was very unsettling to realise that his wrath was caused not because I had tried to have sex with his wife, but because I'd *failed* to have sex with his wife.

'If you want to come here and fuck my wife that's one thing, but if you do then you have an obligation to make a decent job of it, otherwise piss off and stop wasting everybody's time.'

'I wanted to come here and do an interview with you, if you must know.'

'God,' he said, 'why do I have to deal with such unimaginative people? It's a perfectly simple idea. You pump Victoria, making a decent job of it, then as soon as you've finished I burst in, pull you off and take over. Doesn't sound like such a complex idea, does it? But all you want is a bloody interview. Now you've gone and ballsed-up everything.'

57

'*I*'ve ballsed–up everything?'

I thought for a moment of adopting a tone of high dudgeon and offended principle, but no, it wouldn't have suited me. I gathered up my bags and my tape-recorder and sloped out of the hangar, looking, I imagined, like an ashamed puppy. The husband's anger showed no great signs of abating, but it seemed self-contained and I realised he wasn't going to attack me. I walked past him on the way out, rigorously avoiding eye contact.

I had to struggle to get the sliding doors open. I went to my car, trying not to break into a frightened run. I felt in my trouser pocket for my car keys, and I realised, with a kind of cold, amused horror, that they must have fallen out on to the concrete floor while my trousers were unfastened. I was contemplating leaving my car and going home on foot when Victoria came running up to the car jangling my keys. She was no longer naked, and now that I saw her in daylight I discovered that I found her very attractive.

'Your keys,' she said. 'I'm sorry you couldn't get an erection.'

'I don't know if I am or not,' I replied.

She looked puzzled but I couldn't be bothered to explain.

'As a matter of fact,' I said, 'I've never had that happen to me before.'

I meant that I'd never been unable to summon an erection when I'd wanted one, though it might equally have applied to the whole or any part of the scenario.

'Don't worry,' she said. 'It happens to me all the time.'

I could believe it.

'Let's meet again,' she said. 'Soon.'

I grunted something non-committal and went home. It hadn't been an exactly profitable afternoon; sexual humiliation, a waste of petrol and no interview. Still, it was better than sitting in my room pretending to be a writer.

'All right,' said Jim, 'test me.'

'All right,' I said. 'Go ahead.'

He began.

'Egbert, Ethelwulf, Ethelbald, Ethelbert, Ethelred, Alfred, Edward the Elder, Athelstan, Edmund, Eadwig, Edgar, Edward the

58

Martyr, Ethelred the Unready, Edmund Ironside, Canute, Harold I, Hardicanute, Edward the Confessor, Harold II, William I.'

'Very good,' I said. 'But you missed Eadred.'

'Damn and blast.'

'Even so, it's still very good.'

'Very good isn't good enough. And I've hardly started on the dates.'

'You've got to walk before you can run.'

'I've got my first public appearance in less than a week you know.'

I knew only too well. Jim's first public appearance seemed modest enough; the first round of a quiz taking place in a local pub called the Bricklayers' Arms, to find after many rounds, both of the quiz and of drinks, the Brain of the Bricklayers'. Jim was taking the contest with the utmost seriousness, so much so that we had abandoned our weekly outing to the pub and instead I was helping him to do some cramming.

'You *are* going to be there, aren't you?' he said.

'I wouldn't miss it for the world.'

I meant it.

'All right,' Jim said, 'give me ten minutes with the dates, then test me again.'

I passed the time by flicking through volumes of *The Books of Power*. My belief that they would sit in a dusty corner of Jim's mobile home had proved totally incorrect. In fact they occupied pride of place, set on the dining table in the centre of the living-room, accommodated in their custom-made melamine bookcase. There were eighteen volumes, each alarmingly thin, together scarcely occupying a foot and a half of shelf space. Their bindings were as gaudy as the colours of exotic ice-cream, each one different; strawberry, lime green, peach, chocolate. Embossed down each spine was the volume number along with one letter of the title. Thus volume one had a 'T' on it, volume two an 'H', volume three an 'E', and so on to spell out *The Books of Power*. Volumes four, ten and thirteen remained blank to provide spaces between the words.

I pulled out volume five and riffled through it. My eyes were bombarded with ham-fisted drawings, maps and diagrams, in colours as lurid as the bindings. There were some out-of-register photographs of Edinburgh, Edward Elgar and T. S. Eliot. My eyes fell on the entry for 'England'. I was a little surprised to find it in this volume rather than under 'Great Britain', and I wouldn't have expected to find it illustrated by pictures of John Mills, a steam-roller, the 1966 World Cup team and a Bakewell tart. I decided to read it from beginning to end. It didn't take very long.

England swings like a pendulum do. There'll always be one. England, anybody's England. There is some corner of a foreign field that is for ever it, but what do they know of it who only it know? England expects. It is a happy land. Oh to be in it.

Beefeaters, ravens, the bloody tower.

Richard III had a hump (1483–5).

Elizabeth I was a virgin.

Alfred burned the cakes.

Richard I had a heart like a lion.

Much of this is conjecture.

Raleigh and his bowls. Shakespeare and his Globe. Nell Gwyn and her oranges.

A sense of history: the castles and stately homes, the coaching inns, the cruck houses, the deck-access tower blocks.

The culture: bawdy Chaucer, romantic Keats, marvellous Chatterton, so-so Colley Cibber. Music: Elgar (1857–1934). The visual arts: one in the eye for the British public – Henry Moore and David Hockney.

Some important dates: 1066, 1914, 1952.

The food: the sandwich, sirloin and pease pudding, spotted dick and custard, fish and chips, cakes and ale.

Entertainment: once the English made their own – Morris dancers, the maypole, pearly kings and queens. More recently the Sex Pistols and Tim Rice.

English comedy: *Every Man In His Humour, Punch,* pantomime, *Carry On* films, Whitehall farce, Ted Langley (oh God help us).

Two famous acts: Toleration. Settlement.

One famous bill: Reform.

Three unsung Prime Ministers with titles: the Earl of Wilmington, Viscount Goderick, Baron Grenville.

One famous English vice: *le vice anglais.*

World War One: trenches, appalling casualties but some damn fine poetry.

World War Two: the blitz, sleeping in the Underground, VE Day – dancing in the streets. The GIs, over here and all over everybody.

The climate: worth talking about.

Ethnic mix: the Celts, the Picts, the Danes, the Saxons, the Romans, the Normans (not in that order). Today: racial harmony – the Tykes, the Geordies, the Cockneys, the Kentish men and the men of Kent. You can be any colour you like so long as it's not black.

The landscape: green and pleasant.

The clothes they wore: the Wellington boot, Nottingham lace, cloth caps, moleskin trousers, clogs. *See* BRUMMEL Beau.

Some lovable rogues: Cromwell, Jack the Ripper, Guy Fawkes, Dr Crippen, Ronald Biggs, Christopher Marlowe (1564–93), Mary Queen of Scots.

Sport: cricket, soccer, darts, snooker, rugby, jolly hockey sticks. How English can you get?

The English character: reserved. Except at pantomimes, football matches, wedding receptions, in pubs and clubs, on picket lines, at New Year sales, at the bingo, at the seaside, on coach parties.

Some English types: jolly jack tars, men in bowler hats, middle-aged women who go shopping in fluffy carpet slippers, butlers, yokels, dour northerners, laughing policemen, cheery postmen, cheeky kids. (All these are dying breeds.)

Henry VIII: fond of changing wives and religions. He had his reasons. Who can blame him? He looked not unlike Charles Laughton.

An Englishman's home, a stiff upper lip, backbone, a sense of fair play, the Dunkirk spirit, a heart in the right place.

The Armada, the Crusades, the Opium Wars. Who were the real winners? The strains of Empire. The loss of America. Lawrence of Arabia: a rum sort of cove.

Some great cities: Bristol, Liverpool, Manchester.

Some hell-holes: Pontefract, Blackburn, Stevenage, Tamworth.

Some weighty topics we shall not be dealing with here: feudalism, the Black Death, the British Constitution, Lollardry, the Star Chamber.

Some famous English obsessions: Ireland, public schools, contempt for the French.

Democracy: suffragettes chained to railings, that woman who threw herself under that horse.

A tradition of radicalism: Wat Tyler, the Luddites, the Peterloo Massacre, the Tolpuddle Martyrs.

Two famous revolutions: the Agrarian. The Industrial.

England gave us the English language, and her television isn't as bad as it might be.

She has much to be proud of.

I looked over at Jim who at that moment had his eyes closed in concentration.

'Is this meant to be a joke?' I said. 'This is gibberish.'

He opened his eyes and looked at me as though he couldn't possibly imagine what I was referring to.

'This entry here for England,' I said, 'it's just garbled nonsense. You're going to have a hard time learning anything from this.'

Now he looked wounded.

'What's wrong with most encyclopedias', he said, 'is that they present information in a dry-as-dust manner. No more! *The Books of Power* change all that and make learning simple and fun. Learning no longer becomes the province of the bookish academic. Thanks to *The Books of Power*, education has life and colour, broad sweeps of fact accompanied by local impressionistic detail.'

'Impressionistic it certainly is,' I said.

'Anyway,' said Jim, 'leave me alone until I've learned these dates.'

Admittedly the dates in the 'England' entry had seemed accurate enough on the few occasions when they appeared, and certainly Jim's list of kings had been perfectly sound, but I still had my doubts about *The Books of Power* as things you might learn anything from.

I turned to another volume and looked up 'Collecting'. There was no such entry, though there were a few mordant comments about 'The Collective Unconscious'. Then I looked up 'The Middle East'. It read, 'I don't understand what's going on in the Middle East. Frankly I don't think anyone does.' That was all *The Books of Power* had to say about the Middle East. Conciseness and honesty are no doubt things to be prized in a reference work, but this was a little severe. Then I looked up 'The Novel'.

THE NOVEL
Don Quixote, *Moby Dick*, *War and Peace*, *Ulysses*; these are the great novels. I haven't read any of them. Probably you haven't either.

Lately, they say, novels have been about the collapse of narrative, discontinuity and linguistic decay. Oh really? You try telling that to Jackie Collins.

Your standard novel is about 80,000 words long. In other words, if you wrote a thousand words a day, every day for a year, you'd have written 365,000 words, i.e. about four and a half novels. Any damn fool can sit down and manage to write a thousand words a day. Ergo writing novels is, as the English say, a piece of piss. Why don't you try it?

Rasselas – that's a good read.

I was smirking over this in a superior sort of way when Jim announced that he was ready to be tested on the dates of his kings.

'Egbert 802–39, Ethelwulf 839–58, Ethelbald 858–60, Ethelbert 860–6 . . .'

And so on. He got every one right.

Before I was a full-time writer I always used to say that working was my hobby. Like anyone who becomes a writer, I did the usual round of shit jobs; gallery attendant, gardener, hospital porter. Unlike a lot of aspiring writers I didn't regard work as some terrible affront to my art and dignity. I found it interesting. It was material. I found the jobs a rich source of anecdote. I didn't take them seriously. As soon as I started taking any of them seriously I stopped enjoying them and then I stopped doing them.

The jobs were interspersed with spells on the dole, and when all else failed I went back to working behind a bar. I worked in all sorts of places, from the seediest of pubs to some quite glossy hotels. Then I made up my mind that if I was going to have to do this kind of work from time to time I might at least try to make life more comfortable for myself. So I decided to learn how to make cocktails. It was a frivolous decision. Once I'd learned I thought I'd get a job in some ritzy watering-hole where drinks were expensive and people might leave tips. I wasn't aiming for the Savoy but I was aiming higher than the spit and sawdust local.

I spent a couple of weeks with books out of the public library learning the recipes for the basic Martinis, Manhattans, Slings, Sidecars, Screwdrivers et al. And I learned a few exotics – the Hawaiian Daisy, the Aberdeen Angus and the Orange Posset. I even committed to memory a few that were so weird I hoped I was never going to be called upon to make them: the Scandinavian Glogg, the Rum Fustian and the Irish Cow.

My knowledge was entirely theoretical. Though I'd learned how to make these drinks, I'd never actually done it. I couldn't have afforded to fill my bedsit with kümmel, parfait amour and guava nectar even if I'd wanted to.

But it worked. My studies paid off. I got a job in a cocktail bar in Covent Garden, called the Gold Cadillac (which I also happened to know was the name of a drink made from crème de cacao, galliano and cream). My knowledge was well in excess of requirements. Each table in the bar had a menu of about a dozen cocktails on it, and most of the customers stuck to those, but I think it gave the management a feeling of security to know that one of the barmen could rustle up a Newton Apple Cocktail, should the need arise.

It wasn't a bad job. I thought I looked quite the part in my white shirt and black bow-tie, with a towel over my arm and a shaker in my hands. The customers were okay, the same combination of all-right people and complete shits, and in roughly the same proportions, that I'd met in every other job I'd ever done. That was how I met Rachel. She was a regular in the bar, and at the time I thought she was one of the all-right people, but that opinion comes in for constant revision.

She used to come in after work with a group of people from the agency, and I talked to her and the others in my best, cheery barman

63

manner. I never saw her as the girl of my dreams, much less as a potential spouse, but she was an attractive and friendly face. She was easy to talk to. Then one night she came in alone. That wasn't so unusual. This was London in a liberated age. She told me she'd had the worst day of her working life, and would I mix her a drink that would speed the onset of oblivion. Six Schussboomer's Delights later we were the very best of friends, and the old magnetism or electricity or chemistry was flowing. The bar wasn't busy and we talked a lot, telling each other highly edited versions of our life stories. I could tell she was relieved I wasn't 'just' a barman. It was the start of something big, if you could call my marriage big.

Later that night we went to bed together. We liked it. We became regular, then permanent, lovers. I continued to work in the bar. My writing wasn't going very well, but that was nothing new, and nevertheless my life seemed good. I had a girlfriend, and a job that I enjoyed. In fact I enjoyed the job so much that I started to take it seriously, and that's probably where I went wrong.

If you work behind a bar you have to put up with bores. The type of bar determines the type of bore. There are the ones who are boring about football, the ones who bore you by telling you jokes. There are the beer bores and the whisky bores and the wine bores. And there are the people who tell you your beer's off or you're giving short measure. It's an irritation but you know it goes with the job so you try not to let it get to you. However, the man behind the cocktail bar finds himself on the receiving end of more boredom and complaints than it's right to expect anyone to tolerate.

You get people who order something disgusting with crème de menthe and Benedictine, drink half of it, then complain that it's disgusting. You get the ones who come in and demand a drink with some outlandish name you've never heard of. You say you've never heard of it. They laugh derisively, ask how you can call yourself a barman if you don't know *that*, then you discover they don't know what it is either but they heard the name in an old Rita Hayworth film. Then there are those who order an apparently simple drink, like a Bloody Mary, and when you've made it they tell you that a *real* Bloody Mary has to be made with Zubrovka, the way the Cossacks drink it.

Mostly I could cope with it, but one day when I was taking things particularly seriously I suddenly *couldn't* cope any more.

As soon as the bar opened a couple came in. He was old enough to be her father, if not her grandfather. He looked as though he must have spent a good few decades slouching from one cocktail bar to another. I took an instant dislike to him, but the girl obviously adored him and he was certainly out to impress her.

They took seats at the bar and he said to me, 'I *think* I'd like a Dry Martini.'

'Aren't you sure?' I asked.

'Frankly, no. I mean that it all depends on how it's made and who's doing the making.'

I knew that there was a fair bit of mystique about the Martini, about the ratio of gin to vermouth, what kind of gin to use, whether to shake it (the wisdom is that you don't because shaking bruises the gin, but this strikes me as absurd – gin is robust, unbruisable stuff in my experience), whether to chill the glasses, whether to use orange or Angostura bitters, etc etc. It's a subject you can get very boring about.

'I'm the one going to be making it,' I said.

He looked me over.

'You'll do,' he said.

'And I'll make it any way you tell me to make it.'

'Where's the sport in that?' he said. 'No, you make us two Dry Martinis your way and I'll tell you if you've done it right.'

I shrugged. I made two Dry Martinis in the recommended house style. I took a glass pitcher, half-filled it with ice, added four parts gin to one part vermouth, added four drops of Angostura bitters, stirred it well, then strained the drinks into two cocktail glasses. I put an olive in each, then presented them. The man looked at the drink, took a sip. He didn't appear to like what he tasted but he downed the drink in two swallows and said, 'That wasn't the worst Dry Martini I've ever tasted, but it was close.'

He slapped some money down on the bar in payment.

'If it was so bad,' I said, 'don't pay for it.'

'I believe in paying for what I drink however bad it is.'

I expected him to get up and walk out, but he ordered another two Dry Martinis. The girl had barely touched her first.

'And this time,' he said, 'no olives, no bitters, stir it in the glass, make the proportions seven to one, make sure the vermouth is Noilly Prat, and maybe then you'll be getting close.'

'Are you sure you can trust me?' I said.

'Sure. It's child's play. Just do it the way I tell you. By the end of the evening you'll have got the hang of it.'

It was a long evening. In between serving the other customers

I made a series of variations on the Martini theme for this guy. I became familiar with the Naked Martini, the Trinity, the de Luxe, the Gibson, the Perfect, the Gordon, the Somerset and the Queen. We could have had the International but I was clean out of absinthe. I was initiated into the mysteries of the vermouth rinse and the vermouth spray, and told of barmen who merely *show* the vermouth to the gin. I was lectured on the significance of bitters, the twist of lemon peel and the cocktail onion.

I had to admit, reluctantly, that he knew a thing or two about Martinis, and all night he kept up a stream of anecdotes about Martinis he'd had throughout his life, in Raffles Hotel, in Harry's Bar, at the Café Royal with Ernest Hemingway. His girlfriend took it all in with damp awe.

I suppose it could all have been thought of as colourful and interesting, but I didn't think of it that way. I hated the bastard. I couldn't stand his arrogance and superciliousness. I couldn't understand what sort of kick he could possibly be getting by giving a hard time to some barman he'd never met before. Worst of all, he didn't seem to sense my resentment. I was as icy and as sarcastic as the job would allow, but he didn't notice. I think he thought I was being dry and ironic, and entering into the spirit of the thing. He kept calling me 'old son', and every now and again he'd say grandly, 'We'll make a good bartender of you yet.' Before long I despised him with a murderous passion.

He could hold his drink though. He kept putting away the varying combinations of gin and vermouth, and though he became more garrulous and unbuttoned as the evening wore on, he certainly didn't get drunk or incoherent. Which was a shame. I was hoping he'd keel over in a drunken stupor and crack his head open on the brass foot-rail.

As it got towards closing time I couldn't stand it any longer.

'This next one's on the house,' I said. 'I'll pop down to the cellar and get you something special.'

You'll have guessed. I went down to the cellar, taking a mixing-jug with me, and I pissed in it. I took it back up to the bar and while the guy's attention was elsewhere I made a drink that was two parts piss, one part vermouth, with a hefty squeeze of lemon juice to hide the smell.

He looked at the drink, noticing its yellow colour.

'What is that?' he said. 'Are you using real Dutch geneva or is that yellow Chartreuse?'

'Taste it,' I said. 'Then you tell me.'

He looked at the drink. He sniffed it.

'Aren't you having one yourself?' he asked.

I shook my head. He picked up the drink as though to put it to his mouth, then in one easy, casual movement, tossed it in my face. I smiled. I still had a jug of my piss. I let him have the lot. A mêlée ensued. The man himself was too dignified, or possibly too old, to hit me, but the girl made up for it. She climbed over the bar and started punching me. I wasn't too much of a gentleman to hit back, and after a struggle we fell to the floor, into a pool of melted ice and broken cocktail glasses.

That was the end of my career as a cocktail maker. At the time I thought it was worth losing my job for. Now I'm not so sure. Now I get embarrassed when I think about it, but that doesn't stop me telling people about it. After all, it's a good story.

Elaine knocks briskly on the door of the big house. It is a warm evening. Midges dart and bite under the overhanging trees and around the bushes. The sky is tinged the colour of a cigarette smoker's fingers. She has her brief-case with its sample pages. She has her patter ready. Victoria's husband opens the door. He is an unlikely wearer of Bermuda shorts and Hawaiian shirts. His thickly padded arms and legs, flecked with grey hair, look shockingly naked. He views the prim, well groomed young woman on his doorstep with good humour and without suspicion.

'Don't tell me,' he says. 'You're here to sell us a set of encyclopedias.'

She bursts into well rehearsed tears.

'Hey,' he says, 'things aren't that bad, are they?'

Elaine sniffles and nods her head in a way that suggests they are.

'Then you'd better come in and have a drink.'

He shows her into the conservatory; an elegant, billowing Victorian structure in need of some repair. The slender mullions are warped, and here and there rotten. Some of the panes of glass have spidery cracks through them. Plants grow, but not in any profusion: a powdery old vine, a couple of bay trees, boxes of unflowering orchids. But there are rattan chairs, an antique wind-up gramophone and a fridge for wine, all of which work perfectly.

'It's been a really bad day,' she says. 'Sorry.'

'No problem. Have a drink.'

'I shouldn't, but I will. Thank you.'

'Sit down.'

She sits on one of the chairs, rather nervously and stiffly on its edge, her brief-case held squarely across her lap.

'I've never met an encyclopedia-seller before,' he says as he hands her a big glass of Muscadet, frosted with cold. 'Tell me about it.'

'There's really not much to tell,' her tears stopping. 'I go around knocking on doors. I pretend I'm doing a survey. I ask a lot of lame questions about education, and the idea is that the questions lead you logically and inexorably to the conclusion that you need a set of encyclopedias.'

'They must be great questions.'

'No. They're very lame questions, and everybody can see through them, well perhaps not everybody, but anyone with a grain of intelligence.'

'How long have you been doing it?'

'Too long.'

'How many have you sold?'

'Not many. I wouldn't mind, but they're really good encyclopedias. They're terrific if you've got kids.'

'We haven't.'

'Or even for everyday reference.'

'Spare me,' he says.

'Sorry.'

Victoria saunters into the conservatory. She shows no surprise at finding her husband talking to an unknown woman. She pours herself a glass of wine. She winds up the gramophone and sets the needle down on the brittle, black seventy-eight. A brassy Charleston rattles through the horn. Victoria drapes herself around a spare chair and looks at the sunset.

'So do you get a wage or is it all commission?' her husband continues.

'All commission. I haven't made anything this week. I've only worn out my shoes.'

He looks at her shoes. They don't appear to be very worn.

'So how will you live?'

Elaine shrugs. She tries to look endearing, brave, helpless. She thinks she's getting a generous amount of sympathy here.

'Victoria, haven't you ever thought of having a set of encyclopedias?'

'No,' she says.

'I could show you a few sample pages,' Elaine says, snapping open her brief-case and reaching her hand inside.

'No, I trust you,' Victoria's husband says. 'I suppose the one good thing about your job is that you get to meet a lot of people.'

'Well, I try to sell them encyclopedias. That isn't quite the same thing as meeting them.'

'But even so, you see how they live. You go into their homes. You get to talk to them.'

'Well, yes.'

'I bet you meet some real eccentrics.'

'Not really, no.'

'You see, Victoria and I collect people. People are so interesting and so different and varied. Of course we don't own them and keep them, not like collecting butterflies, but we do like to make contact with new and different people.'

'Right,' she says. 'I know what you mean.'

'Do you? Good. How much do you want to sell us a set of encyclopedias?'

'Very much indeed, but I wouldn't want to sell you a set unless you really wanted one. I wouldn't want you to take it out of sympathy for me.'

'Let me put it another way. What are you prepared to do in order to sell a set?'

Elaine doesn't quite know what he's getting at, though she suspects that she might, though she hopes that she doesn't.

'I don't know exactly,' she says.

'Would you be prepared to sleep with us?'

Her soft features harden. Her molars lock to show a sinewy, angry jaw-line.

'I'll pretend I didn't hear that,' she says.

'But you did hear it. Let's not deceive ourselves. You're cordially invited to have a little sexual romp with us. Why not? We're pleasant people. We'd take the appropriate precautions. I'm sure you'd enjoy it. And then we'd buy a set of encyclopedias.'

She sits prissily upright on her chair, as though her skeleton has suddenly become extra rigid.

'These aren't any old encyclopedias I'm selling,' she says. 'These are *The Books of Power*.'

She pauses as though this should mean something to them. It doesn't.

'They're a rich and noble work of scholarship. What you're suggesting is low and disgusting and, frankly, people like you shouldn't be allowed to have access to works like this even if you wanted it. You're not worthy.'

Elaine closes her brief-case. She stands up. She turns her back on the Havergals and lunges out of the conservatory, into the garden and down the long driveway. The conservatory rattles with surprised, mocking laughter.

'Ah well,' says Victoria, 'I've always felt a little unworthy.'

Mike Gombrich parks his newly repaired Corvette in a lay-by on the A636. It is an unlovely spot but that doesn't concern him. He has some thinking to do. He knows that isn't going to be easy. He was once quite good at thinking but over the last few years he's deliberately weaned himself off the habit. Buying and selling has become pure instinct rather than reasoning; and all the other things he might once have thought about – politics, religion, art – have been banished from the usable bit of his mind. There was a time, and he's made damn sure that none of his current circle are aware of the fact, when a new issue of the *Times Literary Supplement* or the *New York Review of Books* might have sent him into a frenzy of cerebration, note-taking and checking of references. It was a long time ago. He's deeply grateful that all that's behind him now. But even so, however much you fight against it, a time comes when a man has to do some serious thinking, and he's finding it torture to get back into the groove.

He breaks himself in gently by thinking about his car. It looks fine now, as good as ever, and so it should. He had to pull in a number of favours to get the job done quickly and to the right standard. Nobody would ever know it had been vandalised, but *he* knows of course, and he still feels the car is sullied. Perhaps that's how some husbands feel when they know their wife's slept with somebody else; but he doesn't want to think about that, not yet.

He's fitted a supposedly impregnable alarm system to his car, locking wheel-nuts, an immobilisation device, but he realises that all the technology in the world can't stand in the way of some little

70

twat with a Stanley knife. Why can't somebody invent a force field to surround your car when you leave it? The field would lie, say, two inches from the surface of the car, and would form an invisible, impenetrable barrier. It would stop people reversing into you as well. If you were feeling particularly evil you might turn up the field and give an electric shock to any invader, the seriousness of the shock somehow being linked to the strength of the attack.

Or failing that, how about a mind-control device? You'd turn it on when you parked your car and it would pump out harmless but irresistible hypnotic beams, chasing all thoughts of autotheft out of approaching criminal minds. Again you might be able to turn up the power and make the villain turn himself in, or start a religious conversion, or mutilate himself and jump off a high building.

Mike Gombrich realises that he might be less paranoid, and his car less likely to be assaulted, if he drove a battered old Talbot or Escort van or Land-Rover, and increasingly he wouldn't be averse to the idea; but mostly he drives a flash car as a rolling advertisement for Killer Kars, and paranoia is part of the agreement. The car is also a great asset when it comes to pulling birds.

There has been no shortage of women in Mike Gombrich's life, not since he changed course, started the successful business and acquired the trappings that go with it: the car, the flat, the clothes, the video, the cameras, the stereo, the sun-tan, the antique bed. Most of these are not paid for but the girls don't know that, and even if they did he doesn't think it would make any difference. He knows what girls like. A certain *sort* of girl, he admits, but after all we live in a material world.

But Victoria didn't need any pulling; and that is what he's really come here to think about. Mike has always liked to think of himself as an erotic adventurer, but it's been brought home to him that he isn't actually very adventurous. He would say that he believes in trying most things once, but he sees now how little he has tried. Of course there are all sorts of things he wouldn't want to try – all the obvious ones that are painful and disgusting, and no doubt a hundred and one other things that people no doubt do but which he can't even imagine, the sort of thing they get up to in London. But a threesome with a beautiful young woman and her husband, free from any trace of queerness, that surely isn't so bad, is surely worth trying.

He has found it necessary to convince himself that such an idea isn't bad because that idea, the fantasy of this sexual liaison with Victoria and spouse, has become overwhelmingly attractive to him.

71

He tries to imagine Victoria's husband. He has to be rich if he can afford to collect cars, and perhaps also to be able to keep Victoria, and presumably he isn't physically repellent or else Victoria wouldn't have married him, though you can never be certain of that. Women marry some unlikely men.

Mike isn't sure how best to approach this business, nor what the next step should be; nothing too crude or direct, perhaps if he could run into the two of them in a restaurant or bar. They'd have a few drinks to lower their inhibitions, one thing would lead to another, and the whole event could happen naturally with some sense of spontaneity. It would be sophisticated and easy. And even if he didn't enjoy it very much at the time, it might be interesting to look back on, and it would definitely be an experience. Mike is all in favour of experience.

Mike likes to ask his girlfriends to give him a little something to remember them by, and when they ask what he suggests a pair of their knickers. Some refuse, but not many.

He has observed that there is no way of predicting which women will wear tiny, lacy, exotic wisps of underwear, and which will wear large, wholesome, frayed passion-killers. It doesn't seem to relate to their personalities or their libidos. Some don't wear any at all, but there are very few in this category. Over the years he has put together an impressive drawerful of used ladies' underwear. It may not have a lot to say about the history of fashion or the nature of female sexuality, but it speaks to him.

Sometimes, in fits of maturity, he thinks he ought to grow up and throw away, or at least stop adding to, his collection; but he's never had the heart. They're great mnemonic devices, and in some cases he'd have forgotten the girls completely if he didn't have the knickers to jog his memory. He wonders what sort Victoria wears. He'll enjoy adding them to his collection whatever they're like. But did he ought to ask for a pair of her husband's as well?

I was in the underground carpark at the local giant Sainsbury's; a wide concrete plateau, cut with thick, square pillars and gradations of grey light. I was going back to my car with a trolley-load of tinned food, white bread, own-brand whisky and lager. It was a weekday afternoon and there were lots of spaces in the carpark. I'd parked in the middle of an empty row, well away from any other cars, but while I'd been shopping another car had parked next to mine. This new car had come to rest untidily, slewed diagonally across two spots. It was an Alfa Romeo Spider, but that meant nothing to me then. I had no way of knowing that young women in sportscars were trying to track me down to underground carparks.

Victoria was sitting in the car, fully dressed this time. The car was as perky, as glossy, as fundamentally unserious as she was. She waved to me and I waved back half-heartedly. I looked around to see if her husband was spectating from some concealed vantage point, not that I was going to give him anything to watch.

'Aren't you domesticated?' she said.

I loaded my groceries into the boot of my car. I couldn't see what was so domesticated about what I was doing. If a person's going to eat he has to go shopping. Going shopping also meant that I didn't have to sit at my desk pretending to write.

'That's me,' I said. 'A real housewife.'

'Don't you have a real wife to do that sort of thing for you?'

'I have a wife but she doesn't do that sort of thing.'

She perked up in anticipation of my describing some novel and exotic domestic arrangement, but all I could say was, 'Separated.'

'No girlfriend?'

'No.'

'No servants?'

'Not even a butler.'

She smiled. I slammed the boot of my car. I opened the driver's door. I was about to get in and drive off, but Victoria had other ideas.

'I've come to take you away from all this,' she said.

'I like it here,' I said, but I could tell she didn't believe me.

Cruising and playing the radio with no particular place to go is normally my idea of a very bad time, but I agreed to take a ride with her. I didn't know why. She drove badly but with great originality. I've always noticed that something protects cosmically bad drivers. They somehow escape the prangs, scrapes and dents that beset the rest of us moderately bad drivers. I told myself to relax.

'I'm sorry about the other day,' she said.

I nodded, avoiding the automatic urge to say, 'Never mind,' or 'Think nothing of it.' I did mind, and I wanted her to think something of it.

'These things happen,' she said.

73

'Not to me.'

We were heading out of town. The houses were getting bigger and less tightly packed. There were more trees and a higher speed limit. She had a clear stretch of empty road. I felt safe for the moment. She accelerated, the engine whined, and I was pushed back in my seat.

'What sort of people do you collect?' I asked.

'Nice ones. That is I try to find nice ones. Sometimes I choose badly. Sometimes there isn't very much choice.'

'And your husband?'

'He collects cars.'

'That's not what I meant.'

'I know that's not what you meant. Sometimes I collect lovers for his benefit. Sometimes I collect them for my own.'

'I don't think I understand your relationship with your husband.'

'I'm sure you would if you thought about it.'

'And I don't think I want to be collected.'

'But you're not sure.'

'I'm sure I don't want to be collected for your husband's benefit.'

'But if it were just for mine?'

'I'd have to think about it,' I said.

'Think about it.'

I tried to think about it as we passed the city boundary and she squirted the car through some tight Peak District bends. I had fleeting impressions of what it might feel like to be 'collected', to be labelled and catalogued and assigned a place in a display cabinet; and this was quickly followed by images of taxidermy – to be fixed in some characteristic 'life-like' pose, stuffed, mounted, given false eyes and a perpetual glassy stare. You can imagine how attractive I found it.

I suppose women who go around asking strangers to sleep with them or with them and their husbands must develop a thick skin. They ought to be used to rejection. Yet as I sat beside her in the car, sensing her enjoyment of the drive, she seemed somehow young and vulnerable, and I had a terrible urge not to hurt her. I'm not kidding you, though perhaps I was kidding myself. Perhaps that was the first indication that, knowing almost nothing about Victoria and not exactly being delighted by what little I'd seen of her habits, I was starting to like her. Even so, I don't think I'd have agreed to sleep with her, start an affair or whatever you want to call it, if it hadn't been for what happened next.

74

She was attempting to overtake a tall, square, baker's van on a blind corner. She pulled out, changed down, and was nearly past the van when another car came chugging round the bend, heading straight for us. She braked very hard. The car swerved and pitched back to the left-hand side of the road. We survived but the sudden braking caused the glove compartment to flip open. Sunglasses, lipsticked tissues, a chocolate-bar wrapper, an empty cigarette packet, two ten pound notes, a tampon and a thick hardback book pitched out on to my lap. The book was Thornton McCain's *The World Seen Through Plexiglass.*

'Thornton McCain,' I said.

'He's a genius,' she said.

In that moment I was hers.

Victoria drove until we came to a little stone-built village. She parked the car and we set off walking out of the village, off the road, along damp, peaty paths until we found ourselves on top of a gentle but exposed moor, where we attempted to make love.

Victoria was the first woman I'd been with since my marriage left me, and though I felt sex ought to be one of those robust skills that didn't evaporate through lack of practice, I still felt rusty. And even if I hadn't felt rusty, this open-air venue, complete with heather, puffballs and sheep droppings was not calculated to help me give of my best, any more than the hangar had been.

Victoria lay down on a particularly sharp and rocky bit of terrain.

'Are you comfortable there?' I asked, thinking she couldn't be.

'It's fine.'

'Isn't it a bit hard?'

'I always enjoy being between a cock and a hard place,' she said.

The place, however, was the only thing that *was* hard. Again, I couldn't get an erection. I tried. Victoria did as well. God knows the spirit was more than willing, and the flesh got all kinds of encouragement, but still nothing happened. We tried for as long as seemed polite and reasonable, then we went back to her car.

'Nice car,' I said.

'I bought it for my husband. He didn't like it.'

That's right, conversation didn't come easily. I didn't know what to say. I resisted the temptation to apologise, but I was certainly sorry about things. I never for a moment thought that Victoria would want to 'work things through'. I expected her to dump me at some inhospitable roadside and drive off into her own world of sportscars and joyous, carefree successful coupling. I was surprised and pleased that she wanted to come home with me. She said she wanted to see where I lived.

I could tell she wasn't impressed by my house, but then who would be? She insulted its design, its furniture, its carpets. 'This is awful. How can people live like this?' I told her it wasn't easy.

We went, after a while, to my bedroom. It was dishevelled and a little rank, and unprepared for sensuality. Victoria insisted that I draw the curtains and make the room as dark as possible. That seemed surprisingly coy of her, but she explained, 'It's so that I don't have to look at that wallpaper.'

We tried again. This time I felt a lot more relaxed and comfortable. I was playing at home, after all. Victoria enjoyed herself, and I think I had a considerable part in that, and I couldn't say that I had a miserable time either, but I still couldn't get it up. I tried getting angry with it. Victoria tried coaxing. I tried to reason with it. Victoria tried to take it by surprise. Nothing.

Victoria was very sympathetic and seemed neither concerned nor pissed off by the dysfunction. 'It's not a problem,' she said, though I wasn't sure that she meant it, and I wasn't sure that she was right, but I was glad that she said it. It was the right thing to say and it made me like her all the more. In fact I suspected that I already more than liked her.

I was well aware that I shouldn't get involved with somebody when I was 'on the rebound', definitely not someone who was married, and probably it was a bad idea to get involved with someone like Victoria at all, in any circumstances. But damn it all, I liked her, she appeared to like me, she'd made the first move, we had Thornton McCain in common, and even if we weren't exactly good in bed together, we were trying hard. Why shouldn't I have been allowed to feel some affection for her?

We spent the rest of the afternoon and evening in bed, interrupted by trips to the off-licence and the Indian take-away. Occasionally I was haunted by visions of her husband slapping a ladder against the front of the house and climbing up to peer through a crack in the curtains, or smashing his way into the bedroom to tell me I still wasn't doing it right. I couldn't have argued with him.

Whatever Victoria's objections to seeing the walls of my bedroom, she finally turned on a bedside light and (pretentious and/or corny

76

though it sounds) she read to me from *The World Seen Through Plexiglass*.

As I was falling asleep, with her voice and Thornton McCain's words seeping into my head, I asked her if she had to get back to her husband. I was dreaming before she answered.

She was still there in the morning. I woke up and watched her sleeping. The room was warm and musky. Any anticipated complications and disappointments seemed a long way off. But things weren't as they seemed.

There was a knock at the front door. It was a quiet, unassuming knock, and it was the right sort of time for it to be the postman, so I put on my dressing-gown and went breezily downstairs, feeling content and faintly rakish. I opened the door and found that my caller was Victoria's husband. He was no smaller than he'd been before, but he was a lot less imposing. He was no longer loud, and he no longer blustered. He looked profoundly upset. His face was red and bloated, as though he hadn't slept and had been crying. His hands were shaking.

'Is Victoria here?' he asked.

I should have said, 'Victoria who?' but I didn't have the presence of mind, and in any case her car was parked in front of my house.

Instead I said, 'She is, yes.'

'Would you mind if I came in?'

The request was so polite and unassuming that I didn't refuse. He asked if I'd be kind enough to give him a cup of coffee. I led him into the kitchen and put on the kettle.

'Victoria's upstairs,' I said.

'I thought she would be,' he said sadly. 'Do you think I might see her?'

It seemed a reasonable request.

'Of course,' I said. 'I'll go upstairs. I'll get dressed. I'll tell Victoria you're here. She'll probably come down. Help yourself to coffee.'

I returned to the bedroom. Victoria was still sleeping with one long, bare leg hooked outside the sheet. I tried to wake her.

'Your husband's here,' I said.

She was too asleep to hear. I shook her and repeated the news. Then she was instantly awake, and furious.

77

'That's the bloody limit,' she said. 'That really isn't playing the game.'

She got out of bed, very determined, very angry and very naked. She darted past me and went downstairs to give hubby a piece of her mind. Even before she got to the kitchen I could hear her start her tirade.

'Look, you bastard, this simply isn't *on*. You know the rules as well as I do. You don't come barging into someone else's home playing the heavy husband.'

Then the kitchen door slammed and it went very quiet. I dressed very slowly, giving them time to say or do whatever it was that they might think needed doing or saying. I was hoping that any threats or recriminations wouldn't involve me. I even thought of doing a runner. But, after I'd let a decent time elapse, self-respect demanded that I go down to the kitchen and do the manly thing, whatever that might be. Perhaps I would find out when I got there.

I knocked on my own kitchen door, and after a long pause was told that I could enter. Victoria's husband was seated at the kitchen table with two mugs of coffee in front of him. His big elbows were slumped across the table and his arms, shoulders and head formed one continuous, drooping curve. Victoria was standing beside him, stroking his hair and cheeks. He looked at me with wet, canine eyes.

'Look,' I said, 'I don't know what sort of marriage you two have. It strikes me as very strange, and I think really it's probably better if I don't know all the details, and I know it may be a little late for me to say this, but I really don't want to be involved. All right, you might say I'm already involved . . .'

They let me carry on that way for a while, apparently too preoccupied to stop me, but at last Victoria said, 'He's not here about that.'

'Oh,' I said.

'Victoria is a free agent,' he said. 'I'd never interfere in her affairs.'

'Good,' I said, involuntarily.

'I'm here because I needed to see her. I couldn't stand to be alone. I'm afraid I've had a bad night. I haven't slept. I don't suppose I could have some toast?'

I told him he couldn't. All my groceries were still in the boot of my car which was parked at Sainsbury's. He was bitterly disappointed. It was one more damned thing.

'I'd been out for the evening and I got home a little after midnight. I'd had a few drinks, and I have this habit, after a few drinks, of going to visit my cars. I sit in the XK 120 and have a nightcap. I find I do some of my best thinking there. I went into the garage and . . . oh, Jesus!'

Slowly, with much interruption for sobbing and head-shaking, he told me of the scene that confronted him: windscreens smashed, instruments pulled out of dashboards, paintwork scratched and daubed with paint-stripper, tyres and upholstery slashed, engine oil and petrol doused all over the cars.

'I've spent the night in a kind of fever,' he said. 'I was with the police for hours. I made a start, trying to clean up the mess, then I realised I couldn't, just didn't have the heart. And Victoria wasn't there, and it crossed my mind, oh God, how ignoble of me, I thought somehow Victoria might have left me and done this as an act of revenge.'

'You poor thing,' she said.

'I know how ridiculous that sounds, but I was going out of my mind.'

'I was in bed here with Steve the whole time.'

'Thank God for that. Then I thought that *he* might be the culprit.'

He turned to me, his whole presence asking for forgiveness. I felt a little reluctant to forgive someone who was referring to me in the third person.

'I gave you a hard time the other day,' he said. 'I was a fool. Please accept my apologies.'

'All right,' I said.

'Is there really nothing at all in this house that I can eat?'

I searched the cupboards and came up with some old cream crackers. He seemed to find them somewhat infra dig, but he devoured them nevertheless.

It wasn't exactly *déjeuner sur l'herbe*, but I could see how to an outsider it might look like a paintable scene from Bohemian life. There was the naked female model, the large chunk of a man in the centre of the composition vacuuming down his breakfast, and then there was this third figure: me. What part did he have in the picture, standing as he did on the periphery, sketchily drawn, not fully realised?

'I want to know what it means,' Victoria's husband said. 'Is it some act of revenge by an unknown enemy? Is it against me personally? Or is it that some people can't tolerate the existence of beauty, order, creation? Who did it? Who are these people? Anarchists? Nihilists? Or are they simply yobs?'

I didn't offer an answer.

'I'm not saying my collection was perfect,' he continued, 'but it was interesting, it was worthwhile. A lot of time, money and love went into it. If nothing else, it was mine.'

'I'm sorry I never really saw it,' I said.

'And now you never will.'

'But it can be rebuilt,' said Victoria. 'The damage can be repaired. There'll be the insurance money.'

'It will never be the same,' he moaned. 'Never. I don't suppose there's any brandy in the house?'

'No,' I said.

'There's some in the car,' he said, motioning vaguely towards the outside world. 'Would you be good enough to get it for me?'

Like a good servant I went out to his car, a pricey, sober, executive car, and returned with a bottle of brandy. He twisted off the top and poured brandy down his throat. Then he said he had to be going. He was barely in a state to walk, much less drive, so Victoria had to drive him home.

'I'm sorry to break up the party,' he said.

Victoria got dressed, then she kissed me gently on the mouth while he watched, then she went to play chauffeuse. She said I'd see her again very soon, and I believed her, not least because she'd left behind her Alfa Romeo Spider, complete with keys.

Jim's appearance at the Bricklayers' Arms wasn't, in the end, a complete disaster, but it came close. I had never expected him to emerge from it covered in glory. He'd only had his precious encyclopedias for a short time, and even if he'd learned everything in every one of them, I still suspected he wouldn't know enough to win a quiz at his local pub. On the other hand, I imagined the questions wouldn't be so very difficult, I thought the competition from the other participants wouldn't be too stiff, and even if everything went totally wrong and he made a complete fool of himself, there wouldn't be too many people there to see it.

The quiz was taking place in the evening of the day which had begun with my opening the door to Victoria's distraught husband. I drove Jim to the Bricklayers' in Victoria's car since I hadn't been to collect my own. If he recognised it he didn't say so. Probably his mind was on other things. On the way there, I tested him on the wives of Henry VIII, British Prime Ministers of this century, and the dates of famous English battles. Of course I didn't know any of these things, but Jim had written out the information on tiny sheets of paper which I had on the dashboard of the car, and checked as he recited from memory. It didn't make driving easy.

The Bricklayers' had made a brave attempt to create a party atmosphere. There were balloons, a length of bunting, and a hand-painted red and yellow sign announcing 'General Knowledge Quiznite'. The bar staff and the customers were less than festive.

Nobody needs to tell me about the miseries of being a barman, but somebody's got to do it. The problem is that the people who end up doing it are always the wrong ones. The people behind the bar at the Bricklayers' were mean, heavily built and tattooed, and (as Ted Langley would probably say) some of the men were just as bad.

We went into the 'Concert Room' where the quiz was to take place. There were two tables set up at the end of the room, each table with three chairs behind it, one for each of the six contestants, and between them was a black, plastic swivel chair for the question-master.

The question-master made himself known. He was something at the local radio station, but not, I thought, anything much. He seemed unsure whether to adopt the manners of a disc-jockey, a headmaster or a KGB interrogator. To be on the safe side he had managed to adopt the least appealing mannerisms of all three, being simultaneously matey, schoolmasterly and sinister.

'Hi,' he said. 'Good to know you. Great to have you aboard, Jim. Sit down over there, give your hair a comb, straighten your tie. I shall be asking the questions. You will answer clearly and concisely and only your first answer will be accepted.'

He told Jim that all contestants were entitled to a free drink, but only after the contest. Jim was jangling with nerves. I put a double whisky into him. He was reluctant to take it, fearing that alcohol might impair his razor-sharp responses, but I convinced him that he might be sharper still if he could stop trembling and twitching. The drink didn't do much good. In fact, long before the quiz started I too had caught Jim's nerves.

The other contestants and a few spectators arrived. The competition looked stronger than I'd anticipated. I wasn't sure what kind of people I'd expected to find taking part in a quiz at the Bricklayers' Arms (bricklayers possibly) but four out of the other five contestants – one woman, three men – looked like serious, bookish know-it-alls. They looked to me like librarians, teachers or civil servants. They looked as though they'd have considerably more general knowledge than Jim, though I knew that looks can be deceptive.

Jim was not at home in such company, but he looked a lot more at home than did the sixth contestant, a young lad in jeans and a ripped tee-shirt held together with anarchy badges. He scarcely looked old enough to be allowed in the pub. He was skinny, punkish, wispy. His face was bland, big-eyed, stunned.

By the time the quiz started the room was full of spectators, far more than I'd expected. A few were noisy and partisan, but I'd have guessed that most were there out of curiosity. The question-master, having donned a lurex jacket, did the introductions, with much forced schoolmasterly humour and with disturbing, sinister overtones. He made continual, deeply inept attempts to put the contestants at their ease.

The first question went to Jim. He gripped the table in front of him as though he wanted to pulverise it. Even before the question was asked his mouth opened and closed, and I could see his tongue darting around his mouth in search of a bit of saliva that might allow him to speak. The question was, 'What was the title of Mel and Kim's first hit single?'

Jim's face froze with disbelief. He was speechless. He shook his head to say that he didn't know, and the question went the round of the librarians, teachers and civil servants, who didn't know either, and finally it went to the skinny kid, who *did* know.

That was essentially the pattern for the rest of the evening. The questions were entirely about pop music, TV comedy, TV soap opera, TV personalities, sport, showbiz and royalty. Neither Henry VIII nor any of his wives got a mention. Jim got two answers right in the course of the quiz. He knew that Stephen King's 'Christine' was a car, and he knew that the 'walking encyclopedia of comedy' was Ted Langley. The know-it-alls got fairly slim pickings too, but the skinny kid seemed to know everything. He answered correctly every question he was asked, picked up endless bonus marks, and strolled in a very easy, unruffled winner.

As the contest progressed I saw Jim's fear and panic disappear, to be replaced by a resigned indifference as it became clear that he was unlikely to be able to answer any questions at all. Then, towards the end of the quiz, he became irritated, restless, and finally began to pulse with anger.

His mood didn't change even when the contest ended. He left his seat and went to claim his free drink at the bar. The question-master was there waiting to be served and he turned to Jim and said, 'Never mind. It's not whether you win or lose.'

Jim said, 'That's a very stupid remark, even by your standards.'

'Sorry I spoke,' the question-master said.

'I'm sorry you spoke too,' Jim came back at him. 'In fact I'm sorry I ever got involved with this travesty.'

'There's no point being a bad loser.'

'I've never been confronted by such stupidity, such banality, such empty-headed Philistine nonsense.'

'What's the matter with you?' the question-master asked, still thinking his mateyness might save the day. 'You swallow a dictionary or something?'

Jim was above being bated.

He continued, 'This contest was advertised as a general-knowledge quiz. To any intelligent person that suggests there'll be questions about history, politics, culture, philosophy and science. All we've had here tonight is a battle to decide which of the six of us has the most puerile mind.'

I thought that was a bit hard on the kid who'd won. I didn't think his mind was necessarily puerile. Just because he seemed to have an encyclopedic (and I make no excuse for using that word) knowledge of popular trivia didn't mean that he didn't know about other things as well. I also thought that if the questions *had* been about history, politics, culture, philosophy and science, Jim might not have fared much better than he had. Nevertheless, I thought Jim was a real hero. He said something he thought needed saying, and he said it well. He was calm, dignified and infinitely superior to his surroundings.

A mean, heavily muscled, tattooed man behind the bar said, 'If you feel that way about it you can forget your free drink.'

Jim smiled sweetly at him.

'I wouldn't use your beer to give a pig an enema,' he said, very loudly and clearly.

I wasn't sure that everybody who heard knew what an enema was, but a lot of people laughed, if not because they understood the insult then because of the beautiful way it was delivered. It was an exit line, in fact, as Jim walked out of the pub, swiftly yet unhurriedly, and without any hint of a flounce.

In the car, as we drove to a different pub, Jim was less heroic and self-assured.

'What a terrible night,' he kept saying.

'I don't know,' I said. 'I wouldn't have missed it for the world.'

'What am I supposed to do? Fill my head with a lot of crap about soap operas and pop groups?'

'Of course not.'

'Maybe I should. Maybe that's the only way I'm going to advance my ambitions.'

'Are these your ambitions to become a TV personality and opener of supermarkets?'

'Partly. Not only that.'

'It wouldn't have advanced your ambitions much even if you'd won.'

'That's true,' he said gloomily. 'And it wouldn't have got me any nearer Elaine, the woman of my dreams.'

'Oh, her.'

He said, 'I started out thinking that if I bought the encyclopedias from her, that would be enough to make her like me. I think it probably did. After all, she nearly agreed to have a drink with me, and she didn't entirely rule out the possibility of seeing me again. But it's not enough.

'As I see it, the only sure way to make her sit up and take notice of me is to absorb all the information in *The Books of Power*, use it to change my life and become a somebody.'

'I don't know, Jim,' I said. 'I really don't know.'

'She's the best thing that's ever happened to me.'

I was tempted to say that was because nothing much had ever happened to him; but I was glad that I didn't.

A couple of days passed and I didn't hear from Victoria. Somehow I hadn't got round to picking up my car from Sainsbury's and I'd taken to driving around in Victoria's Alfa. I had no very good reason for doing this except that I had become gently enamoured of Victoria. I wanted to hear from her, speak to her and see her again, and driving her car was a poor but honest substitute.

The car was rapidly becoming familiar and I drove along moderately to the manner born. I was driving into town. The traffic was heavy and I didn't have much opportunity to play the boy-racer, but as I arrived at a red light a car pulled up beside me, and my first impression was that he wanted to race. He looked as though he'd win. The car was some kind of hot, wicked-looking, black Corvette, but the driver didn't look competitive. He wasn't gunning his engine and sneaking forward, in fact he was waving at me in a cheerful way and gesturing for me to pull over to the side of the road. I didn't recognise him. I didn't know what he could possibly want with me. As a rule I would think it's safer not to pull over to the side of the road to debate with the drivers of hot, wicked-looking cars, nevertheless, when the lights changed I pulled away slowly and parked as soon as I was across the junction. The Corvette pulled in behind me.

We were outside a reproduction furniture shop that had most of its stock out on the pavement: settees, tables and standard lamps set up like a living-room.

In distant retrospect I suppose it ought to have been obvious to me that the man in the car was Mike Gombrich. After all, Jim had spoken about him at length and had certainly mentioned that he drove a rather wild automobile. But even if I'd known who the driver was that wouldn't have helped me to understand the conversation we were about to have.

I stayed in my seat while he got out and came sauntering up to talk to me. It was what I'd have done if the police had stopped me. His manner, though, was not at all police-like. He was trying very hard to be breezy and friendly.

'So you're Victoria's other half,' he said.

I saw no reason to formalise my status with Victoria, so I said, 'You could say that. How did you know?'

'The car.'

'Right.'

'How are you finding it?'

'Takes a bit of getting used to.'

'But it's worth it,' he said.

'I hope so.'

'It's the best present a bloke's ever had.'

'Well, it certainly came as a surprise.'

'You're a lucky man. She's a beauty.'

So far I hadn't been entirely sure whether we were talking about the car or Victoria. I assumed that if I persevered it might become clearer, but it was only when he said, 'She's told me all about you,' that I knew he couldn't be meaning the Alfa.

I didn't know what Victoria had been up to in the last few days, and it didn't seem impossible that she might have been talking about me to this man, though I couldn't imagine what she might have been saying.

'Marriage can be such a strait-jacket,' he said.

'You can say that again.'

'It's good to know that not everybody wants to stay in that strait-jacket.'

'Sure.'

'That's why I admire people like you and Victoria.'

It was at this point that I began to think I was talking to a rich maniac; rich because of his car, maniacal because he wanted to stop a complete stranger and discuss motoring and marriage. However, he clearly didn't regard me as a complete stranger. Perhaps any friend of Victoria's was a friend of his.

'We must get together,' he said. 'Soon.'

'Why not?'

'We'll go out to some ritzy little watering-hole and have a really good time.'

I thought my days of having really good times in ritzy little watering-holes were long past, but I didn't like to spoil his enthusiasm.

'And then,' he said, 'and I know you're the kind of man I can be frank with, then I'd like the pair of you to come back to my place and we'll have that threesome.'

I wondered if the manly thing would have been to punch him in the mouth and threaten to horsewhip him. I couldn't help feeling, in some old-fashioned Toryish way, that sexual manners had gone too far in the wrong direction when unknown men stopped you at traffic lights and invited you and the person you had only ever been to bed with once, and then not very successfully, to a bout of troilism. Fortunately the engine was still running. I slipped the car into gear and started edging into the traffic.

'Must dash now,' I said. 'Interesting talking to you.'

'Hey, can we fix a time and place?'

'I'm fairly busy for the foreseeable future.'

'What's the matter?'

'Nothing's the matter.'

'You act like you're offended. It was your bloody idea, not mine.'

A gap appeared in the traffic. A bus driver flashed his lights and let me in. There was just a hint of tyre squeal as I accelerated away, leaving the maniac standing in the road looking confused and disappointed. I kept looking in my mirror and it was a long time before I was sure that the Corvette wasn't following me.

I continued my research.

In April and May 1988, following the death of Andy Warhol, Sotheby's New York held an auction of his belongings. The English *Daily Telegraph* covered it under 'Social News'.

There were plenty of paintings in the sale, Jasper Johns' 'Screen Piece', 'Sail Boats' by Lichtenstein, a portrait of Warhol by David Hockney; but this was not essentially a sale of fine art. Also in the auction were Indian blankets, movie posters, vending machines, tin toys, a carved wooden alligator, and lots of artwork from the covers of *Stag, Men Only* and *True Action*. It all got a lot of attention and the majority of it sold for well above estimate, but most of the real hysteria was reserved for the cookie jars.

At some time in the 'sixties Warhol had bought a couple of hundred ceramic cookie jars in the shape of Little Red Riding Hood, various black caricatures, policemen and preachers. He bought them for about two dollars each from a company on Second Avenue called Pieces of Time.

Now it may seem bizarre to buy two hundred cookie jars, but this was as nothing compared to the eccentricity, not to say insanity, of the people who bought the jars at Sotheby's auction.

The only people who got to buy them in quantity were a Mr and Mrs Gerry Grinberg, in fact they cornered the market. They bought 145 of the two-dollar cookie jars for a total of 198,605 dollars. They became the proud owners of a collection of cookie jars collected by Andy Warhol.

Somebody called Jim Judelson was at the auction and decided to see how high the Grinbergs were prepared to go. He bid against them for Lot 868 – consisting of two jars and a salt-and-pepper shaker – and managed to beat them, but only by paying 23,100 dollars.

As the auction continued people paid extravagant, exorbitant sums of money for plaster busts of Napoleon, money-boxes in the shape of

Campbell soup tins, lots of inept paintings of prostitutes and male hustlers. The catalogue called this stuff 'collectibles', which is an American word for junk.

Of course, what the buyers were getting was not an object but a relic, a little something to remember Andy Warhol by. A cookie jar was as good a relic as anything else.

Apparently Warhol had the good sense to keep these collectibles in the storeroom at the back of his house so that he didn't have to live with them or look at them, but even so the mere fact that he had bought them and owned them was enough to imbue them with the sort of Warholian spirit that made them desirable.

The *Telegraph* said, 'It was not so much a collection as an assemblage – a sprawl of taste to suggest that Warhol had not the remotest discipline as a collector,' but the *Telegraph* would, wouldn't it?

I say, Good for Warhol. I'd have been a little disappointed if the Warhol estate had consisted of a few well chosen, supremely fine connoisseur's pieces. It was in the nature of the man, or at least in the nature of the image of the man, that he accepted dross. He turned indiscrimination into an art. You wouldn't want a man who saw the aesthetic possibilities of a Brillo box to be a collector of unimpeachable good taste.

I have also heard that Warhol had a vast collection of pornography, and of Polaroids of famous people in the nude. These weren't in the catalogue. I wonder which discriminating collector got those.

Victoria returned.

Just as I'm not sure what most marriages are like, I'm not sure what most affairs are like either. What do people do when they're having an affair? Do they run through exotic landscapes? Do they meet in smoky places? Or what?

Yes, it began to look as though Victoria and I might be having an affair. She eventually came back to collect her car. She drove me to the Sainsbury's carpark where my own car had remained all this time, my groceries rotting in the boot. Victoria insisted we have a brief, feverish attempt to make love in the underground carpark. It failed, which obviously didn't please me but I took that as a sign from Victoria that we were going to attempt to become lovers on a regular basis.

'I'm very sorry about the other day,' she said. 'My husband's normally so reasonable.'

'He has a lot to be reasonable about. Have the police found who wrecked his cars?'

'Of course not.'

'What does your husband do?'

'He likes to watch and . . .'

'For a living.'

'He's a bookmaker.'

'Really? He doesn't look flash enough.'

'He lives in a big house. He has a swimming-pool. He collects cars. He has me. Isn't that flash enough?'

'I expect bookmakers to wear loud suits and trilbies and carry big rolls of fivers.'

'Wrong stereotype. He just makes lots of money out of a lot of dim people. Do you know how he makes a lot of money? From people who don't bother to collect their winnings. They have a small each-way bet at low odds and the horse comes in third. Their winnings only amount to about fifty pence and they can't be bothered to claim it. Imagine tens of thousands of customers doing that. It adds up. But I suspect you don't want to talk about my husband.'

'Right.'

We went to bed together several times. It was fun, but I still couldn't get an erection.

Being in a plodding frame of mind I'd looked up impotence in one of those unauthoritative, semi-pornographic dictionaries of sex. There, amid the definitions of irrumatio and ipsation, before intercourse but after illegitimacy, I found my problem.

I learned that impotence comes in two brands: primary and secondary. I was pleased to find that mine was the latter, more common, more curable variety. What was required, the book told me, was sympathy, ideally from a sympathetic partner (which I liked to think I had) or, failing that, from a sympathetic doctor or therapist (which I didn't have and didn't think I could cope with). The dictionary also offered the opinion that the condition caused the partner to suffer as much as the impotent male. This I doubted.

When Victoria and I weren't failing in bed we sat in my house and talked, and when that became unbearable we sat in her car, or went out to pubs and wine bars and restaurants and talked there. Sometimes I would express doubts about her 'lifestyle'.

'I don't want to sound like a spoilsport,' I said, 'but isn't there a certain amount of risk attached to the way you conduct your sex life?'

'I'm not a fool, you know,' she replied. 'I move with the times. I practise what is laughingly known as safe sex; barrier methods, no exchange of fluids. Okay? Happy?'

'Happier.'

Safe sex. I considered my own malfunctioning equipment. It didn't come much safer than that.

Or sometimes, it had been known to happen, we might talk about books.

'Don't you think we should write to Thornton McCain,' she said, 'and tell him it was one of his books that brought us together?'

'No, I don't.'

'He'd probably be delighted to get a fan letter.'

'I'm too old to write fan letters,' I said. 'I'm too old to be a fan.'

Here's another old joke. I'm sure Ted Langley has it in his collection. A little boy and a little girl are playing doctors and nurses and showing each other their parts. The little boy, no doubt playing the doctor, proudly shows off his penis and says, 'I've got one of these and you haven't.' But the little girl isn't impressed. She points at her own parts and replies, 'I've got one of these so I can have as many of those as I like.'

I'd heard it before, but I still laughed when Victoria told it me.

'So how many of "those" have you had?' I asked.

'You wouldn't want to know,' she said. 'Would you?'

'I'm not sure. I think I would.'

'Why?'

'Idle curiosity.'

'Is that all?'

I really didn't know. Perhaps the curiosity was morbid rather than idle. Perhaps I just wanted to see how serious a collector she was.

'Are we talking about more or less than a hundred?' I asked.

'You're as bad as my husband.'

'Your husband doesn't need to ask how many. He's there for most of them, isn't he?'

She laughed, and I laughed as well, though I wasn't at all sure that it was a laughing matter. It seemed weird and unhealthy to me that a husband should encourage his wife to take lovers, weirder still

90

for him to want to participate or watch. I wasn't sure how weird or unhealthy it was of me to want to know the chapter and verse (or at least the page numbers) of her exploits. Partly I could justify it by saying it was part of a general wanting to know her better. I was interested in everything about her; her background, her childhood, her tastes and prejudices, but none of these things seemed so pressing as wanting to know the extent of her promiscuity.

'I'm not some dull little nymphomaniac, you know,' she said.

'I know that.'

'I happen to believe in variety, that's all. I don't like to be stuck with the same old thing day in and day out.'

'Is your husband the "same old thing"?'

'Anything becomes the same old thing if you repeat it often enough. That's why it's best to keep changing. You wouldn't want to wake up every morning next to a hunchback or a sixteen-year-old surfer or a twenty-five-stone wrestler, but once in a while it's irresistible.'

I didn't much like the idea of Victoria sleeping with hunchbacks, surfers or wrestlers. Or perhaps I didn't like the idea of sleeping with someone who'd slept with hunchbacks, surfers and wrestlers. At times I thought she was probably exaggerating, even that she was making the whole thing up; or perhaps that was only what I wanted to think.

Perhaps I should have been grateful that I was getting such a powerful insight into the mentality of the collector. Perhaps it would be just what my book needed. But in Victoria's case I didn't want that insight, didn't want to understand; or at least the desire to understand and the desire not to know existed simultaneously.

I didn't know then, and I still don't know now, to what extent you can collect people. In one sense you can't collect people any more than you can collect fresh air or mountains or bird-song. You can't collect what you can't own. Collection demands possession.

Sex, of course, can be seen as possession. People 'have' each other, they talk about belonging to each other. They speak about *my* wife, *my* husband, *my* mistress, and it isn't only metaphorical. But you can't own a hundred different partners at the same time unless you literally have a harem, or whatever the female equivalent would be. Victoria's collection was serial, scattered in time and space, and her 'ownership' kept deliberately brief; and in that sense it probably couldn't be called a collection at all. My theorising meant nothing at all to Victoria. It didn't mean very much to me either.

91

We kept going to bed together. Victoria would arrive unexpectedly at my house with a bottle of champagne or a bunch of flowers. We'd sit around, talk, listen to a record, and then we'd try to make love. We tried hard. We made gallant attempts. And we did all the things that people do in bed together, except that I didn't happen to have an erection at the time. We made the best of a very bad job.

I suspected that I wasn't the only man Victoria dropped in on unexpectedly and went to bed with. I continued to ask dogged little questions about who and where, how often and how many, and Victoria remained tantalisingly unforthcoming on the subject. Perhaps I should have been grateful. Then one night she decided to tell me 'all', and she painstakingly revealed the utter depth and breadth of her collecting tastes.

She began by telling me of the unusual nationalities – a Kurd, a Bolivian, a Lithuanian, a Maori; then went on to religions – a Rastafarian, a Christadelphian, a Mennonite; then unlikely professions – a tree surgeon, a steeplejack, a clock repairer, an arms' dealer. She told me of the unusual places she'd had sex – in trains, boats and planes, on the roof of a moving Land-Rover, in a box at Covent Garden, in the gentlemen's lavatory on the third floor at Harrods.

There were lovers with physical peculiarities, scars and amputations, steel plates in the head and strange growths here and there. There were the simultaneous couplings with trios of rugby fans, string quartets, gangs of scaffolders. There was the occasional whiff of bisexuality, a hint of incest as she slept with fathers and sons or pairs of brothers. There was sex with the very old and the very young, the blind, the deaf, the disabled.

Then there were the perverts and fetishists, the men who needed her to dress like a nun or a traffic warden or a charlady, the ones who were only interested in her armpits or feet, or who wanted to shave her, or sniff her stockings or coat her in chocolate spread. There were the voyeurs and the exhibitionists, the spankers and the transvestites and the bondage freaks. I heard about the orgies and the group gropes, the quickies, the slap and tickles. I heard it all in lubricious, prurient, dirty-mouthed detail. It took most of the evening.

How did I feel about all this? Well, of course, I didn't know how I felt. It would have been easy enough to feel the old regulation male disgust for rampant female sexuality, and I don't deny that I felt a certain measure of that. But I also felt some amazement at her stamina, her determination, and at the catholicism of her taste. She had the staying power of the truly obsessive collector. Possibly I was also extremely envious of her. She was having precisely the kind of sex life she wanted. I wished I could have said the same.

I wasn't sure how I fitted into all of this. I didn't feel that I was nearly exotic enough to merit a place in such a collection. And, certainly, given the sweep and the urgency of her collecting instincts, I was flattered that she had enough time to try to coax me through my limpness. Perhaps she liked me.

When she'd finished the story of her sexual life and times she looked at my limp cock.

'Sometimes when I tell men about my exploits they get really horny.'

'Perverts,' I said.

The phone rang.

'Hello Steve.'

'Hello again, Rachel.'

I said it in a less antagonistic tone than I normally used for speaking to Rachel. She had Victoria to thank for that.

'Are you well?' she asked.

'I am, surprisingly enough.'

'Good. I'm ringing to say that if you don't come and collect these things of yours soon I'll have to throw them away.'

'What things?'

'The letters and photographs. You remember?'

'Oh, those.'

'They're really cluttering up the place.'

'Really? How much stuff is there?'

'Well not that much but that's not entirely the point. The point is, I think I'd prefer it if there weren't any of your possessions in my flat. We're supposed to have made a clean break.'

'So throw my stuff away.'

'That doesn't seem right.'

'It seems perfectly all right to me.'

'Not to me.'

'The other thing that occurs to me, Rachel, is that if you really want to make a clean break mightn't it be better if you stopped phoning me all the time?'

'I don't phone you all the time,' she said angrily. 'I only phone you once in a while.'

'It must only seem to be all the time. But you could stop phoning me even once in a while if a clean break's what you want.'

'I don't want to stop phoning you,' she said, and then went very quiet.

I knew it was my turn to say something but I wasn't going to make it that easy for her.

'I suppose in fact,' she said, 'I don't really want to make a clean break. I phone you because I want to talk to you, and I'm reduced to this nonsense about your old letters and photographs because I feel I need an excuse before I can ring.'

'I'm sorry,' I said.

'Perhaps if you were a little less hostile I wouldn't feel that I needed an excuse.'

'If I was less hostile you'd be ringing every day.'

'Would that be so terrible?'

'As things are now it wouldn't be the best.'

'What does that mean? How are things "now"?'

'I'm sort of involved with someone.'

'Someone permanent?'

'Permanent's a long time. I've never known anybody to be permanent.'

'Is it anyone I know?'

'Who do you know in Sheffield?'

'I thought it might be someone you'd mentioned.'

'I haven't ever mentioned anybody.'

'All right. So how did you meet her?'

'Through my work. She's a collector.'

'Of what?'

I had to think quickly. I said, 'Paintings.'

'What sort of paintings?'

'English. Water-colours. Victorian. Landscapes.'

'I didn't know you were going to be writing about English Victorian water-colours.'

'Neither did I. That's the joy of research. It's a voyage of exploration.'

'I hope she's good for you.'

'So far.'

'And is she the reason why you don't want me to phone you any more?'

'I didn't say that.'

'Good. I'm glad. I'll phone you again soon then. Don't worry, it won't be every day.'

Before I could make some mordant comment or even say 'Okay,' she'd put down the phone. I wasn't sure if I'd won or lost that little exchange. Perhaps Rachel and I had moved on to some new phase where our telephone conversations weren't only about winning and losing. But perhaps not.

I continued to go drinking with Jim, and we continued to talk about whatever was on our mind, sometimes not much. I didn't mention Victoria to him. He and she seemed to inhabit separate planets and I wanted to keep them apart. And of course I didn't mention my impotence, but that didn't mean that we didn't talk about sex.

Jim said, 'I've been thinking I'm in the wrong job.'

This had occurred to me before but I didn't immediately see what this had to do with sex.

'The way to really get a lot of women', he said, 'is to become a driving instructor. You're with the girl in an enclosed space. She hangs onto your every word. She wants to learn. She wants to please you. She does what you tell her.

'Girls always get crushes on their teachers. You can touch them on the arm if you want to help them get full lock on. You can touch their legs to demonstrate the importance of clutch control.

'And there's all the symbolism – the movement, the speed, the endless manipulation of the gear lever. You're in her power because she's driving, but you're the boss and you've got dual control. Yes, I bet driving instructors get a lot more than their fair share, and only because of the job they're doing.'

I didn't feel I knew much about the sexual possibilities open to driving instructors. The man who'd taught me, over a decade ago, had been a sixty-year-old white supremacist in a Cortina. I preferred not to think about his sex life.

'The rest of us', Jim said, 'have to rely on more ingenious methods.'

Whenever I turned up at Jim's mobile home it was never a simple matter of him getting in the car and driving off. Each time I arrived he'd be in the middle of learning a new section from *The Books of Power*. This was always extremely urgent and we couldn't go out until he'd finished. So I spent what seemed like very long periods killing time in Jim's living-room, and more often than not I found myself leafing through the volumes Jim wasn't studying. I almost came to enjoy some of them. It was adolescent of me, but I looked up 'Sex'.

SEX
A big issue.
What people do in the privacy of their own mouths is nobody else's business.
Nymphomania: a plot device invented by the writers of one-hand magazines.
Lesbians: nobody likes lesbians more than I do – so long as they let me watch.
Marriage: St Paul reckoned it prevented fornication and he wasn't wrong.
The female orgasm: rarer than rocking-horse orgasms.
The Pioneers: Havelock Ellis, Sacher-Masoch, de Sade, Freud, Kinsey, Krafft-Ebing, Marie Stopes. Would you really want to sleep with any of these people?
(N.B. Alfred Charles Kinsey began his career as a zoologist. In seventeen years he collected, measured and classified between two and four million gall wasps. Some would think this symptomatic.)
Fetishism: shoe fetishism de-feets the object.
'Rectum' is Latin for straight. Ironic, no?
Sex change: a sex change is as good as a rest.
Impotence: ignore it and it may go away.
Oral Sex: the girls of Thailand refuse to perform oral sex, claiming it is against the laws of Buddha. Western women come up with less spiritual excuses.
Music: a powerful aphrodisiac. Who put the KY in funky?
Sex education: you can't believe everything you read in books.

I did think, briefly, that I might be able to do a bit of research on Kinsey and his millions of gall wasps, but thought the information was very likely to be wrong.
Next I looked up 'The Automobile'.

THE AUTOMOBILE
Hero or villain? A potent source of freedom, mobility and self-definition, or an ecological disaster and mass killer?
Karl Benz, Sir Herbert Austin, Lord Nuffield, Colin Chapman, Lee Iococca.

The Scarab, the Gas O'Car, the Whippet, the Mosquito, the Gaylord, the Testarossa, the Minx.

Or perhaps a Barthesian equivalent of the Gothic cathedral. Pull the other one, Roland!

'Pull the other one' is very much my own reaction to large expanses of Roland Barthes. I like to have my prejudices reinforced as much as the next man. I was starting to feel better about *The Books of Power*. I wondered what they might have to say about Karl Marx.

KARL MARX (1818–83)
The man who put the Marks in Marxism.

He rejected the idealism of Hegel. *Das Kapital* is a monumental work. He ruled the International with an iron hand.

The class struggle, the dictatorship of the proletariat, to each according to his needs, dialectical materialism, surplus value, commodity fetishism, a spectre is haunting Europe, nothing to lose but your chains, the opium of the people, the first time as tragedy, the second time as a sit-com.

Wasn't keen on the bourgeoisie, but who is?

He led his wife a dance.

He was a master, but he didn't have all the answers.

That was enough for one session. I was closing the volume, about to put it back, when a familiar name leapt out at me from the top of one of the pages.

THORNTON McCAIN
An outsider in English and American letters: and outside is probably the best place for him. Today, few would claim his writing was either interesting or relevant, and they're not wrong.

Started out young and derivative with *The Foxhole*, and ended up weary and avant-garde with *The World Seen Through Plexiglass*, not such a hot title in our opinion.

Later works revel in a kind of hallucinatory dislocation – could be seen as a response to twentieth-century malaise and moral chaos. Could be he doesn't know what he's doing.

Too cynical and decadent to be a child of the 'sixties, but that doesn't stop him seeming like a left-over from another age.

A true anecdote: some time in 1967 Thornton McCain was sitting in a pub in Bristol in the company of Tom Stoppard, Harold Pinter and Vivien Merchant. Pinter went to the bar and bought a round of drinks. McCain tasted his pint and said, 'This beer's piss.'

That was, alas, typical of the man.

Some readers relish the difficulty of his novels, most find them too much like hard work. Nobody likes hard work.

Anyone wishing, despite these clear warnings, to paddle in the muddy waters of Thornton McCain might like to read *The Bullet Leaves the Gun*. Then again they might not.

I didn't know what to make of that. It seemed odd that McCain should be included at all. A quick look through the volume showed that Arthur and Henry Miller and, for that matter, Maugham didn't rate a mention. But why include him only to abuse him? There was also this problem of a book called *The Bullet Leaves the Gun*. How come I'd never heard of it before? I hadn't seen it mentioned in the dictionary of authors I'd consulted in the library, nor did it appear in McCain's books under 'other titles'. I wondered if Victoria had ever come across it. Did this mean it was a recent work? Was McCain still writing? I looked in vain for a date on *The Books of Power*. What did they know about Thornton McCain that I didn't?

I was thinking about this when Jim announced that he was ready to go to the pub. He was delighted to see that I'd become engrossed in the volume.

'Good stuff, isn't it?' he said.

'Yes,' I said. 'In a way.'

'You see how *The Books of Power* make learning fun?'

'Yes,' I said. 'They're genuinely unputdownable.'

Jim smiled.

In the shop where I'd first bought a book by Thornton McCain I came across a record called 'Eve's Droppings'. It had a collage on the front featuring images of, among other things, a Swiss chalet, the Bayeux Tapestry, a unicyclist, a bubble car, an Aga cooker, a haggis and the Dalai Lama. It looked like my kind of thing. The sleeve didn't give much away about what I was likely to find on the record. The tracks on side one were called 'Eve's Droppings Parts 1 to 8', and on side two there were 'Eve's Droppings Parts 9 to 32'. But it was in the bargain bin so I decided to take a chance.

I got it home, put it on my stereo and listened. In so far as it resembled anything I'd ever heard before, I suppose it wasn't entirely unlike a sound effects record. It started innocently enough with the noise of traffic, footsteps on gravel, a variety of doors opening and closing, but then it started to get out of hand.

There was hideous feedback, machinery recorded at distorting volume, out-of-tune pianos, people gibbering in unknown languages, explosions, dreadful wet, fleshy noises, animals screaming in pain. But many of the noises were completely unidentifiable; scraping, sucking, smashing noises, perhaps mechanical, perhaps from some inner part of the body, but all sinister and alarming and reproduced with disgusting clarity.

Inspecting the inner sleeve I read, 'All these sounds come from the Eve Leviticus Collection. For more information contact Eve Leviticus at this address: – '

Of course, I had to contact her. She lived at a very smart address near Fitzroy Square in London. I wrote to her. I explained my book and after we'd exchanged a couple of letters we agreed to meet. I took the train to London, walked from St Pancras to her home, and found myself ringing the bell of a basement flat in the bottom of a tall, Georgian house.

The person who answered the door was in her teens, plump, greasy haired, uncoordinated, having elements of the school swot and of a member of a motorcycle gang.

'You were expecting someone older,' she said. 'Come in.'

This was Eve Leviticus.

'My parents didn't christen me Eve Leviticus,' she said. 'I'd rather not say what name they gave me, but when you get to a certain age you realise you can change these things. My parents live upstairs. They have the whole of the rest of the house. I stay out of their way. They're rolling in money. They don't like me very much. I can understand that. This is the best arrangement.'

'Pleased to meet you,' I said.

For all the house's elegance, the basement was dark, damp and inhospitable. There were no carpets, no lampshades, no signs of comfort. A distended campbed and two plastic stacking chairs were the only furniture. There were items of recording equipment strewn around; microphones, mixers, recorders, decks and speakers, but they all looked very old and basic.

I'd become used to seeing people's collections displayed to their best advantage, but this collection was one to be heard not looked at, and the basement was full of cardboard boxes containing countless tapes and cassettes, in no discernible order.

I tried to explain what I was doing, and make some small talk, but she wasn't very interested. She behaved as though she gave interviews on a fairly regular basis. She was, however, extremely keen to play me some tapes.

'All this is better when you're on drugs,' she said. 'Acid is ideal, dope's okay, even barbiturates if you're desperate.'

I told her I wasn't desperate. She played me a tape. It was what you might call industrial noise. There were mechanical slammings and grindings, unsilenced exhausts, the sound of circular and chainsaws, the hammering of metal on metal. It was a succession of unlovely noises, all played back at painful volume, but it might have just about passed as *musique concrète*. Eve Leviticus sat listening to it with an intent, enthusiast's ear.

'Did you record all this yourself?' I began to ask, but she hushed me into silence.

When the mechanical row had finished she said, 'Of course I recorded it all myself. There'd be no point otherwise.'

'You go into factories, on to construction sites, that sort of thing?'

'That sort of thing. You'll like the next tape,' she said. 'It consists of silences.'

She didn't lie. The tape passed through the heads but no sound emerged. From time to time there seemed to be a slight change in the acoustic quality of the hiss coming from the speakers, but I could have been imagining that.

'There,' she said some time later. 'All those silences were recorded in different parts of the world – the Sahara, Namibia, the Outback, and the final one was recorded in an anechoic chamber at the University of Maryland.'

'You get around,' I said.

'My parents don't mind paying for me to travel. They're trying to compensate. Also they're trying to get rid of me.'

The next tape was of bodily noises. Eve explained how different the belch of, say, a Tamil tea picker, is from, say, that of a Carlisle lorry driver. Nobody could disagree. Thus I sat through ten or fifteen minutes of belching and swallowing, rumbling stomachs, sneezing, coughing, hawking, retching and farting. I was prepared to believe that a true expert would have been able to detect geographical and social, and no doubt medical, differences between the various noises, but it was much of a muchness to me.

'That last sound you heard,' she said, grinning happily, 'that was of somebody emptying their colostomy bag.'

I found it hard to know what kind of facial expression to adopt while listening to these sounds. Eve's own expression was somewhere between rapt attention and bliss, and she was probably too caught up in it all to care about how I was reacting.

We moved on now to a miscellany of noises from lawnmowers, ascending lifts, rain on a tin roof, a variety of flushing toilets, and what she assured me was a pig being slaughtered. Occasionally there was the sound of an unusual musical instrument, a serpent or a glass harmonica, but Eve Leviticus had never recorded anything so formal as a tune or melody.

She played me a tape called 'Sounds from a massage parlour', full of slapping and groans. There was a recording that she said had been made in an operating theatre during a caesarian delivery of Siamese twins, and a recording made by radio microphone attached to a cat falling from a fourteenth-storey window.

There were the sounds of muggings, stabbings, obscene telephone calls, dog fights, the ramblings of incoherent drunks from all parts of the world in all sorts of languages, an orgy taking place in a flat in Peckham Rye, and the sound (and she had to explain this one) of a body's sphincters going slack at the moment of death.

'Why?' I said.

'Huh?'

I realised I probably sounded like somebody's father, though not presumably like Eve's, but I said, 'Is this all really very healthy? If you want to record things shouldn't you be out capturing the sounds of bullfrogs or steam-engines or the local garage bands?'

'In Fitzroy Square?'

She had a point. Even so I said, 'I think you may be a very sick girl.'

'So tell me something I don't know. Tell me something the teachers and doctors and counsellors haven't told me already. Of course I'm sick. I come from a sick family in a sick society. You'd be sick if you were in my position. What are you going to say about me in your book?'

'That you're very sick, I suppose.'

'I'd like a royalty.'

'In that case I could very easily decide not to say anything about you at all.'

'It's not the money. It's that I want to assert my professional status, not rely on my parents.'

'I can see your point.'

'At least buy one of my recordings.'

She offered me a variety of recordings that she'd compiled. They were on cassette and had stomach-turning if eye-catching covers. They had titles like 'Radio Noir', 'Domestic Animals in Pain' and 'Deliria of the World'. They didn't in the main sound like things I'd want in my house, but in order to show willing I bought something called 'Oral Sex in Stereo'. Side one featured twenty minutes of cunnilingus, side two featured twenty minutes of fellatio. She recommended that I hear it on headphones to enjoy it at its best.

Another day, another test drive, another young female customer. She is besuited and businesslike and looks as though she'd have a company car. It is Elaine. She saw Jim on the forecourt but managed to prevent him seeing her as Mike Gombrich took her out in a Volvo 1800, the sort the Saint used to drive.

'It's sporty,' Mike says. 'Lovely lines. Nice free-revving engine.'

She overtakes a Ford Sierra with effortless ease.

'And reliable?' she asks.

'If you want my opinion, far too much importance is attached to reliability these days . . .'

Mike Gombrich does his spiel. She appears to be listening attentively. She drives comfortably with total relaxation. Mike doesn't fancy her. She's too cold and brusque, but that could be an act.

'Pull over into that lay-by. I'll buy you a cup of coffee.'

'I don't know if I should.'

'What's the problem?'

'Oh, nothing. At least I don't suppose having a cup of coffee will make it any worse.'

She pulls into the lay-by. He goes to the van selling snax and returns with two cups.

'Comfy driving position,' he says, slapping the leather seat.

She agrees.

'Will you use the car for work?'

'I don't know.'

'What kind of work are you in exactly?'

'Market research.'

'Yeah?'

'It's quite interesting really. I wonder, no, I know I shouldn't ask, but would you have time to answer a few questions?'

This isn't on, Mike thinks. This is breaking some unwritten agreement. Still, he wants to be obliging while ever there's a sale to be made. What harm can it do? So he agrees and they go through the questions about education, knowledge and finance.

'So *you* would be interested in a simple, easy, cost-effective, infallible way of increasing your knowledge?'

'No.'

'But you just said . . .'

'I've already got a set.'

'A set?'

'Don't get innocent. Encyclopedias.'

'So you've seen through my little ruse. All right, so you have a set of encyclopedias, but you'll have nothing like *The Books of Power*.'

'Say that again.'

'*The Books of Power*.'

His face becomes suddenly set and solid, a dangerous expression that she can't quite read, but knows that she definitely can't trust.

'I'm afraid this is your unlucky day darling.'

She sticks to her plan. Her face falls. She looks as though she's about to weep.

'A set of *The Books of Power* is exactly what I *have* got. Now get the fuck out of my car.'

'What?'

'You heard me. Get out. You're walking back. I mean it.'

She can see that he does. She can see that tears aren't going to work this time.

'Aren't you over-reacting?'

'No.'

'All right, I admit I was in the wrong. I was stupid to try selling to another salesman, but you can't blame me for trying, can you?'

'That's not what this is about. Get out. Now.'

'You pig.'

She gets out. He slides into the driver's seat and drives away sedately, calm with anger. She continues shouting 'Pig' at him long after he can possibly hear. She wonders if he really does have a set of *The Books of Power*. He doesn't look the type, and she didn't think anyone had ever bought a set before she started selling them door-to-door. She can't see why he got so angry. If he isn't angry that she tried selling to another salesmen then what *is* he angry about? She turns towards the tea van. She makes herself begin to cry. She walks over and says to the man behind the counter, 'Hello, I'm conducting a survey into educational resources and I wonder if you'd mind answering a few questions.'

In any other setting Mrs Edwin Rivers would have seemed a very lean woman, but when seated next to her husband on my settee she looked well fleshed and overblown. Their son, in his early twenties, nervous, gum-chewing and rodent-like, and in his father's opinion good for nothing, stood menacingly by the bay window refusing to sit down. When I'd first answered the door and found this trio unexpectedly on my doorstep, I thought for a moment that the beer can collection must have been found, husband and wife had been reconciled and they had come to share the good news with me. Yet even a cursory look at their faces showed that they were a long way from being reconciled.

'I'm Mrs Edwin Rivers,' she had said. 'I think we'd better come in.'

It was a Sunday morning. I hadn't washed or shaved. I was in the living-room surrounded by newspapers, and the stereo was blasting out something unsuitable, though not as unsuitable as 'Oral Sex in Stereo'. They were lucky to find me dressed. I turned down the music and they turned down my offers of tea and coffee. It was obvious that Mrs Rivers meant business.

'My husband owes you an explanation,' she said.

'But', said the son, contemptuously, 'he's too much of a coward to give you one himself so we're going to have to do it for him.'

Edwin looked pained yet resigned. He stared intently at my patterned carpet.

'First of all,' said the wife, 'he'd like to apologise for dragging you all the way down to Coventry on a wild-goose chase.'

Edwin nodded in agreement.

'It was hardly his fault that the collection went missing,' I said.

'The collection didn't go missing,' she replied.

'I'm glad to hear that.'

'The collection didn't go missing because there wasn't ever a collection.'

The son could see that I was looking puzzled, so he took over the narrative.

'This toe-rag, my father, likes to pretend he has the world's finest collection of beer cans. But he doesn't. He doesn't have *any* beer cans. He never has had any. He never will have any.'

'But . . .' I said.

'He rents a room to store this non-existent collection,' his wife said. 'He's spent good money having shelving put in. He loves to talk to people about his collection. He tells them all how wonderful it's supposed to be, but talk is all it is. His precious collection only exists inside his head.

'That's why he makes such a song and dance about not letting anyone know where it is, and about being reluctant to show it to anyone. Most often it stops there. But every now and again he meets someone like your good self and takes them to that room in that awful house and pretends that the collection's been stolen, and that we're responsible.'

She made an expansive, motherly gesture that embraced her son.

'A lot of women wouldn't stand for it, but I do because I care about him.'

'I care about him too,' the son said.

'I know you do,' said his mother. 'Apart from this one quirk Edwin is perfectly normal and not a bad husband and father at all, and since we love the man, we put up with his quirks.'

Mother and son beamed with what they obviously considered to be well justified pride. I was finding the room airless and oppressive.

The son said, 'But we think it's a bit much when he involves people like you and that's what we've brought him to apologise for.'

'But why does he do this?' I asked, as though Edwin wasn't there.

However, Edwin now was able to speak, as though a great weight had been lifted. He said, 'There's much that we still don't know about the human mind.'

'You can say that again,' I replied.

'Does this mean,' Edwin asked, 'that I won't be featuring in your book?'

I thought perhaps he might feature in an appendix entitled 'Collecting: pathological aspects'. Jim had told me stories about life on the used-car lot, where bogus high-rollers would stroll in and order ten thousand pounds' worth of motor car, only for the salesman to discover that the putative buyer was penniless and the money no more real than Edwin's beer cans.

I could just about understand the psychological need to swank around in an expensive car pretending to be rich and powerful. I couldn't understand the psychological need to pretend you had a beer can collection.

'I may still be able to find a place for you in the book,' I said.

'Oh good,' said Edwin.

'You've made him very happy,' said his wife.

'But you'll have to answer me one question,' I said, addressing Edwin.

'I'll try.'

'He'll try.'

'Why don't you start a *real* beer can collection?'

The carpet became unbearably fascinating to him again.

'It's easy enough to start,' I said. 'You don't need much outlay. You can walk into your nearest off licence and start your collection immediately.'

'You've asked a very good question,' Edwin said. 'And I don't have a simple answer, but perhaps I might say this.

'Yes, it would in one way be possible and easy to start such a collection. But what sort of collection would it be? Would it be fine and extensive? Would it be full of rare items and special finds? Would it be one of the world's great collections? Could it ever be as big, as grand, and as comprehensive as I would want it to be? Would it ever be as good as the collection in my head?'

Then he was silent until finally he said, 'No, it wouldn't.'

I'm sure you know the story about Oscar Wilde coming through customs, being asked if he had anything to declare and replying, 'Only my genius.'

This has always struck me as a real pain-in-the-arse thing to say. I'm sure customs men have a lousy enough job without some smug, wise-cracking, Irish aesthete making it worse. It's also struck me as a very poor line. I'm sure that if anyone except Oscar Wilde had said it, it wouldn't have been remembered at all, but Wilde was a famous wit, so his sayings get recorded and repeated even if they weren't actually very witty.

I wonder why lines and stories get linked to famous people. Any smart remark about sexual inadequacy, God or death gets attributed to Woody Allen, whether he said it or not. Anything to do with sexual adequacy gets attributed to Errol Flynn. Anything that puts down children and promotes alcoholism goes to W. C. Fields. When they can't think of anyone else to credit with a *bon mot* it goes to Groucho Marx, Samuel Johnson, Bernard Shaw or Oscar Wilde.

Why are the words and stories of famous people perceived as more interesting, funnier and cleverer than those belonging to the rest of us?

Sometimes different famous people get attributed with the same story. Errol Flynn was also going through customs once and had to fill in an immigration form. Where it asked for 'Occupation' he wrote 'Sex', and where it asked 'Sex' he wrote 'Occupation'. Riotous eh? It's probably apocryphal, and it would work just as well if you told it about Mick Jagger or Jack Nicholson. It wouldn't work so well if you told it about Steve Geddes, Thornton McCain or Jim.

Jim's efforts to become famous and find true love were, in a funny sort of way, progressing. After his first night at the Bricklayers' Arms things could only get better, and they did. He continued to enter pub quizzes. I didn't go to every one of them. I sometimes had better things to do, like see Victoria, but not often, so I went to quite a few and he seemed to be faring increasingly well. He didn't win any of the quizzes but he often finished a good second or third. Partly things were improving because he'd learned how to pick the right sort of contest – the ones that didn't only ask questions about pop music and television – and partly it was because he was picking up a lot of actual general knowledge.

I was frequently surprised by some of the things he knew. I was particularly surprised because everything he knew he'd learned from *The Books of Power*, which I still considered a very dubious source. Perhaps their real power was that they enabled you to do well in quizzes.

Once I'd attended a few quiz nights I began to recognise some of the contestants. There was something of a circuit. Many of the same people went from pub to pub, week after week, competing against the same opposition, sometimes answering the same questions.

The skinny, punkish kid who'd won that first time at the Bricklayers' Arms was a regular competitor. I never saw him lose. He was every bit as knowledgeable about history, literature, politics and geography as he had been on the other topics. He was always the one they had to beat.

Jim persevered doggedly, doing better all the time, but never looking likely to win.

'I'm getting there,' he'd say. 'One of these days I'm going to be a winner, then it'll all start happening for me.'

I tried to point out, gently, that it hadn't all started happening for the skinny kid. He was as pumped full of general knowledge, and as adept at winning quizzes as most of us could ever imagine being, yet he hardly seemed overburdened by the trappings of fame and success. He didn't appear on television or open supermarkets. He didn't seem to have attracted the girl of his dreams.

I suppose we all fantasise that at some point in the future our worth will be recognised and we'll be famous. We'll be seen as 'characters'. People will want to write our biographies and make documentaries about us. Our perfectly ordinary childhoods and adolescences will become significant and fascinating. Our friends will be interviewed and they will recount the many wry and portentous things we did and said. Our lives will be transformed into rich funds of anecdote. Maybe, if we're lucky, the wry and portentous words and stories of others will be attributed to us.

This, I'm sure, is what Jim wanted. He wanted attention, in the same way that Edwin Rivers wanted to be in the book. Jim wanted to be good at something besides cleaning cars, good at something that would make him a celebrity. I sometimes thought he might be better employed committing a famous murder than studying *The Books of Power*, but what did I know?

Jim did, however, make it on to radio. It was only local and only a phone-in, but he thought it was a step in the right direction. The quiz seemed unnecessarily complicated, being somehow based around horse racing and double and treble bets. I listened to an hour of it and never quite got the hang of the rules.

Jim's appearance was brief.

'And now we've got Jim on the line,' said the presenter. 'Hello Jim.'

'Hello.'

'Speak up, Jim. We all want to hear you.'

'Hello.'

'That's it. And what do you do for a living, Jim?'

'I clean cars.'

'I wish somebody would come and clean mine. Tell me, what's the secret of getting a car really clean?'

He thought for rather longer than local radio finds acceptable but finally said, 'Love, I suppose.'

'Well, it makes the world go round doesn't it? Who's your favourite pop act, Jim?'

'I don't know really,' he said, then added hopefully, 'the Beatles?'

'Right. All you need is love! An oldie but goodie. Okay Jim, you understand the rules, now here's the first question. In what country was Vincent Van Gogh born?'

'Holland,' said Jim.

'Hard luck, Jim. The correct answer is the Netherlands.'

'But that's . . .'

'Sorry about that. Pity you weren't with us longer, Jim. We'll have our next contestant right after this record.'

Apparently the phone lines to the radio station were jammed for some time by callers pointing out that Holland and the Netherlands were one and the same place, but by the time this news had filtered through to the presenter, and by the time they'd got through to Jim again he was in such a huff that he wouldn't have taken any further part in the quiz even if they'd begged him, which they didn't.

Jim liked to think this was the kind of tantrum a star might throw. I wondered if he might be able to gain a reputation as a sort of Bobby Fischer of the general knowledge world, a wild temperamental maverick. I wondered if this was the stuff myths are made of, but I seriously doubted if anyone made myths out of general knowledge contestants. They are not the sort of characters that people want to tell anecdotes about.

I felt the book wasn't going very well, though since I'd never written a book before I didn't know how a book felt when it *was* going well. I'd completed a fair number of interviews with collectors. The interviews were on tape and I'd then laboriously created typescripts from the recordings. I didn't mind that it was laborious, in fact that made me feel better because it seemed that at least I was working hard.

So I had a stack of tapes, a growing pile of unprocessed manuscript and a couple of big notebooks filled with jottings, scribbles, and a few attempts at flowing prose; a collection of sorts. I felt consoled that there was some concrete evidence of the work in progress. Material was being accumulated. Things were moving forward. It ought to have been easy to summon up a little optimism, but it wasn't.

I'd get up every morning, have a big breakfast, watch some morning television, more than was good for me, skim the morning paper; putting off as long as possible the moment when I had to climb the stairs to the spare bedroom, sit at the typewriter and try to be a writer.

Occasionally I had Victoria to distract me, but not often. And when I did see her, I asked if she'd ever heard of a Thornton McCain novel called *The Bullet Leaves the Gun*, but she hadn't. Sometimes the post brought a welcome interruption; some letter that demanded instant action or a reply. On a bad day even a gas bill would do. On a cripplingly bad day I would even hope that Rachel might ring.

Once in a while things would come through the letter box that could be construed as inspiring. In the junk mail there'd be a leaflet urging me to buy 'A Complete Self-Contained Classical Music Collection' available on six albums for under twenty-five pounds. I would agonise for half an hour or more about the meaning of the words 'complete' and 'self-contained' when applied to a collection. Then I would bash away at the typewriter, debating whether collecting was a process of inclusion or exclusion. Then I'd read it through, decide that it was pretentious rubbish, throw it away and have lunch.

The free papers were sometimes great sources of material. They often filled an idle couple of column inches with details of somebody's unlikely collection. I started cutting them out and sticking them in a scrapbook.

'Phil and Lorraine Fouberts of the Druids Inn have thrown down a challenge to everyone in Sheffield.

'With a total of 321 different miniatures they believe they have the largest collection in the area, but would like to hear from anyone who disputes that.'

Or:

'The Castle Museum in Norwich has gone potty and snapped up the world's largest collection of teapots. After paying £120,000 for the 2,600 exhibits they'll need a good strong cuppa.'

Or

'A Barnsley woman has collected more than 3,000 jelly moulds in the past decade, in every shape and size, made from pewter, copper, tin, glass, ceramic and plastic, according to Rowntrees Jelly which celebrates its 65th birthday this year.'

These items didn't set me agonising or heading for my typewriter. Mostly they depressed me. I pictured some sad Barnsley woman with nothing in her life but jelly moulds. Perhaps I shouldn't have been depressed. There were surely much sadder Barnsley women, those with *nothing* in their lives, not even jelly moulds.

I suppose the fact that I kept coming across collectors might have cheered me about the likely future reception of the book. If there were so many people out there who collected, maybe there were a lot of people who'd want to read a book on the subject. But I wasn't sure about that. Most of the collectors I'd met didn't have time for theory or for anybody else's interests. They were too busy being obsessed with their own subject. That depressed me too, and when you're depressed you tend to think that your book isn't going very well. Equally, when your book isn't going very well everything is depressing.

Jim returns to his mobile home after another unsatisfying day. A couple of weeks ago Mike took a Frog-eyed Sprite as part of a complicated part-exchange deal. The car was a mess and Mike didn't really want it. It was always going to be a bugger of a job to get it looking halfway decent, even for good old Jim.

But the Jim who works for Killer Kars today is no longer quite the good old Jim. He has evolved. He's become a new model. He still works hard enough, puts in the hours, doesn't swing the lead, and nobody blames him that the Sprite still looks a mess after a half a day's solid graft. It would have taken a miracle to get it looking good, but the old Jim would have performed that miracle.

He never thought it would happen but he's bored with his job. There are times when he thinks he can't take it for another day, not for another hour or minute; and then he thinks of Elaine, and somehow he survives.

Yes, it's sexual fantasy that gets him through the day, though that sounds a little coarse and bestial, a little too physical. Jim fills his head with rosy imaginings about himself and his saleswoman. Certainly there's a sexual element. He doesn't envisage a love that's entirely chaste and cerebral, but he does imagine a form of love-making that is noble and undifferentiated, seen through gauze, without hard edges or gross details.

This fantasy often extends beyond the working day. Now, as he enters his mobile home, turns on the television in the living-room and gets himself a beer, Elaine is still much on his mind. So much so that when he looks out of the window and sees a woman crossing the lawn, he almost mistakes her for his dream girl. But then he realises that she isn't the kind of person you can mistake for anyone else; that hair, that suit, that efficient but easy deportment. Therefore it *is* her.

His first instinct is to dash out and fall on his knees before her, but that might lack subtlety. Perhaps she's visiting some of the other inhabitants of the mobile homes, trying to sell them encyclopedias. Well, if she wants a testimonial . . . He catches sight of his face in the wall mirror. He wishes he'd washed his hair this morning, or at least his face. He runs a hand over the stubble on his chin and is about to make a search for his electric razor when she knocks on the door.

So she's come to see him. God, he feels unprepared for this. Still, she'll have to take him as he is, stubble and all. Perhaps she's come because she feels exactly the same way about him as he does about her. Perhaps she's decided to take the initiative. He hopes so. It will save him a lot of bother. But maybe that isn't the reason she's come. But why else?

He realises that opening the door to her will be the first step in finding out. He does so. He invites her in. She is more formal than when he last saw her. She sees *The Books of Power* given pride of place on Jim's table and seems pleased.

'How are you enjoying them?' she asks. 'Although that's not a question I really need to ask because I'm certain that you're enjoying them immensely.'

'That's right.'

'I'm sure you're finding them useful and educational and terrific value for money.'

'Right. Would you like a beer?'

'No thanks. Not when I'm working.'

Jim's spirits dive.

'Before long', she says, 'you'll wonder how you ever lived without them, and certainly you won't ever want to be without them again. In the fascinating fields of history, physics . . .'

'It's all right,' says Jim, 'you don't need to convince me. *The Books of Power* have already changed my life.'

'I'm pleased to hear it.'

'I'm going to read every single word and, if possible, commit every single word to memory.'

'That sounds ambitious.'

'I hoped you'd be impressed.'

'I'm glad that you're happy with your purchase. We like to make sure that our buyers are satisfied.'

'I am.'

'It's part of our after-sales service.'

'You won't find a more satisfied customer than me.'

'Good. However, if you're so satisfied I'm a little disappointed that we still haven't received our first payment from you.'

Jim looks shifty and crestfallen. So, already his beautiful dream of love has been besmirched by money.

'I can't understand that,' he says. 'I definitely put the cheque in the post.'

'Did you?' she asks.

'Well, I'm fairly certain I did.'

'If you really did, then clearly the cheque has gone astray in the post. You'll have to write another one.'

'Yes. No problem. It's just that I'm waiting for a new cheque book.'

'Please Jim,' even in these circumstances it's a thrill for him to hear her speak his name, 'don't think you can fuck about with *The Books of Power*. They're the genuine article and the genuine article always costs. If you couldn't afford them you shouldn't have ordered them. But you did order them, you signed the agreement and now you have to come up with the payments.'

'I will, honestly. It's been a bad month.'

'I don't care, Jim. I don't care what sort of month it's been. An agreement is an agreement. If you really don't have a cheque book I'll be happy to accept cash.'

'Well . . .'

113

'You see, Jim, I'm here trying the gentle approach. If that doesn't work there are other ways of collecting debts.'

Jim slinks into the kitchenette, opens a cupboard, opens a tea caddy, shakes tea leaves from five neatly rolled ten-pound notes. He takes them back to Elaine and proffers them; not quite the love token he had in mind.

'Is this enough?'

'It's enough to be going on with.'

She takes the notes, unrolls them, holds them up to the light to check their authenticity, puts them in her wallet. She takes a pad from her brief-case and writes out a receipt for Jim. Perforations tear savagely as she rips it from the pad. Jim accepts it with a quiet dignity.

'I'm sorry,' he says.

'That's all right. So long as it doesn't happen again.'

'I'll see that it doesn't. I'm sorry we got off on the wrong foot.'

'It's nothing personal,' she says.

Jim thinks something has to be done or said here. He is at least as faint-hearted as the next man, but for once he decides to risk making a fool of himself.

'I don't want you to be angry with me,' he says. 'I don't want you to hate me.'

'I don't hate you exactly.'

'And I don't hate you. In fact I like you. I like you a lot.'

He waits, hoping she might say that she likes him too. But that's hoping for too much. When no such statement comes he sees he must press on alone, and hopes that he doesn't appear desperate. Desperation, he knows, is never very attractive.

'I like your encyclopedias,' he says. 'I think they're great. I feel we could be good friends. Would you let me buy you a drink?'

Her face is not friendly. She is not going to say yes. Yet she appears sympathetic, concerned even. It looks as though she may be about to give him some 'good advice'.

'Jim,' she says, 'I don't want you wasting your money on drink. I want every spare penny you've got going to pay for *The Books of Power*.'

'Then why don't *you* buy *me* a drink?'

Even as he's saying it he knows this is a mistake. He knows that you don't make girls fall in love with you by asking them to pay for your drinks. He has lost. A moment later she's gone. He still has the receipt, written in a slim, elegant script; something of her. There is a

114

beer can in his hand. He takes a defiant swig. Why shouldn't he spend his money on drink? He settles down with *The Books of Power*. He'll show her. He'll show everybody.

Mike Gombrich doesn't recognise the voice on the phone, though he knows he ought to. It is a voice that announces itself as Victoria's husband, and though voices are never quite the same in life as they are in the earpiece, he realises that the person speaking to him is not the man in the Alfa to whom he made an indecent suggestion. He wonders if someone is trying to make a fool of him, or, more worryingly, if he may have made a fool of himself.

'The thing is, Mr Gombrich,' says the voice.

'Call me Mike.'

'The thing is, I've got some cars to sell.'

'We're always interested in buying interesting items,' he says. 'You say "some". How many exactly?'

'The whole lot. My entire collection. About twenty.'

'I see.'

'Probably you don't, but I wondered if you'd be prepared to come to the house, look at the cars, and see if you can make me an offer.'

Mike thinks he detects sexual innuendo there but prefers not to read too much into it, not now, not yet, not if he made a fool of himself on that previous occasion. He makes an appointment for the next day.

He leaves his Corvette behind, he's not sure why. This would surely be the time when he ought to be trying to impress with things automotive. He goes in the firm's van. He's not sure, either, why he wants Jim to come with him, but he does. Partly it's because Jim knows the territory, having already seen the collection and assured Mike that it's a good un. Partly it's because there's safety in numbers, and he feels some need of safety, and he hopes it will be harder to make a fool of two people than of one.

They set out together, Jim driving, Mike slouched into the far corner of the cab. They have a camera with them, a notebook, a trade guide to classic car prices, even though Mike claims to know most of it by heart, a full tool kit, inspection lamps, jacks, axle stands. Mike also has a pack of condoms with him, though he

115

hasn't told Jim about that and he doesn't seriously expect to get a chance to use them. Today is reconnaissance.

'I really would rather not be going,' Jim says after they've covered a mile or two.

'What are you scared of?'

'I'm not scared of anything, but there's a lot of work I could be doing back at the garage.'

This Mike seriously doubts. He knows that Jim's standards have slipped, and he wouldn't mind knowing why. He knows that Jim is preoccupied. For one thing he spends every lunch and tea break reading. This is out of character. And he does it in a secretive, furtive way. Mike has no idea what he's reading or what he's up to, but he has never thought of Jim as a bookworm, and he doesn't like the change. He disapproves strongly. He'd find it easier to understand if Jim was only preoccupied with love or money.

'So,' says Mike, 'you didn't fancy this bloke's wife.'

'Not really, no.'

'Why not? What was wrong with her?'

'Nothing wrong. Just not my type.'

'What's your type?' Mike asks, thinking there is probably no such thing.

Jim says, 'Cool, efficient, intellectual, cultured.'

Mike hopes that Jim is being waggish, but he can't tell with Jim any more. They can see the big house now. Jim turns into the drive, taking the van slowly towards the house, ever more slowly, ever more reluctant to arrive, but arrive they do.

A very big man is seated on a bench at the edge of the lawn. He is wearing old clothes and his feet are bare. He looks up as the van arrives but doesn't seem very interested. They can't be sure that this is Victoria's husband. From his appearance he could be the gardener or possibly some tramp who's wandered in from the road. Nevertheless, they approach him and he knows who they are and is expecting them, and he asks them to follow him round the side of the house to the big blue hangar. His gait is plodding and weary. There is an air of sadness and defeat about him and yet, Mike decides, he does somehow look like the sort of man who would own this house and might have collected twenty classic cars. And yes, he looks the sort of man who might be married to Victoria. He looks more the part than the man in the Alfa did. So who the hell was *he?*'

Mike wonders what it would be like to find yourself in the same bed as Victoria and this man – crowded, he thinks. The man's bulky and fleshy and a bit old, but after all, it's not as if Mike would be touching him or anything, God forbid.

They enter the hangar through the small side door. Immediately there's a reek of petrol and immediately Mike and Jim see why. The cars have been left as they were when Victoria's husband first discovered them after the break-in. He has changed nothing. He has padded among the débris, leaned against a mutilated wing, surveyed the scene for long, morbid, tearful hours, but he's made no attempt to clean up the mess.

Mike Gombrich is horrified. He can empathise. He remembers how bad he felt when the Corvette was vandalised. This must be the same feeling to the enth degree. He wonders if there's a connection. Wrecked though the machinery is, there's no denying the quality. These are real thoroughbreds, real collectors' items, and that's why it really hurts.

'Fucking hell,' Mike says.

Jim looks at the mess and suspects that the job of cleaning up this place might defeat even him, even if he was in peak form, even if he really cared.

'What happened?' Mike asks.

'Yobs. Maniacs. I don't even want to think about it.'

'I know what you mean.'

'I just want to get rid of them all, get rid of everything.'

'Are you sure?'

'Absolutely certain.'

'Are any of them still driveable?'

'Possibly, if they haven't had their sumps drained and their tyres slashed and their steering wheels and gear levers pulled out. But I'd rather not talk about it.'

Mike walks up the centre aisle, the cars facing him. They stare at him through broken headlamps. They have dumb, twisted radiator grilles for mouths. Mike has never been a great one for zoomorphism but he can't escape the impression that he is walking among fine but wounded beasts. He treads warily, avoiding pools of oil and broken glass, wing mirrors and pieces of trim ripped from the cars.

He says, 'You'll understand that I wouldn't exactly want to buy them as they stand.'

The big man nods sadly.

'But there might be some kind of deal we could do,' Mike adds.

'I need a bit of help,' Victoria's husband says. 'I feel paralysed. I need someone to take control, do what's necessary, take them away,

117

get rid of them, sell them. You can restore them or sell them for scrap, do what you like, but I can't face doing any of it myself.'

'I see,' says Mike. 'With what kind of financial arrangement?'

'You can name your own terms.'

This is an offer he knows he can't refuse. This is a deal he ought to want. He ought to be salivating. There are some wonderful machines under all this destruction, infinitely better than his normal stock. Selling this little lot, just having his name involved, would improve his business status and edge him into a bigger, higher league. That ought to be what he wants. He can't understand why he feel so unenthusiastic at the prospect.

'Can we go outside?' Victoria's husband says. 'I can't stand to be in here any longer.'

They leave the scene of destruction and step outside. Together they pace the lawn.

'I've been doing a lot of thinking,' Victoria's husband continues, 'about why I'm so upset, and I think I've worked it out.'

Jim and Mike's faces show that they're unlikely to be fascinated by this, but he is perhaps not as sensitive to the needs and desires of others as he once was.

'My collection wasn't so very much,' he says, 'but it was a small, ordered, civilised corner in a very hostile world. What is life, anyway?'

Jim and Mike shrug to show that they have no idea.

'Life seems to me to consist entirely and increasingly of forces over which we have absolutely no control. We all want control of our destinies, but if we're honest with ourselves we know we can't get it. So we try to build some small kingdom over which we rule. It could be a family. It could be a corner shop.

'That's what my collection was. When I used to spend time in there with my cars, cleaning them, doing a bit of servicing, admiring them, I thought I was king of all I surveyed. Foolish, I know. There's been an insurrection of reality.'

Jim and Mike nod sagely. They wait until they're sure he isn't going to say anything else. Jim thinks he might change the subject.

'Is the wife keeping well?' he asks.

'My wife is unchanged.'

Mike thinks this must be a good thing, though present circumstances have driven immediate hopes of erotic gratification from his mind. He's thinking, with no great pleasure, about how to tackle the job ahead, which of his contacts he'll need to use, what specialist skills

118

and services will be required, whether he has any regular customers he might be able to talk into buying one of these cars. There's also the problem of where to begin.

Leaving the victim on the lawn he returns with Jim to the cars in the hangar. He takes photographs. They'll make good 'before' shots. He notes down makes and models, whether the damage is cosmetic or structural, which ones need trailering, how long restoration would take and how much it might cost. He is well out of his depth here.

He tells Jim that he doesn't want to rush into this. The first job will be to attack the mess, have a good clean up so they can see precisely what they've got on their hands. How does that appeal to him? It doesn't appeal to Jim at all, and he can't hide the fact.

They leave Victoria's husband with the promise that at least one of them will be back before long, and then they can really get down to business. As they leave he has resumed his former position on the bench, a gloomy piece of statuary presiding over the garden.

Mike and Jim don't say much to each other on the way back to Killer Kars, and once they arrive Mike gets in his Corvette and drives home for the day. He is a confused and troubled man. Though usually free of both paranoia and introspection he is today worried by both. First his car is vandalised, then his sexuality takes an unexpected turn, then his best employee loses his touch, then he himself loses, if not his touch then at least his taste for the business. And does this have something to do with the wrecking of Victoria's husband's cars, and does everything in some way involve that little cow selling the encyclopedias? Even if it isn't anything more than coincidence he still doesn't like it.

He parks his car, goes into his flat and knows right away that something is wrong. The front door doesn't seem to have been forced and there's no sign of any ransacking but he knows immediately someone has been in. He can see that his stereo and video are still there and some instinct takes him into the bedroom. Even there nothing looks out of place, but he slides open the bottom drawer of his mirrored wardrobe, the drawer in which he keeps his collection of women's underwear, his erotic souvenirs, and finds the cupboard is bare.

There is a story about P. G. Wodehouse's first meeting with W. S. Gilbert. It appears in *Bring on the Girls* by Wodehouse and Guy

119

Bolton, but I have to admit that I came across it in *The Oxford Book of Literary Anecdotes*, which will give you some idea of the rigorousness of my research methods.

Wodehouse, aged twenty-one, and in his words 'a shrinking floweret' was invited to Sunday lunch at Gilbert's home, in company with fourteen other guests. He was relieved by the size of the party because he thought that would make it possible for him to sit quietly and go unnoticed.

Gilbert was known as a raconteur, so halfway through the meal he began to tell a story. It was a shaggy dog story, drawn out to great length, building up anticipation for the punchline which was delayed as long as possible. When, at last, Gilbert got to the moment when the punchline was due to be delivered he took a long pause for comic effect. However, the quiet and thus far inconspicuous and very nervous Wodehouse thought that the story was over. Wanting to be a good audience he let out a burst of laughter that was initially forced, but once it had started it became uncontrollable, hysterical, going on for several minutes. By the time Wodehouse had stopped laughing the other guests had started to talk of other things and Gilbert never got the chance to deliver the punchline.

Gilbert looked daggers at Wodehouse and appeared to be about to do him some injury. Wodehouse was terrified and also ashamed that he'd made such a fool of himself, and had completely failed in his attempt to remain inconspicuous. The only consolation available to him was to think that he had the distinction of being the only man ever to stop W. S. Gilbert telling a funny story.

I like this anecdote a lot. It is a funny story about a man failing to tell a funny story. The punchline is that Wodehouse prevented Gilbert delivering the punchline. By destroying one anecdote Wodehouse creates another.

I can see how this is a tale for our times, about the breakdown of narratives, or perhaps, more properly, a tale about narratives about the breakdown of narratives. I expect Ted Langley wouldn't have been much amused by it. He probably wouldn't even have bothered to file it.

Thornton McCain, incidentally, does not figure in the *Oxford Book of Literary Anecdotes*.

★

'Everything's lot easier if you're very thin and black suits you,' said Victoria.

By 'everything' she meant deciding what to wear. We'd spent the night together at my house still erectionless and now, the morning after, she was inspecting my clothes with some distaste and disapproval. My 'wardrobe' consisted of three pairs of jeans in various states of fade, half a dozen shirts that were neither casual nor smart, two shapeless sweaters, a slightly Italian-cut jacket, a good old battered leather jacket, and a suit I could still wear if I needed to, though its style was at least five years out of date. I had the usual miscellany of shoes, socks and knickers, and half a dozen ties. That was all. It seemed enough.

'We need to smarten you up,' she said. 'We need to make you more hip.'

I wanted to be obliging. I agreed to go shopping. First we tried the Oxfam shops and the secondhand clothes shops. I've never had any objection to secondhand clothes in principle, but tracking down something I'd want to wear from one of these shops seemed to require more time and foraging instinct than I possessed.

Victoria would hold up some large, plain, cotton shirt with a frayed collar and say, 'How about this?' I would object to the frayed collar. Then she'd find a satin cowboy shirt with lassoes embroidered across the breast pockets. Then a velvet waistcoat that must have been just the job circa 1967. Our trawl of the secondhand clothes shops of Sheffield landed us a painted silk tie and a burgundy trilby hat ('The sort bookmakers wear,' Victoria said). They both struck me as perfectly good, stylish items for someone other than me to wear. Nevertheless I bought them. It seemed to make Victoria happy. Then we hit the menswear and department stores.

'My husband's got thousands of ties,' she said, apropos of nothing.

'Don't tell me he collects them.'

'No. They just sort of breed.'

I couldn't imagine finding a thousand ties that I liked. I couldn't imagine finding half a dozen.

Choosing clothes in the new shops should have been easier. They might not have been so Bohemian and chic, but at least they came in a better range of sizes. Only clothes for giants and dwarves seemed to have found their way on to the secondhand market.

We spent a couple of hours looking at new clothes. After much heart-searching and increasing inertia on my part I bought a pair

121

of black tee-shirts. I wasn't very thin and I wasn't sure that black suited me, but it pleased Victoria, and by then that was all that mattered.

By the end of the afternoon we had seen, considered and spurned enough men's clothing to keep a small Third World nation snappily dressed for the next decade. I was struck, hardly for the first time, but with renewed impact, by how little of anything I wanted to buy. Much of the time it seemed inconceivable that *anybody* would want to buy the tatty, ugly junk we'd looked at. Yet presumably people did buy this stuff otherwise it wouldn't be in the shops. The merchandise that they stocked provided a commercially based, yet psychologically accurate, profile of people's needs and tastes.

As we moved from shop to shop, buying nothing, liking nothing, it was as though we were looking at exhibits in some terrible museum of the present day. And though we had only looked at clothes, I suspected it would have been the same if we'd been looking at carpets or curtains or crockery or furniture. The exhibits were utterly arcane. They came from a society I didn't begin to understand; fragments from a lost civilisation. What kind of maniac would put together a collection like this?

It was another night when I had nothing better to do than watch Jim perform at a quiz night. He didn't do badly but again he was beaten by the skinny kid. Jim didn't seem particularly down-hearted. While he went to the bar I got talking to the kid. He was still wearing his tee-shirt held together by anarchy badges. I didn't know if I was being crazy but something somehow clicked. I pointed at the badge.

'Are you interested in anarchy?' I asked.

He shrugged. 'Yeah.'

'And how does that interest show itself?'

I knew I sounded absurd. He looked at me as though he agreed.

'I don't go around trying to smash the state if that's what you mean,' he said.

'What about bus shelters and phone boxes?'

'I'm not a bloody vandal.'

'Or collections of cars?'

'What are you talking about?'

'It's all right by me,' I said. 'I don't mind if you wreck a few systems.'

'You're the one who's wrecked.'

I wasn't, but I didn't argue.

'There's nothing very anarchic about winning general knowledge contests,' I said.

'That's right,' he said. 'I'm not an anarchist, I'm an anal retentive.'

Ah yes. I knew that Freud had a lot to say about the oral and the anal. I didn't particularly understand what it was he had to say, but I knew that the anal type wants to keep his faeces to himself. He wants to organise, regiment, retain. He is your archetypal collector. It occurred to me that a possible subtitle for my book might be, 'Anal Retentives I Have Met', but I thought it wasn't snappy enough.

However, finding a snappy title for the book was the least of my problems. The simple fact was that I had ceased to be deeply fascinated by collectors and their quaint, touching eccentricities. I'd had a bellyful. I didn't need to hear any more about the origins and manifestations of their obsessions. I didn't need to read any more books or track down any more articles. My research was complete. I had more than enough material. I had arrived at the point where I ought to have been able to start the actual writing of my book. So why couldn't I?

I didn't know why. But I didn't worry about it at first. Writing a book was a daunting task. It was therefore no surprise that I was daunted. That was par for the course and only to be expected. The difficulty could surely be overcome. A moment would surely arrive and I would seize it, make a start, and the whole work would flow easily from me in a most un-anal-retentive way. It was only a question of getting in the mood and finding some impetus. I was stupid enough to believe all this crap.

Next morning the phone rang. I answered it. I said, 'Why do you keep phoning me?'

Rachel said, 'We've been through this. Because I want to.'

I was never able to stop Rachel doing anything she wanted to do. I was never able to stop anybody.

'I thought we'd agreed we were still going to be friends,' she said.

'Friends ring each other once in a while. There was a time when we said we were always going to be friends.'

'I don't remember saying that.'

'You only remember what you want to remember. You said it all right.'

'I probably nodded non-committally.'

'You said it. You were nicer to me in those days.'

'That's it,' I said. 'I was a really nice guy in those days, now I'm just a brute. I don't see why you keep ringing me when you know I'm such a brute.'

'Because I know you don't mean it.'

She seemed to have won some sort of victory by insisting that I was a better person than I pretended to be. I had no defence against those sort of tactics.

'How's your book?' she asked.

'Rotten,' I said. 'It's stagnant. It's putrid. It's sitting there decaying, causing a bad smell.'

'It sounds as though you'd rather not talk about it.'

There was no denying that Rachel had certain intuitive gifts. I expected they came in very handy in the world of advertising.

'How's your girlfriend?' she asked.

'Fine. How's your work?'

'Frantic as ever. You don't really want to hear about it, do you?'

'Not really.'

'As a matter of fact we're starting work on an account that may turn out to be something of a first.'

'Oh yes?' I said, turning my listening faculties to neutral.

'It looks like we're going to be doing a major campaign – for a set of encyclopedias, would you believe? It makes a change from lager. We're doing ads for newspapers, magazines, television, the works. It ought to be the biggest splash anybody's ever made with any kind of book, let alone an encyclopedia. The problem is, we need an angle and so far we haven't found one. And there's another problem, the product has a very naff name: *The Books of Power*.'

Suddenly I was listening, and I was wishing I'd started to listen earlier. 'Did you say *The Books of Power*?'

'Don't tell me you had a set by your bed as a child,' she said.

'No, but I know someone who's got a set now.'

'Well, it proves somebody must be buying them. How do they rate on customer satisfaction?'

'Off the scale.'

'Huh?'

'He thinks they're the best thing in the history of the world.'

'Really?' she asked.

'No kidding.'

'Have you looked at them?'

I admitted that I had.

'They're not the best thing in the history of the world, are they?'
she said.

'No.'

'In fact I thought they were fairly piss poor.'

'That's no doubt why you decided to take on the account.'

'Spare me the integrity, Steve.'

'I thought you liked my integrity. Listen. I may have an idea.'

'I've heard your ideas on advertising.'

'An idea for your campaign. An angle.'

'*You* have an idea for a campaign?'

I didn't rise to that. I said, 'You run a series of nationwide general
knowledge contests. You could link it up with a newspaper or a
television company, and all the questions you ask are from *The
Books of Power*. You could get all kinds of celebrities involved and
the winner gets . . .'

'A free set of encyclopedias?'

'No,' I said. 'I think the prize needs to be a bit more up-market.'

'These things *are* up-market. You know how much a set costs?'

I told her I did. I could tell she didn't like my idea much, which
was a shame, at least for Jim. I felt sure he'd be a certain winner,
and that looked to me like his best, possibly his only chance of
stardom.

'The problem with competitions', Rachel said, 'is that people like
the ones where they don't have to do or know anything and stand
to win a million. A nationwide general knowledge contest sounds
too much like hard work.'

'So you're not going to use my idea.'

'No, but I've heard worse. I hear worse ideas every day from our
creative department.'

'I'll expect paying if you use it.'

'You don't count. You're family.'

Poor Jim. At least I'd tried. My conversation with Rachel ended.
It had been rather less antagonistic than usual. We made some
nebulous reference to meeting up in the unspecified future. We

125

might even have sounded like friends. My views on advertising remained unchanged.

In the greater scheme of things I tend not to believe much in progress. I don't think things get much better. The sum total of misery in the world seems to remain about constant; though I don't deny that there is some occasional, localised relief. However, comparing small things to great, progress was suddenly made with a vengeance in my own small domain the night that my impotence disappeared and Victoria and I 'did the business'.

We'd been out to see a film, a film in which none of the characters seemed ever to have been troubled by anything so un-Hollywood as impotence, and we got back to my house at about ten-thirty. We went to bed. We petted heavily, my penis didn't stiffen, and Victoria, as ever, displayed great stoicism.

Then, as on a previous occasion, she began to read aloud from Thornton McCain. I've said before that McCain's writing is sometimes scurrilous and erotic, and Victoria chose that passage from *The Bottle Blonde* where the heroine, Fee Magnusson, is seduced by the albino brother and sister. They get themselves locked in a department store overnight and perform a different, depraved sexual act in each department. I think it had as much to do with Victoria's way of reading as it did with the words themselves, but one way or another, after she'd read a page or so, I found myself formidably erect. I was amazed.

It was too good an opportunity to waste. Victoria threw the book aside and leapt on me. It crossed my mind that this new tumescence might be a fragile thing and ought to be treated with extreme care and delicacy; but I was being over-cautious. At long last the erection was here, and it looked like it was here to stay. Naturally it waxed and waned a little in the course of the night, but it was more than serviceable whenever it was called upon, and it was called upon a great deal. I did my best, better than my best, to make up for all those previous failures, and Victoria seemed to be more than delighted with the new state of affairs. Why wouldn't she be? In between extremely accomplished love-making we dozed gently, but seldom for very long, and I expect I had a smirk set across my face for most of the night, caused by pride, pleasure and yes, localised relief.

126

'I always said Thornton McCain was a genius,' said Victoria.

In the morning we successfully made love again before she had to leave and go back to her husband. I felt duly exhausted and extremely pleased with myself. Victoria assured me that our success had been well worth waiting for, and I said I couldn't wait to try it again. She said I'd have to, but I didn't read anything into that at the time. As far as I was concerned the secondary impotence had been banished and now we could get down to the serious business of pleasure.

We had only ever seen each other at infrequent, irregular intervals, and I tended to wait for her to ring me, because I didn't want to phone her house and risk having to talk to her husband. He probably wouldn't have been troubled by it but I would. Nevertheless, I was surprised, given the tremendous erotic breakthrough we'd just made, that a whole week passed and I hadn't heard from Victoria. I assumed she'd be keen to sleep with me again. At the very least I thought she'd be curious to see whether the breakthrough was permanent. Personally, I had no real doubts. Some psychological and physiological ravine had been crossed and I felt I was safely on the other side and that there would be no going back. I felt that a complete cure had, by whatever mysterious means, been effected, but that didn't mean I wouldn't feel better once we'd made love again.

I soon got fed up with waiting for the phone to ring, so despite my misgivings I called Victoria's number. I got her husband, naturally. He was civil enough, said that Victoria wasn't home at the moment and I said, Never mind, I'd try again later. I didn't leave a message. This happened several times. By now two weeks had passed and I was starting to get seriously paranoid. I thought something was going on. I thought her husband was probably behind it. I thought somebody owed me an explanation. So I rang again and got her husband again.

'Look, there isn't a problem here, is there?' I asked.

'What sort of problem?' he said suavely.

'I don't know. Is Victoria ill or something?'

'No, she's not ill.'

'And she hasn't gone away or something?'

'No.'

'So are you stopping her coming to the phone maybe?'

'Don't be absurd,' he said.

Yes, it did sound absurd when I put it into words. Victoria was not the sort of woman you could prevent from coming to the phone if she wanted to.

'Tell me to mind my own business,' her husband said, 'but it sounds to me as though she really doesn't want to speak to you.'

In all my paranoia that wasn't actually one of the possibilities I'd thought of, and I still didn't seriously entertain it. How could she not want to speak to me when we were suddenly so good in bed together? I didn't believe it for a moment. Then a few more days passed and I still hadn't heard from her, and I had to start considering it as a real possibility, even if it was a possibility that made no sense.

I wanted to do something. I wanted to make some gesture. I couldn't quite see myself marching up to her front door and demanding an explanation but I thought that was probably what I ought to be doing. I ought to have been dramatic, forceful, passionate, but I was none of these things, so I hung around seething with hurt, getting more and more angry and frustrated, feeling ever more like a victim, though I was not sure a victim of what.

Then I *did* see Victoria and it was by accident and I was completely unready and unrehearsed for the grand emotional scene that I felt was required. We ran into each other in the magazine section of W. H. Smith.

'Victoria!' I said.

She looked at me uncertainly. Perhaps she didn't have her contact lenses in. She greeted me as she might have greeted a harmless but distant in-law.

'What's going on?' I said.

'Nothing much. I was looking for a copy of *Vogue*.'

'Why haven't you rung me?'

'I was going to. I just never got round to it.'

'But why were you never there when I rang?'

She shrugged. It was part apology, but it had a good measure of indifference in it too.

I said, 'I thought we had a pretty good time when we were last together.'

'We did.'

'I thought you might want to repeat it.'

Her look told me that she didn't want to repeat it. Not now. Not ever. I was in utter confusion.

'Why not?' I asked. 'What's going on?'

'This really isn't the place.'

She was right. Next to us two young heavy metal fans were

128

thumbing through music magazines and listening to our conversation. We moved to the stationery department.

'It's just one of those things,' Victoria said.

I had no idea what she meant.

'What can I say?' she went on. 'Once is enough. You always knew I was a collector. I'd never slept with a writer before. Now I have so it's time to look for something else.'

'I don't believe this.'

'Besides, it's one of the house rules, one of the things my husband and I have agreed on. He doesn't care who I fuck so long as I only fuck them once.'

'What?'

'That way he knows I'm not going to get involved and leave him.'

'I thought we were already involved.'

She gave me a look that I wasn't clever enough to interpret. I wanted it to mean that she felt as involved as I did but was fighting not to show it. But perhaps it meant that she thought I was stupid ever to have felt any such thing. Then another thought belted me across the face.

'Are you saying that if I'd managed to get it up that first afternoon, that would have been it?'

She nodded.

'Christ. So all the time I was impotent,' the word seemed to echo round the shop, out of place amid the double entry books and the pen and pencil sets, 'I was prolonging our relationship.'

'Yes.'

'And in being able to make love properly I was ending it?'

'That's right.'

'Jesus.'

I felt like kicking or smashing something. No doubt there are those who would have kicked or smashed Victoria, but I'm no brute, and I had to content myself with picking up a desk diary and beating it feelingly against the edge of a metal shelf.

'Why didn't you tell me any of this?'

It was a stupid question and she didn't bother to reply.

'I don't have any right of appeal on this one, do I?' I said.

'Of course not.'

I was caught between the desire to storm out dramatically and the desire to stay and slug it out with some vile, wounding tirade. But I couldn't think of anything to say, and the shop was too crowded to allow a successful storming out. I shook my head in a rather studied gesture of sadness, loss and incomprehension. It didn't impress Victoria.

She said, 'I don't suppose you *did* destroy his car collection, did you?'

It took me a while before I realised what she was talking about.

'I was with you at the time,' I said. 'How could I?'

'I'm not sure. Perhaps you could have got somebody else to do it.'

'Oh sure.'

'It was only a thought.'

'The only collection I'd like to break up is your collection of lovers.'

'You're very sweet.'

We never performed the great emotional scene. How could we in W. H. Smith? Before long I had nothing more to say. I didn't want her to go but I had no way of keeping her. I had nothing to bargain with. I'd lost my status as a desirable collector's item. I wanted to change her mind but I had no powers of persuasion. She was her own woman. We are all our own people. That's most of the problem.

I had never for a moment thought that my affair with Victoria was any version of the real thing. I'd always known it wasn't going to last. I'd always known that Victoria would eventually go in search of new finds. I'd never had the vanity to think I was the prize of anyone's collection, least of all Victoria's, and I knew I wasn't the one item that made all further collecting unnecessary.

All the same, as everything else in my life seemed to be becoming redundant or malignant, Victoria had meant more and more to me. Increasingly she had seemed like all I'd got. It didn't feel very good to be reminded, of what I'd known all along, that I hadn't got her at all.

I felt angry, hurt, bitter, betrayed, deceived, rejected, used – all the usual things; and I felt worst of all because I knew I had no right to feel any of those things.

Ted Langley is thrilled when the carrier's van pulls up outside his house and the delivery man presents him with two boxes of what he takes to be computer hardware. In a way he's glad that his wife's out shopping so that he can have the pleasure of unpacking all to himself. The boxes are smaller and heavier than he's been imagining, but that doesn't disappoint him. No doubt this is because of miniaturisation and technical wizardry.

He carries the boxes into the living-room and places them on the large, low coffee table. Prior to unpacking them he prepares himself a cup of tea, a plate of bourbons and a supply of cigarettes to intensify the pleasure.

Ted doesn't know much about computers but he's started to learn. He's got hold of a couple of books on the subject, and as far as he can see his demands aren't that great. A fairly simple system ought to be enough for his purposes. He hopes he hasn't bought something in excess of his requirements. He needs a system with a moderately large memory to contain the vast database of jokes. He'll have to type in each one, probably in some abbreviated, shorthand form. At first he thought he'd have to give each one a category or a code, but he's learned that won't be necessary. Once the jokes are in, all he'll have to do is operate a word search to locate the jokes he wants. If he's playing a one-night stand at the end of a pier in a holiday resort in Wales, he'll tell the computer to search for 'Wales', 'Pier', 'Seaside', 'Holiday', and 'Landlady', and get it to print out all the jokes in which those things appear. This will then give him his night's script. Easy.

This very night he's doing a show at a club in Doncaster. This morning he went through his card files and he has now assembled tonight's script. With luck, this hallowed process will soon be redundant. The riffling through cards, the endless cross-referencing and re-filing, the problem of lost or misfiled or damaged cards will be a thing of the past.

It feels good to know that he's harnessing technology to his own creative ends, good to know that he's a man of his time, slightly ahead of his time as far as the world of comedy is concerned. Other comedians still jot down jokes on the back of envelopes and in school exercise books. This will give him a much needed edge.

Scattering bourbon crumbs and cigarette ash, he begins to unpack the boxes. He is expecting matt plastic surfaces, plugs, leads, discs, screens. He is not expecting a set of *The Books of Power*. The first box contains volumes one to nine. The other box contains the rest.

Clearly there's been some sort of packing error at the warehouse. They must keep their computers and the encyclopedias side by side, and some disenchanted employee's sent him the wrong one by mistake. Incompetent but typical. Ted is bitterly disappointed, but he'll get on the phone to them right away and sort it out.

There's no packing note or return address on the boxes so he gets out the agreement he signed. He sees that the name at the head of the document is BOP Services. There's an address but it's only a post office box, and there's no phone number or name of anyone to complain to. He spends a barren and infuriating fifteen minutes with directory enquiries. He smokes a couple of cigarettes. It looks as though this problem may have to be sorted out by letter, and he's not very good at writing letters, and it's going to take time, and if anybody thinks he's paying the return postage on these encyclopedias they've got another think coming.

He looks at the agreement again and sees that it refers throughout to 'goods' and not to any specific product. It's not possible, is it, that he inadvertently *did* sign up to buy a set of encyclopedias? Suddenly it looks all too possible. The lying little bitch! Seething with disgust and rage, he thinks he may very possibly have been very severely had. He looks at the books and the packing material. He kicks them around for a while, knocking over the coffee table in the process, but they yield too easily. There's not even any satisfaction there.

Fury steams and bubbles inside him. He would like to destroy someone or something. Ted Langley is not much given to walking, but these are extreme circumstances. He slams the front door behind him and sets off for the local park, as though his own house is too small to contain his anger.

He's supposed to be sharp and clever. He's not supposed to get conned. They haven't heard the last of this. He'll sue. Nobody messes Ted Langley about. He'll track them down. He'll get his money back. He'll get what he's entitled to.

He's wrong. He won't. By the time Ted reaches the park and sits down by the children's playground, the cigarette that was in the ashtray on the coffee table that he knocked over will have started a small fire. The cardboard boxes and the polystyrene packing will be the first to ignite. Flames will spring from them and lick at the table and carpet, then spread to the upholstery of the settee. In a few minutes, long before any signs of the blaze are visible from outside, fire will be scurrying up to the first floor of the house, into the bedrooms. Flames will gnaw their way into the wood of his custom-made filing cabinets. The wood and the

132

cards will burn easily. The house will become an inferno. In ten minutes or so Ted Langley's need for a computer will be utterly destroyed.

The pub is hot and packed, and the jukebox is playing hits of the early 'seventies that make conversation difficult. Another quiz is over and Jim has finished second again to the skinny kid. Nothing new in that. It was a close contest this time but Jim never really thought he was in with a chance of winning. He knows he still has a lot to learn. The kid, whose name Jim can never remember, despite having heard it dozens of times now, is magnanimous in victory and has bought Jim a pint.

'Good contest,' the kid says.

'Yes,' says Jim, unconvincingly.

'Didn't you enjoy it?'

'I got a lot wrong,' he says. 'There was a lot I didn't know.'

'I got a lot wrong too.'

Jim can't remember him getting any wrong at all, but he nods in agreement.

'And you know what?' the kid says. 'I've been watching this. When you and me are in a quiz together we always get different things wrong, never the same things.'

Jim hasn't noticed this, but that's not such a surprise. Once a quiz has started he concentrates so hard that he misses most of what goes on around him.

'Yes,' says the kid. 'You know things I don't. I know things you don't. We have different areas of specialisation and different blind spots.'

Again, Jim hasn't noticed that the kid has any blind spots at all, and Jim certainly has no area of specialisation. Jim thinks the kid must be leading up to something.

The kid says, 'So what I'm saying is, let's pool our resources. Let's form a team.'

'Huh?'

'We'd be unbeatable together. We could enter team quizzes and play against those general knowledge fruit machines. Together we could clean up.'

'But you seem to be cleaning up on your own.'

The kid looks sad and vulnerable, and younger than ever.

'You're not making this very easy for me,' he says. 'Yeah, all right, so I'm cleaning up. I'm a real know-it-all. Yeah, I win every quiz I enter. And you know what? Sometimes I deliberately get answers wrong so that I don't look like a complete smart arse.

'But so what? There's no virtue in it. There's no real skill in it. It's not as if I've ever had to work hard at it. I've just got one of those minds that stores a lot of rubbish.'

'It's not rubbish,' says Jim.

'Well maybe not all of it, but a lot of it. And not much of it *means* anything. Information just accumulates in my head, that's all.'

'I envy you,' says Jim.

'Oh Jesus, look, what I'm saying is, it's lonely. I'd like a bit of companionship. I'd like a friend. I thought you might feel the same.'

Jim doesn't know how he feels. Sure, he's lonely. And if he linked up with this kid he could start winning quizzes instead of finishing second or third. But winning isn't everything. In fact, when it's put to him like this, he realises winning isn't anything. He isn't in it for the winning any more, though no way is he in it for the joy of taking part. Once he was in it to try to impress Elaine, but that sounds silly to him now. He realised, he's not sure when, how hard Elaine is to impress. Mike Gombrich could probably do it, but not a mere mortal like him. He's given up hoping. He's surprised to find he has no regrets.

Somewhere along the line Jim has become a true obsessive. He has become obsessed not so much with knowledge itself as with knowing the contents of *The Books of Power*. His performance in quizzes gives him some rough indication of his progress but ultimately he feels this too will pass away. And it looks as though the need for companionship may already have passed.

'I'll think about it,' he says to the kid, but they both know he won't.

The show, Ted decides, must go on. His house is consumed, his jokes gone, his wife (who came home from shopping to find the house a blackened ruin) is sedated but still hysterical. His life is shredded, but he still wants to go out in front of a few hundred Doncaster folk and be funny.

He sits in the dressing-room in a cocoon of confusion and despair. He is also in an advanced state of drunkenness. He has eaten two whole Madeira cakes and washed them down with a bottle of vodka. He feels only slightly better for it. The club's manager has told him he needn't go on.

'They'll be disappointed, of course,' he says. 'You're a very popular attraction. They want to see you. But they'll understand. Nobody expects a man to go on stage and give his best when he's just lost his house.'

'I don't give a toss about the house,' Ted says. 'It's the jokes.'

The manager doesn't understand, and perhaps it's as well. Ted insists he'll be appearing as advertised. Quite what he'll do when he gets on stage is another matter. He can't remember which jokes he selected that morning. In fact he'd be hard pressed to remember any joke at all at the moment, but he hopes that once he gets on stage everything will be all right.

On stage now, a matron in red leather is singing a version of 'Memories' and the crowd hasn't rioted. They must be a good audience; pliable, docile, easily pleased. This is what Ted needs tonight.

He dresses for the stage. His tie won't lie straight and there's some kind of sugary stain on his jacket's breast pocket, but if the audience really loves him they'll forgive a few faults in his clothing. It's the whole man they're getting here.

He feels no nerves or excitement as he waits to go on. He's only going out there to do what he's done thousands of times before, and even if he isn't as good tonight as he ought to be, he believes his basic professional instincts will see him through. There's the matter of what material he's going to perform, but it's too late to think about that. He hears himself being introduced. He's on.

He's slow crossing the stage and getting to the mike, and when he gets there he stands silently for a long time with his hands in his pockets, looking up at the lights, down at his feet, off into the wings. It is some time before he looks at the audience. He gives a start as though surprised to find them there. The house lights are bright. He can see individual faces. They usually blend into a collective whole, an undifferentiated gathering that constitutes the house. But now he can see each set of features and each expression.

Fortunately most of the faces are smiling. Some people are even tittering. They're enjoying the spectacle of this large, blundering man, standing unsteadily at the edge of the stage and inspecting

135

them. They find this funny. He opens his mouth as if to say something but thinks better of it. They find this funnier still.

'A funny thing happened to me on the way here this evening,' he says, then pauses. It looks like a fine piece of comic timing. 'But I'm buggered if I can remember what it was.'

He laughs a lot at his own joke, if joke it is, amused by some inner, private reference. He thinks things are going well. This could be a good night after all.

'I came from a very poor family,' he says. 'We were so poor when I was a kid, we didn't have any money.'

Then he is in full flow. The human encyclopedia of comedy begins to disgorge his treasure. But the jokes are garbled. He gets halfway through a joke then sets off on another, down dark mental pathways, making connections between newly wed couples, removal men, Irish navvies, hairdressers and double-glazing salesmen. The punch lines don't come, or they come in clusters, but detached from any joke. It is all free association, a kind of surrealism. Fragments of stories, catchphrases, halves of one-liners, ad libs, heckler stoppers, puns, all come spilling out.

'How do you make a Swiss roll? She was only the milkman's daughter. A man goes into a chemist's shop. Take my wife. And the vicar says. I wouldn't say my mother-in-law was. Two melons in a string bag. My dog's got no nose. No, it's just the way my trousers hang. So she turns to me and says.'

He doesn't pause much for breath, nor to let the audience respond. He delivers a collage of formulae and set-pieces, of doctor's waiting-rooms and football terraces and honeymoon suites, the sure-fire winners, the rib-ticklers, the thigh-slappers, the old chestnuts.

'Cotton-wool balls. I thought they'd never dry. Not tonight Josephine. I've left the baby on the bus. Don't talk to me about British Rail. How many queers does it take to change a light-bulb? I'm not feeling myself tonight. Yes, but I don't have the inclination. Hello playmates. Shut that door. Two in the front, two in the back. So he goes up to heaven and there's St Peter at the pearly gates. Bloody English weather. Bloody women drivers. Bloody teenagers.'

It is quite conceivable that there is an audience somewhere who would have hailed Ted Langley's act as a kind of breakthrough. They would have perceived its deranged frenzy as a form of liberating deconstruction. This audience, however, is not in attendance at this Doncaster club on this particular occasion.

136

But there is one member of the audience, someone who has the knack of being in the right place at the right time with the right equipment, who is enjoying the spectacle beyond all expectations. It is Eve Leviticus. She is seated in the front row, a tape-recorder concealed about her person, bootlegging the show for posterity. She knows she's got a real gem, a real classic and collector's item. She's glad she came.

Still burbling, still pressing on with his act, Ted Langley is dragged from the stage after no more than ten minutes. Amid some booing, much bewilderment, and a little applause, he takes a bow and goes down to his dressing-room where he continues to perform to the manager, the backstage staff, to the dressing-room walls, and to himself in the mirror.

'In like Flynn! Tampons. Johnnies. So there's this Chinaman. Nuns. Pakis. The tax man. Senna pods. Tripe and onions. Sporrans. Knicker elastic. Scunthorpe. So anyway, Madame de Gaulle says that what she's really looking forward to is a big fat cock.'

By the time the doctor arrives Ted Langley is reciting monologues and singing comic songs about marrows and winkles; and before he is finally drugged into silence he has run through impersonations of James Cagney, Marlon Brando and Meryl Streep, and done a comic dance with an ashtray and two paper cups.

On stage, in Ted Langley's absence, the matron in red leather is performing her act again. It is not going down nearly so well this time. Someone tells her to have some singing lessons. Various people instruct her to get them down.

Later, Ted Langley is comatose and alone in the dressing-room. Having spewed out all the collected débris of a lifetime's comedy he is utterly still and empty. The manager pops in to make sure he hasn't died or smashed up the room. Ted smiles at him weakly. The manager is relieved.

'Hey Ted,' he says, 'have you heard the one about the choirboy, the nun, the mastiff, the sidecar and the bath full of baked beans?'

Like a fool, I tried to 'throw myself' into my work. It was no good. It would be dignifying things to say that I had writer's block. There was no great traumatic or creative log-jam. It was just that I got up every morning and I could find three million things to do that were more interesting and pleasurable than trying to write.

Most of the things were fairly mundane: washing dishes, listening to the radio, reading the newspaper from cover to cover, masturbating. Anything was better than having to write. And, of course, I spent a fair amount of time thinking about Victoria. Not that there was very much to think.

Occasionally I would hijack myself and force myself to go to my desk, face a blank sheet of paper and try to fill it. That only brought on ennui, nausea and the urge, frequently submitted to, to screw the paper into a tight ball and hurl it impotently against the wall.

The room where I worked had become a museum of meta-exhibits, exhibits about exhibits, a collection about collections. There were my notebooks, tapes and manuscript pages. There were collectors' year books, guidebooks, handbooks, auction catalogues and specialist magazines. On the walls I'd stuck newspaper clippings, letters from the collectors I'd interviewed, postcards, photographs. They crawled up and down the walls like a collage of decaying skin. Every item was a reminder of some collector's diligence and sustained concentration. If somebody could dedicate twenty years of his life to collecting garden gnomes, why couldn't I buckle down and devote a few hours each day to the creation of this blasted book? The room was a dungeon, a permanent accusation. Who could blame me for not wanting to go in there?

I could. I blamed myself a lot. I felt guilty. I felt bad about not doing anything all day. I felt bad about not delivering the goods I'd contracted for. I felt worst of all because I was failing to do the one thing I'd always claimed to be able to do: write.

When it became totally intolerable I rang Alastair. He was my editor. He was supposed to be on my side. Surely he must have had other authors with the same problem.

'I've got a problem, Alastair,' I said.

'I'm sorry to hear that. Is it your marriage still?'

'No. It's the book.'

'Really?'

He sounded surprised, not so much that I was having problems with the book, more that I should be mentioning them to him, whereas if I'd rung up to discuss the state of my marriage that would have been fine.

'I suppose you'd better tell me about it,' he said gingerly.

138

'Well,' I said, 'I think it could be a problem of organisation. I'm having trouble shaping my basic research material.'

This was what I had planned to say. I thought it sounded better than saying I didn't know what the fuck I was doing, and that each time I approached the typewriter I felt sick.

'I want you to know,' he said, 'that we all still feel very positively about this book, and we want you to know we have every confidence in your ability to bring it off.'

This didn't sound like Alastair talking. This sounded like Corporation Man, but I wasn't too dismayed. Maybe this was the pose he adopted to boost the confidence of self-doubting writers.

'I was thinking we might have lunch,' I said.

'But you're in Sheffield, aren't you?'

'Yes, but I'd be happy to come down to London for a chat.'

'It's a long way to come, and my diary's looking rather full.'

'It doesn't have to be lunch,' I said, trying not to plead. 'I could drop in for an hour or so, to talk generally about the book, show you my notes.'

'Well . . .'

It was obvious that he didn't want to see me. I didn't know why. Maybe I was approaching this all wrong. Maybe I had to beg.

'The fact is, Steve, we're having a bit of a shuffle-round. I'm going to be changing roles and taking on the health and self-help lists. It's a promotion of sorts. So I'm not sure how useful it would be for me to get too deeply involved with your book at this stage.'

'What does that mean?'

'It's nothing sinister, Steve. It happens all the time in publishing. Don't worry. There's going to be a new editor doing my job, a great girl called Val, and I know she's going to feel every bit as enthusiastic about your work as I do.'

'But look,' I said, 'it doesn't really matter what job you're going to be doing, I still think you may be able to help me.'

'I'll do my best, but no promises.'

'The fact is, I think it's more serious than not being able to organise the material. I think it really could be . . . well . . . writer's block.'

I was grasping at straws. Yes, I could be accused of over-dramatising, but all I was really trying to do was attract his attention. It seemed to work.

'Really?' he said.

'Yes. I think I may be completely stuck on this one. I wondered, well, do you know of maybe any strategies for overcoming it?'

'No. Frankly I never really thought it existed. I thought it was an excuse writers came up with when they got fed up halfway through a project.'

He was probably right. No doubt plumbers get fed up halfway through re-plumbing a house, or long-distance lorry drivers when they're halfway through a trip, but you don't hear them complaining about plumber's block or lorry driver's block.

'But look,' Alastair said, 'I've got a call from New York on the other line so I must dash. I'm sure Val will be in touch once she's settled in. But don't lose touch. Let's have a beer some time. Good luck with everything. Bye now.'

I went out and had several beers by myself that night. It didn't clear the blockage, but the hangover I had the next day gave me a perfect excuse for not being able to write.

Every morning Jim feels like a fake. He walks to Killer Kars, picks up the company van and drives to the big house where the day's work is done. The work is unappealing and not very satisfying, and it seems to have been dragging on for weeks, but then again, it's not very arduous either.

He puts in his seven and a half hours, and yes, progress is being made, the mess is being sorted out, but it's slow work and he knows he isn't performing at peak efficiency. The worst of it is, he doesn't even care.

He thinks he may have lost his pride; not his pride in himself but his pride in his work. That's because he knows now that this business of cleaning cars is not his real work. He feels above it all. He feels there is a new destiny not far away.

He continues to memorise *The Books of Power*, but he increasingly feels that this is just a discipline, a series of exercises that will make him ready for the next step.

Mike Gombrich turns up at least once a day and asks how it's going, but he doesn't listen to Jim's answers. Perhaps he too has lost his pride. Jim doesn't know why Mike bothers to make the visits. He seems to spend a lot of time sitting around drinking with Victoria and her husband, and perhaps some of it's business, but when Jim sees them lounging by the swimming-pool, opening their third or fourth bottle of the day, he suspects there's more going on than good customer relations.

He doesn't feel resentful that he's working while others play, but he is concerned about Mike Gombrich. If he, Jim, has lost his taste for his job, that's because he senses new things just over the horizon. Mike, however, seems indifferent to his job, without having found anything to replace it. Sitting around swimming-pools is all right, but it's not the real thing.

It doesn't even feel like the real thing to Mike Gombrich. These are just preliminaries, displacement activities while he builds up enough nerve to say, Yes, damn it, he'll do it, he'll go to bed with Victoria and her husband. They have discussed it at some length over several afternoons and now, at last, he is ready.

Victoria is splayed on the sun-lounger, her skin pale, coated in sun-block, though today's weak sun hardly seems like much of a threat. Her husband walks round the pool. He is looking happier these days. He still feels hollowed out by the loss of his collection, but now that Mike Gombrich is in charge of restoring and disposing of it, he can allow himself to feel a little better. He sometimes thinks he might start a new collection of something quite different from cars, but he can't decide what.

He says abruptly, 'So we're all finally ready, are we?'

Mike and Victoria indicate that they are. They stand. Mike gulps down the last of his wine. Victoria pulls a towel round her shoulders. They go into the house, into the warm, enveloping darkness. Mike Gombrich feels nervous yet excited. He senses anticipation and danger. He likes the feeling.

They go up to the bedroom. They undress with their backs to each other and climb into the large oak bed. It is easily big enough for three, possibly for four. It has a carved headboard and a vast duvet patterned with wild flowers. The room is dim, friendly, tidy, not especially sensual. The furniture is old and solid, there are racing prints on the wall. The effect is more of a gentleman's club than of a boudoir.

The duvet is moulded into an undulating landscape as it covers the peaks and valleys created by the three bodies. Victoria, as seems appropriate, is in the middle. Her husband is on her left, one hand behind his head, the other under the duvet, perhaps playing with himself. On Victoria's right Mike Gombrich sits upright, his back against the headboard, attempting to look relaxed and accustomed to this sort of thing.

There is a period of waiting for something to happen, of waiting for somebody else to make the first move, but before very long Victoria makes a number of moves that get the show on the road. Mike Gombrich at first feels uncomfortable at the nearness of her husband's big naked body but this is not too much of a problem. There is, after all, plenty to enjoy.

For a start there is Victoria's body, lean and whippy and dark nippled, and there is what she does with it. He enjoys watching Victoria and her husband. So that's what married love looks like. He's never seen it before. He offers an encouraging hand here and there. He enjoys almost everything.

Sometimes as they arrange themselves in some extravagant sexual posture, Mike finds his arm or thigh rubbing against her husband's body. He supposes he ought to find that creepy and disgusting, but by then he's so aroused that he doesn't. After all, he tells himself, the two male bodies are only coming into contact as they might in a rugby match, or when getting a rub-down from a burly masseur. He knows there's nothing wrong with any of that. So why does he feel that he's enjoying this more than he ought to?

Like some kind of roller-coaster ride, the afternoon is suddenly very quickly over. The ride ends too soon. They finish and wipe off. They get dressed. Victoria's husband thanks Mike rather formally and they have a pot of tea before Mike goes to see how Jim is getting on, and then drives home.

It was early morning. I was awake, out of bed, and sober: that was most of the problem. I was close to despair, though no closer than I'd been quite frequently over the last few weeks. When the phone rang I answered it and heard a woman's voice asking if Steve Geddes was there. I was suspicious, paranoid, deranged, so I said, 'Hold on, I'll go and get him. Who's calling?' She said it was his editor. I said, Okay, and rested the receiver on the floor and let a certain amount of time elapse before picking it up again and saying, 'Hello. Steve Geddes here.' I tried to sound like a man torn unwillingly from prolific literary production.

'Hello, Steve,' she said. The voice was young, effusive, not

142

particularly convincing. 'This is Val. I've taken over from Alastair. I thought it was time we talked.'

'Sorry?'

'I'm your new editor.'

'Oh. Hello . . . Val.'

'I love your book,' she said. 'Alastair's told me all about it, and I think we can really do something with it.'

'Good,' I said.

'How are you getting along with it, anyway?'

'So-so,' I said.

'Problems?'

'Some.'

'That's all right. I can help. That's what I'm here for.'

She was saying the right things. I was tempted to feel optimistic. 'Good,' I said.

'No sweat. In fact, I was having a bit of a brainstorming session about your book and I thought, Yes, collectors and collecting, it's a big subject. It's fascinating, it's got broad appeal, but is it sexy?'

I suspected her question was rhetorical but she paused long enough for me to register my incomprehension.

'You see,' she said, 'if you're not careful, you're going to fill up this book with a lot of Kevins who are into classic cars and beer cans.'

'Yes. That could happen,' I said.

'And, frankly, that's a loser. We want collections that are hip, fun, glossy, *sexy*.'

'Oh,' I said.

'Like jukeboxes or Bakelite radios or false eyelashes.'

'Do you know anybody who collects jukeboxes or false eyelashes?' I asked.

'Not personally, but I'm sure you can ferret them out. You have your contacts, surely.'

'Mm.'

'And, anyway, jukeboxes and false eyelashes are only suggestions. I'm sure you can come up with better ideas than I can. You're the writer.'

'Yes,' I said.

'And money.'

For an hysterical moment I wondered if she was going to offer me extra money – unlikely; or perhaps less money since she herself was providing such a large 'input'. But that wasn't what she was talking about at all.

'People like to read about money,' she said. 'They want to know how much things cost and how much they're worth. They want to hear about items that were bought in a jumble sale for ten pence and are now worth a cool million. There needs to be a lot of that sort of thing in this book.'

'Okay,' I said. It cost me nothing to say okay.

'And Alastair tells me you're interested in the psychological and philosophical aspects.'

'Yes.'

'That's fine, but a word of caution, don't overdo it, all right?'

'All right.' It cost nothing to say all right, either.

'Because in one sense I'm not sure that the words are going to be the most important part of this project.'

I hurled a hostile silence down the telephone. It got lost somewhere along the line.

'I think we're dealing with a very visual project here,' Val said. 'There are all sorts of visual opportunities, and we'd be fools to miss them. I'm sure your descriptions are going to be wonderfully telling, but at the end of the day, people are going to want to *see* the collections you're talking about.'

'But if they can see them, why do I need to write about them?'

'I hear you, Steve. Don't worry. Don't get paranoid. I'm not trying to freeze you out. I don't want to diminish your contribution. No way.'

'Good,' I said.

'But I do have a very talented young photographer who's very excited by the project and wants to get involved. He'll be getting in touch with you soon, and you can chat, give him some names and addresses and he'll start work almost straight away.'

Perhaps I should have been grateful. I was stuck with the book and here was somebody offering me a kind of solution. It wasn't, of course, the solution I wanted, because the real solution was for me to find a way to write what I wanted to write. But it was *a* solution, and I knew I couldn't afford to be too proud.

'In the meantime,' she said, 'I'm very keen to read the first draft.'

How could I tell her there was no first draft?

'It's still a little rough,' I said.

'I don't mind. The rougher the better. I like to get involved as early as possible. So if you'll make sure I have it by the end of the week.'

'Well . . .'

'And once I've had a chance to look at it we'll have lunch, okay? I'll look forward to it. Lovely talking to you, Steve.'

The phone died. It had never taken much to ruin a day's attempts at work, and my conversation with Val had left me completely paralysed. It was a great excuse, even better than a hangover. It was ten-thirty in the morning, too early, by my standards, to start drinking, so I went for a drive instead. It definitely wasn't as enjoyable as drinking.

There had been times when I'd gone driving and discovered all sorts of inspiration. Looking at roads and buildings, the feeling of movement, even the patterns of traffic had, on occasions, triggered off creative impulses. Not today. Perhaps not ever again. The roads, buildings and traffic patterns were flat and without meaning, the movement only a kind of restlessness. If there was anything significant or inspiring in my surroundings I was incapable of observing it.

I drove for what seemed like a long time, but it was only the boredom making it seem that way. I found myself driving down the track to a public dump. A line of cars and vans was unleashing old furniture, garden rubbish, building débris, into a line of yellow skips. Half a dozen big, raucous men were supervising the dumping.

They disposed of oil cans, fridges and cookers, children's bikes, old window frames, black bin sacks that might have contained anything. Each driver delivered the unwanted contents from his vehicle and left briskly looking pleased and relieved; a dirty job well done.

When I got back to my house, less than an hour had passed. I saw that I'd left the front door unlocked. I went in and looked around downstairs. Nobody seemed to have been in. Nothing was missing. Then I went upstairs, checked my bedroom. Okay. I checked my study and it had all gone. The typewriter, desk and bookcases were still there but all my work had been taken; all my research for the book, my notes, manuscripts, reference books, tapes, magazines, clippings, letters. The lot had gone. Some locust of the written and printed word had been through the room and left it barren and devoured.

I had never, in my whole life, felt so pleased and relieved.

★

Jim sits alone in his mobile home. He is only slightly drunk. One hand holds a can of strong lager, the other puts volume eighteen of *The Books of Power* back on its shelf. He lets his hand rest in a loving, fatherly way on the books. He runs his index finger rhythmically back and forth along their spines. There was some old television series where one of the characters, possibly 'My Favourite Martian', could read books just by riffling through them. Jim thinks that would be a pretty good system. Or you could place your hand on the cover, or sleep with the book under your pillow, and all the information would seep effortlessly and permanently into your head. But Jim wouldn't really want to do it that way. There'd be no challenge and no sense of achievement.

He remembers school. He remembers that he could never remember anything. He tried to revise for exams, attempting to re-learn things he had never learned in the first place. That was a long time ago. He was different then. He wasn't stupid. He wasn't even idle, but nothing would stick. It's different now, thanks to *The Books of Power*. He has the knowledge and the power, but he isn't quite sure what to do with them.

The knock on the door is abrupt, hard and threatening. Jim opens the door slowly. There are two men. One is older, fatter, with bad teeth and an old suit. His face is round, his bald head is shiny yet creviced, and Jim detects a smell of beer and onions coming from him. The younger, thinner man with the better teeth is the boss. Everything about him is sharp: his nose, fingers, haircut, suit, his voice. In some circumstances he might appear charming and roguish, but if he was coming to demand money from you he would appear vicious and dangerous as now.

'Jim,' he says, 'you know why we're here.'

Jim doesn't, not immediately. He had assumed that Elaine's vague threats had been precisely that. But there is nothing vague about the man who's speaking. He has a nasty clarity and definition about him.

'The money,' he says. 'The encyclopedias.'

'I see,' says Jim.

'It's very simple,' he says. 'You give us the money and we go away. If you don't give us the money we break a few things and then we go away, but you'll still owe the money, in which case we'll come back again and break some more things. And so it goes on. It sounds like a waste of everybody's time, doesn't it? So give us the money.'

'I haven't got the money,' Jim says.

'In that case, things may not be very simple at all.'

Jim looks around his home to see how many of his possessions are easily breakable. A portable television, a radio, an old cassette player. Nothing much.

'I do think the books are really great,' he says, hoping that perhaps his enthusiasm for the product may soften their hearts.

'That's of no interest to me,' the sharp man says. 'We're from a debt-collection agency. We have no connection with the people who sold you the stuff.'

'Take my word for it,' Jim says, 'they're really great.'

'That may well be true,' the man continues. 'I dare say Rolls-Royces are very nice motors, but I don't go around buying them when I haven't got any intention of paying for them.'

'Okay,' says Jim. 'You'd better re-possess the books.'

'We don't want them back. Nobody does. Who'd want them after you've pawed all over them? We're not in the secondhand book trade. We're in the money trade.'

'Let me show you something,' Jim says.

The sharp man looks impatient.

'Bear with me,' Jim says. 'Do me a favour. Pick one of the volumes off the bookcase, any volume. Open it anywhere at random.'

'Why?' he asks.

The fatter, older man looks sympathetic. He has nothing to lose. He's been in this game a long while. He has all the time in the world. He takes volume nine from the bookcase and opens it towards the back.

'Now what?' he asks.

'What's the entry at the page you've opened?'

'Napoleon.'

'Napoleon,' Jim quotes. 'Napoleon the first, not to be confused with Napoleon the second or third or fourteenth. Able was he, ere he saw Elba. Not tonight Josephine, and in fact hardly ever. At school he was nicknamed the Little Corporal – could have been much worse (see NICKNAMES, SCHOOL, BULLYING). Killed one hundred insurgents with a whiff of grapeshot. He re-arranged the whole map of Europe. Invented the Code Napoleon. Responsible for the Napoleonic Wars.

'Who can forget Austerlitz, his Continental System or the Treaty of Tilsit? He had reckoned without the Russian winter. Gave his name to a pastry, a coin, a card game and a cocktail. He looked not unlike

Rod Steiger. He came up with some great one liners: – "an army marches on its stomach", "England is a nation of shop-keepers", and, less memorably, "Every French soldier carries in his cartridge pouch the baton of a marshal of France." He met his Waterloo in 1815. Quite simply, he was a master.'

He has quoted the entry word for word in every detail. Both debt-collectors are impressed and amused as if they've been shown a good conjuring trick.

'How'd you do that then?' the sharp man says.

Jim shakes his head as though there's nothing to it, but like all magicians he can't reveal how it's done.

'Try me again,' says Jim.

They try him again, several times, on Freud, Poland, Jazz, Rodents, Nato, Poseidon, Polymers. Jim recites each entry with absolute accuracy.

'It's a good trick,' says the sharp debt-collector.

'There's no trick,' says Jim. 'I know it all. I know every word in every volume. The entire contents of *The Books of Power* are in my head.'

'Blimey,' says the other debt-collector. 'It's just like *The Thirty-Nine Steps*.'

The sharp man doesn't know what he's talking about. 'You memorised the whole lot?' he asks Jim.

'Yes.'

'Why?'

Jim thinks of saying something about the quest for knowledge, power and love, but he doesn't feel the two men would be particularly receptive.

'It's my obsession,' he says.

This doesn't explain anything to the two men. They're puzzled. They're thrown. Jim is not the average debtor. They are moving outside their normal sphere of operations. A reversion to type seems called for.

'But that's not why we're here,' the sharp man says. 'We're not here to watch party tricks. We're here for the money.'

'I know,' says Jim. 'But I haven't got any money so I can't give you any.'

He sounds alarmingly serene and philosophical. They are used to wheedling evasions or aggressive sticking in of heels. This kind of equanimity is harder to deal with.

'And even if I had the money,' Jim continues, 'I don't think I'd give it to you.' He starts to smile now. 'Money isn't worth worrying about. Very little is. You can break a few of my things if you like, if it makes you feel better. It won't bother me. They're only possessions. I'm above and beyond all that. I've got the knowledge and the power. What more could I need?'

Eve Leviticus (known to her parents as Emma Rosemary Bligh, also referred to as 'that weird little cow with the tape-recorder') has been having a hard time getting hold of the right drugs. Money is no problem, but she's had trouble making the right contacts. She isn't what you'd call a great socialiser, and she isn't a party girl, and she's never been one for dealing on the streets, so tonight she's doing her best to get out of her head on half a bottle of Bollinger, a few traces of cocaine, and a couple of her mother's tranquillisers. The effect isn't wholly successful or pleasant, but it's different, definitely strange, and when all else fails she's happy to settle for strangeness.

It's a little after ten in the evening. She puts on a short, dark wig and sticks a false moustache to her top lip. She puts on men's clothes and a big duffle coat containing a hidden tape-recorder and microphone. She looks like a plump, weird, little man, but London is full of those. She sets out to record the sounds of the night.

Mostly they are predictable sounds: buses, taxis, traffic, the exaggerated cheerfulness of people in pubs, music spilling from burger joints and Greek restaurants, and trad jazz from a window two floors up.

Eve feels like a spy in a strange city. It's a good feeling. She wonders if that might be her best career prospect. She wonders how you get recruited. She doesn't want to get involved with all that licensed-to-kill routine, no shoot-outs or car chases, but when it comes to a bit of inventive surveillance she thinks she could well be MI5's woman. Camping out in basements, sitting in the backs of vans and limos, phones strapped to her ears, centering needles, fighting against feedback – she'd enjoy that.

She finds herself in Soho. She records a couple of female voices asking if she's looking for a girl, and an old crone in an orange fur coat shouts out, 'Hey, moustache!' but she doesn't answer because that would destroy the purity of the recording, and give away her own female voice.

She arrives at the front door of a hostess bar and makes as if to enter. A dinner-jacketed, brick-built bouncer blocks her way. The bouncer isn't especially aggressive since he thinks he won't need to be. Young lads in duffle coats aren't much trouble as a rule.

'Sorry mate,' he says. 'I don't think you're dressed quite right for this place.'

Eve looks at him sadly and kicks him in the shin. It is only a token kick, not done with much malice, and it can't have hurt much, but she believes that bouncers deal essentially in tokenism. The bouncer is irritated, and astounded that the little wimp in front of him should have the gall to kick him. His first reaction is to beat the shit out of him, but he knows there isn't a lot of pleasure to be had in beating the shit out of wimps, so he simply puts his hand in Eve's face, and pushes hard enough to knock her over. Eve falls. She gets up, takes a run at it, and kicks the bouncer again. He sees it coming and steps aside so that he receives only the most glancing of blows. The kick leaves Eve off balance. The bouncer pushes her again, in the shoulder this time, and Eve falls over again, but now she lands at the bouncer's feet. The bouncer's instinct is to put the boot in, but it would take a harder man than him to start kicking the helpless heap at his feet.

'What's wrong with you?' he says. 'Why don't you get up and piss off home?'

Eve responds by biting him in the calf. This time it hurts, and the bouncer, getting serious, kicks her hard in the chest. Eve slides across the pavement into the gutter, into the path of half a dozen or so lads in football supporters' gear.

It takes them a second to assess the situation, and then they react as a unit, as a demonstration of pack instinct and group mind, and they go for the bouncer. They get him all right, and they also get another bouncer who comes running out of the club to help his mate. The football fans thrash them with a joyful, unaffected delight. They are helping the underdog and righting wrongs. There is no contest.

Afterwards they help Eve to her feet and give her a can of brown ale. She drinks some of it and feels it reacting strangely with the other substances in her system. She still doesn't say a word. They send her on her way, telling her that there'll always be a free drink to be had in Upton Park.

When she's clear of them she checks the recording equipment. It's still working and has recorded everything. It won't be the tape she'd gone out hoping to record, 'Transvestite Teenager Beaten Up By

Bouncer', but 'Bouncer Beaten Up By Football Fans' is surely just as good. She hurries home to play it back.

She is delighted by the thuds and punches and the shouted obscenities, and even the early noises of her hitting the ground and being kicked. There is also, which she didn't notice at the time, the sound of 'You Can't Hurry Love' issuing from the club, and a police siren in the distant background. She plays the recording a couple of times through speakers, then listens to it on headphones. She considers it a classic of its kind, not one of the all-time greats, but nevertheless a classic. She decides to listen to some of her all-time greats.

She rummages through boxes and comes up with a cassette entitled, 'My Parents Having A Fight And Then Screwing'. She slips it into the player and waits eagerly. It seems to be taking a long time to start, and she wonders if the stretching of time might be a side-effect of the tranquilliser, but a lot of real time passes and still no sound. She checks the leads, the player, the deck, the settings on the amp. They all look okay. She takes out the cassette and examines it. Maybe a blank tape got put in the wrong case. But no, it's the right tape, labelled in her own unmistakable handwriting.

She pops the cassette into her personal stereo. Still nothing. She tries a different tape, the one called, 'Ted Langley Loses It On Stage'. Nothing again. She tries out different tapes with different configurations of equipment until eventually, hours later, she has tried out every tape with every possible configuration, and she has not been able to raise a sound.

For a moment she wonders if the football fans put something untoward in the beer they gave her and she's gone deaf through drug abuse, but no, she can still hear the hiss and gurgling of the speakers, she can hear her hands slapping at the controls, and, as she flings tapes and boxes about, she can hear the brittle plastic clatter they make hitting the walls and floor.

She slumps down on the camp-bed and has to admit to herself that someone, or more likely some *thing*, some wicked manifestation of destruction, has been in her room, swept through it wiping every tape, leaving them slick and blank. Eve wishes she had more cocaine or tranquillisers or anything; but this one she has to face more or less straight and sober. It is hell. The rest is silence.

★

151

What the hell is wrong with Mike Gombrich? It's a question anyone might ask, but right now it's a question he's asking himself. It's a morning after. It's early, six a.m., and he hasn't slept much. Beside him a Chinese girl is sleeping. He has never slept with a Chinese girl before. He met her last night in the bar of the sports club. She was nicely muscled and seemed quite exotic despite the Sheffield accent. It wasn't a bad night. She was impressed by his car. They went to a not bad steak house. They went to bed and Mike knows he was his usual athletic, skilled self. A series of nail marks down his back suggests that the girl enjoyed herself too. So why's he feeling so rotten? Why's he so unsatisfied? Why is he lying awake at six in the morning thinking?

As he made love to the girl last night he kept feeling that something was missing. Actually, several things were missing – passion, affection, mutual respect – but he could easily live without those. What he really missed was the presence of a third party. Being in bed with one person was okay, but being in bed with two people (say Victoria and her husband) would have been better. It would have offered more excitement and more possibilities. After his recent afternoon excursion, ordinary intercourse seems a little, well, pedestrian.

He has rung the big house and spoken to both Victoria and her husband and suggested that they 'get together again soon', and he has been told politely and firmly to forget it. He can take a hint, but he's fairly pissed off about it and he knows he didn't ought to be pissed off about it. It was supposed to be a trial, an experiment. It was supposed to be no big deal. So why's he lying awake now feeling unsatisfied and nostalgic? This surely means something.

Does it mean, for example, that he's suddenly become polymorphously perverse? Or a pervert? A closet bisexual? A goddam fruit? Well probably not, but at this late stage in his development, at this particular time in his life, he could do without being troubled about his sexual identity. He already has enough on his plate.

He is not afraid of change. He has changed before. This life he's leading now is completely different from and unconnected with a life he used to lead; the one he doesn't talk about. But he hadn't thought it would ever be necessary to change again. This new life, based on selling and a persuasive way with language, has looked pretty good this last decade. He has always known that cars, sex and money weren't everything, but they were something; and besides, he has always believed, in true Zen tradition, that cars, sex and money are as likely as anything else to be true sources of consolation and enlightenment. It looks to him now as though he may have got that wrong.

In the cold light of morning, as the central heating boiler starts into life, and as the girl beside him begins to snore, Mike Gombrich knows he needs another change.

I didn't call the police about the loss of my research materials. I stayed home. I stopped going out. I stopped shaving and I started drinking more. I stopped seeing people and I didn't miss it. Then I received a series of phone calls that did me no good at all. The first was a voice I didn't recognise. It was young and male, a soft, enthusiastic, cockney voice.

'Hello. Is that Steve Geddes?' he asked.

'Er, no,' I said.

'Can you put him on then?'

'Well, no. He's not here.'

'When's he back?'

'I'm not sure. Can I help?'

'Shouldn't think so, but can you pass on a message?'

'I'll try.'

'This is Jamie. I'm his photographer. Steve and me are doing a book together. We need to have a bit of a chat. Tell him to ring me.'

'Does he have your phone number?'

'No. I'll give it to you.'

He gave me his phone number and I pretended to write it down.

'I've got that,' I said, 'but I'm not sure when he'll be back.'

'Well whenever.'

'He looked like he was going out for a while.'

'Well, tell him I've already started work. I've found a geezer down in Croydon who collects Donny Osmond gear, and I've got another one who's into G-Plan in a big way.'

'Sounds great,' I said.

'Yeah, it's all good stuff. So tell your man to give me a bell. Ta. *Ciao.*'

Days passed and, of course, I didn't return the call. I thought he might ring again but he didn't. No doubt he was too busy snapping G-Plan dining suites from interesting angles.

153

The next call was from Mrs Edwin Rivers.

'I suppose you're proud of yourself?' she said.

'What?'

'You've turned his head completely, haven't you?'

'No,' I said. 'Not guilty. I've never been very proud of myself and I've never turned anyone's head.'

'Very smart. But you've still got a lot to answer for in my book.'

'Me?'

'Who else? Until he met you, Edwin was fine. He was a bit odd but he wasn't too bad. I could live with it and so could he. Then you came along and put all this nonsense in his head about being in a book and he's gone completely round the twist.'

'He didn't have far to go,' I said, and then I thought I was being harsh. 'I'm sorry to hear that.'

'Saying sorry doesn't do any good.'

'All right then,' I said, and I started thinking that maybe I wasn't being harsh at all. 'In that case I'm not sorry.'

'There's no need to take that attitude.'

'My attitude is that I really don't care about you and your gormless husband. All right so he's a nutcase. So what? The world's full of nutcases. Some of them collect beer cans, some of them don't. Your husband's just like everybody else. So what? I don't care. I don't take responsibility. I don't even take an interest any more.'

A noise that I took to be sobbing rippled out of the earpiece.

'He's gone,' she said. 'He's left me. He's gone to live in that horrible little room with all those shelves, And he's started drinking beer and saving the cans, and I don't know what to do. And it's all your fault!'

'No it's not,' I said. 'It's not my fault, but if you want to think it is, if that makes you feel happier, then think it. I don't care about that either. I don't feel any guilt because some twerp from Coventry has left his idiot wife and gone to shack up with a few cans of Skol.'

'I'm at the end of my tether!' she shouted. 'I've contemplated suicide!'

'I think you shouldn't commit suicide,' I said. 'But if you do, that's all right too. I still won't care. And I still won't feel guilty.'

Maybe I was being cruel to be kind. Maybe I thought that by not humouring her I was helping her to pull herself together. But maybe I was just being a bastard. I was even pretty hard on Jim when he rang.

'Hello Steve. Long time no see,' he said. 'Aren't we overdue for a drink?'

'I suppose we are,' I said, wearily.

'A lot's been happening.'

I found that hard to believe. I said. 'Don't tell me you've won your first quiz.'

Jim laughed. 'No, not that. I mean that a lot's been happening in my head.'

'Oh good.'

'And I think I may have done my last quiz. I've moved on.'

'Good.'

'I'll tell you all about it when I see you. And I've been thinking about work and destiny and I've come to some important conclusions.'

It seemed out of character for Jim to have come to any conclusions about anything.

'Why don't we make it Thursday?' he said.

'Okay.'

'Will you pick me up as usual?'

'Okay.'

'About eight?'

'Yeah.'

When Thursday came I didn't go to the site to pick up Jim. I stood him up. It was unfriendly and unnecessary, but I was in an unfriendly and unnecessary state of mind, and I wouldn't have been in the mood to listen to Jim's latest, unremarkable thoughts. I stayed home that night. The phone rang at eight, eight-thirty and at nine. I assumed it was Jim trying to call me. I just let it ring.

And finally there was Rachel. Always, finally, there was Rachel.

'Yes?' I said icily down the phone.

'Hello. How are you?'

'Why do you want to know?'

'Huh?'

'I mean what's it to you?'

'What's the matter? Are you upset about something?'

'What do you think?' I snarled.

'Is it something I've done?'

'It's everything you've done. I don't know why you keep phoning me. I don't know what you want.'

'I want to talk to you. Is that so terrible? I like talking to you.'

'Why?'

'I just do.'

'Is it my wit? My sparkling conversation? What?'

'What's wrong?' Rachel asked.

'Everything's wrong. Everything's just the same as usual, and therefore everything's wrong.'

'Can I help?'

'I don't know. Can you?'

'I can try. If you want me to.'

'How would you try? What would you do? Would you re-structure the universe, or what?'

'Is that what's needed?'

'Yes,' I said. 'That's more or less what's needed.'

'Have you talked to your girlfriend about it?'

'Who?'

'Victoria.'

I was surprised she remembered the name, but pleased.

'No,' I said. 'I don't talk to Victoria about anything any more.'

'Is that what this is all about?'

'Only partly.'

'What else? Your work? Is it going badly?'

'Of course it's going badly. My work's gone completely. It's disappeared up its own backside, but it's okay, I don't miss it. Just like our marriage disappeared up its own backside, and I don't miss that either.'

'That's a shame,' she said quietly, 'because I do miss our marriage.'

'What does that mean?'

'All right, it means that I miss you.'

'That's a very stupid thing to say.'

'Probably. I'm the one who's always saying stupid things, aren't I? I work in advertising, remember.'

'I remember.'

'My work's no picnic at the moment either.'

'So?'

'There have been sackings, more than usual. Everybody's head is on the block.'

'I don't care. I don't want to hear about it. What you do is stupid and absurd and . . .'

'I'm not denying that.'

'And if you had any self-respect you'd get out of it, but you don't have any self-respect, because if you did you'd never have gone into advertising in the first place.'

'Oh fuck off, Steve.'

'Fuck off yourself.'

'What is the *matter* with you?'

'Nothing you can do anything about, okay?'

'All right, Steve. All right, you smug, sanctimonious bastard. All right.'

She slammed the phone down a fraction of a second before I did. I thought of ringing her back to say sorry, but I knew that as soon as I started talking to her again I'd pick another fight. Besides, I wasn't really sorry.

There's a story that Evelyn Waugh received a letter from one of his readers. The reader, who couldn't spell, wrote, 'If I send you my collection of Evelyn Waugh titles with return postage, would you be kind enough to singe them for me?'

Despite Waugh's crabby public image, and despite his distaste for bad spelling, he agreed. The books arrived. Waugh signed them and sent them back. Sometime later he got another letter from the same fan, saying that there'd been a fire in his house, 'and unfortunately your books have now been signed'.

I don't believe this story, but so what? It doesn't have to be an Evelyn Waugh story. You can think of plenty of authors with whom it would work better, but it was told to me as an Evelyn Waugh story.

This is a preliminary ramble to delay saying that after I'd had all these mad phone calls I did a very uncharacteristic thing. I went out and bought some high-quality stationery, came home, went to my empty study, took a sheet of paper from its packet, and wrote the following letter.

Dear Thornton McCain,

I hope you won't mind me writing to you out of the blue like this. This isn't a thing I've ever done before, probably won't ever do again, and I realise I'm far too old to be doing it anyway; but here it is, a sort of fan letter.

I don't pretend to have read every one of your books and I don't claim that my opinion is worth very much, but for what it *is* worth, I think you're a great writer – witty, clever, skilful, moving – all the usual adjectives. I thought you might like to know that at least one of your readers still feels this way. One of your books *The World Seen Through Plexiglass* brought me and my ex-girlfriend together and another, *The Bottle Blonde*, cured me of my impotence. That's more than anyone has any right to expect from an author's work. I have also looked in vain for a book of yours called *The Bullet Leaves the Gun*. I wonder if you can throw any light on its availability.

I feel very embarrassed to be asking you a favour, but I'm going to do it anyway. Would it be possible to have your autograph? Just your signature on a piece of paper would be enough. If this isn't too much trouble (and I'd perfectly understand if you think it is) then you'd be making one of your most enthusiastic readers very happy.

Best wishes,

Steve Geddes.

I put it in an envelope, sealed it and posted it before I could change my mind. I marked the envelope 'Personal. Please Forward' and sent it care of the publisher of *The World Seen Through Plexiglass*, some outfit I'd never heard of, although the *Writers' and Artists' Yearbook* confirmed that they were still in business.

I suppose I might have written a more scholarly letter, that would have sounded more adult and serious, but it would also have been bogus. Let's face it, I was a fan; so a fan letter seemed appropriate.

I wanted Thornton McCain's autograph. I wanted it a lot. But as with all fan letters I suppose I'd written it as a kind of therapy. It felt good to have done something positive. It felt good to know that I could still string a few sentences together. And it felt good to have told McCain that I admired his writing. I hoped that might make him feel good too. If it made him feel good enough to agree to send me his autograph, then so much the better.

Very shortly thereafter I got a letter with a Scottish postmark. Inside was a postcard with his name and address printed on, and typed across the middle of it were the words, 'Fuck off. Thornton McCain.'

I had to smile.

★

I phoned Alastair, my former editor. It was late and I called him at his home. I was drunk and I don't remember every detail of what I said, but I began by telling him that my research had been stolen. He wasn't unsympathetic but he seemed to think that was the price you paid for living in the inner city. When I pointed out that this was going to make writing the book a bit tricky he saw my point, but asked, not unreasonably, what this had to do with him, now that he was in the wonderful world of health publishing. I knew it was time to confess, and confess I did. I confessed to writer's block, to a lack of enthusiasm for the project, to having bitten off more than I could chew.

'For Christ's sake,' he said, again not unreasonably, 'you're not writing *Ulysses.*'

I didn't disagree. He said he couldn't understand why I was telling him all this when he was no longer my editor, and when Val was. I said that was precisely the problem. I confessed to being a coward. I said I found Val deeply unsympathetic and that I couldn't talk to her. I confessed to being scared of her. Alastair, to his credit, understood. He said he knew she had that effect on some people. Did I, when it came right down to it, want him to tell her that I was crying off the project?

'Yes,' I said. 'That's it. That's exactly what I want.'

'No sweat,' said Alastair. 'Well, a little sweat, but I'll deal with it.'

It all seemed so easy. I could have cried. Then, by the next post it seemed, I got a letter from Val. My sense of relief disappeared. I opened the letter. It said 'Without prejudice' across the top and I knew right away I was in trouble.

Dear Mr Geddes,

Given our recent conversation about your book I was a little disappointed (a) not to have received your first draft and (b) to hear (secondhand) that you no longer feel able to complete the book.

What is this shit? Artistic preening or simple incompetence?

As you can imagine, we take a pretty dim view of this kind of amateurism, especially when we've treated you so well, and spent good money bringing in a brilliant young photographer to bail you out.

I dare say you don't have much of a reputation to lose, but believe me, this is the kind of stunt likely to ensure that you never work for any British publisher ever again. At least, if I have my way.

Still, no point being vindictive. Return the advance and we probably won't screw you to the ground for breach of contract.

Incidentally, don't think there's anything personal in this. It's just that we in publishing get a little irritated at being constantly pissed about by third-raters like your good self.

Eh bien.

Val.

I had no way of paying back the advance, and, of course, I should have thought of that sooner. I was deeper in the mire. Previously my problems were of a quasi-artistic kind and therefore quasi-respectable. Now they were simply and crudely financial. This didn't seem like progress. I took another drink.

It was late in the evening. Normally I would have fallen asleep in a chair having drunk too much. But I was awake and I was reading *The Stiletto and I*, which I'd managed to track down in the catalogue of a Plymouth bookseller. The catalogues continued to arrive, and Thornton McCain titles cropped up surprisingly often, though I had never seen *The Bullet Leaves the Gun* listed for sale anywhere.

The Stiletto and I had arrived in the post that morning and since I wasn't even pretending to write any more I had been reading it for most of the day. My expectations had been so high that I was almost prepared to be disappointed, but as I read I was delighted to discover that it was every bit as joyous as I could have hoped for. I'd settled down amid its dislocated paragraphs, its endlessly shifting focus, its ontological questioning of character, when there was a loud knock on the bay window.

I thought at first it might be some passing drunk trying to break the glass, but the knock came again, more quietly this time, and I pulled back the curtain to see the haunted, thin, grey face of Edwin Rivers. He was alone.

I mimed that he should go to the front door, but he seemed rooted to the spot, so *I* went to the front door.

'Are you all right?' I asked.

'No, I'm not.'

Edwin Rivers was not the man I would have chosen to see at that very point in my life but he was obviously in a bad way so I shepherded him into the house. I sat him in an armchair. He was shivering. His shoes and trousers were caked in mud and he seemed, if such a thing were possible, to have lost weight. He looked so bad he made me forget, briefly, my own problems.

'What do you need?' I asked. 'A blanket? Coffee?'

'Give me a beer.'

I had three cans of supermarket lager in the fridge, anonymous, nondescript cans in sickly cream and green colours, bearing some invented coat of arms.

'Do you want a glass?'

'Give it to me straight.'

I gave him a can. He barely had the strength to remove the ring-pull, but he was determined and he managed it in the end. He opened his mouth and poured in the pale, weak lager. His face showed both agony and ecstasy, and he didn't stop until the can was empty.

'You got back your taste for beer,' I said.

'I've got back the taste for life. I realised I couldn't live a lie.'

I was wishing that I hadn't had to abandon Thornton McCain for the sake of this true-life drama, but I tried to be sympathetic.

'I had a phone call from your wife,' I said.

'My wife? My son?'

'Not your son.'

'They were filth, scum, vermin! They made my life hell.'

I was very slightly uneasy about those uses of the past tense. As I said before, I didn't have Edwin down as an axe murderer, but that didn't mean he wasn't.

'When they brought me here,' he said, 'they tried to make out I was mad.'

'Not mad exactly, just a little eccentric.'

'They were lying. I'm no more eccentric than you are.'

I let that pass.

'They said I never had a beer can collection,' he went on.

'*You* said that as well.'

'I was lying. They made me lie. I *did* have a collection of beer cans. It was world class. I *did* keep it in that rented room. My wife and son *did* steal it, and they destroyed it. They made me come here with them and tell you that my collection was only in my imagination. I was under their power. I had no choice. And now she's been ringing you. She's tricky. Very smart.'

I, for one, was not feeling very smart. I felt as though I'd been presented with one of those mind-numbing IQ problems. Had Edwin been lying when he said he owned the collection? Or had he been lying when he said he hadn't? Or was he now lying when he said he'd been lying? Or was he simply telling the truth? Or was he simply demented? It wasn't a puzzle I felt very motivated to solve.

'I've been reading *Aesop's Fables*,' he said. 'It's all in there.'

'Yes?'

'Yes. Foxes, chickens, monkeys, geese, eagles, hares, tortoises. Simple stories with simple but powerful meanings and morals.

'Try some of these for size: the humble poor live safe; the rich are in constant peril. The fruits of labour are a man's real treasure. Those who place their valuables in the hands of wolves must expect to lose them. Don't wait till danger is at hand before making preparations. Naked we came into this world and naked we must leave it. A beer can in the hand is worth two in the fridge.'

I didn't know if this was his subtle way of asking for another beer, but I didn't offer.

'Listen,' he said, 'this is one of my favourite fables. A miser sells all his belongings and with the proceeds buys a gold ingot which he buries for safe keeping. Every day he goes to visit the burial spot to gloat over his wealth.

'However, a workman follows him, guesses the situation and digs up the gold and makes off with it. Next day the miser returns, sees that the ground has been disturbed and realises that all his wealth has gone. He is devastated.

'A passer-by sees him wailing and tearing his hair out and asks why he's so upset. The miser tells him. The passer-by says there's nothing to be downcast about. He should take a lump of rock, bury it, and visit *that* every day instead. To all practical purposes nothing will have changed, since even when the gold was there he made no use of it.

'Moral: possession without pleasure is nothing.'

He smiled at me, looked pleased with himself. I thought possibly he expected me to applaud.

'That's what you ought to be writing,' he said. 'Fables.'

I've never taken very kindly to being told what I ought to be writing. I didn't say anything.

'But you do see what I mean?' he pleaded.

I was too weary of Edwin Rivers to be bothered to tell him whether I did or not.

'Why don't you go home and get some sleep?' I said.

'I can't go home. Never again.'

'Then you'd better stay here and get some sleep. Only for one night.'

'I thought you'd understand.'

'I'm sorry. I don't.'

'At the very least I thought you might include that fable in your book.'

'Wrong.'

He was crestfallen. I thought he might break down. He became very quiet and still, and once it became apparent to both of us that we weren't going to have any more conversation and that he wasn't going to tell any more fables, I gave him a blanket and he went to sleep in the chair.

I went to bed. I didn't sleep well and I got up at about six-thirty. I went downstairs but Edwin had already gone. So too had my copy of *The Stiletto and I* and the two remaining cans of supermarket lager from the fridge. There seemed to be a moral there somewhere.

TWO

The dispersal

'His notes already made a formidable range of volumes, but the crowning task would be to condense these voluminous still-accumulating results and bring them . . . to fit a little shelf.'

George Eliot, *Middlemarch*

Thornton McCain lives in a small, very ordinary but extremely pleasant 'sixties bungalow. It is conveniently situated a little way off the M90 between Edinburgh and Perth. It has picture windows, gas central-heating and cavity wall insulation. It has small, easily managed gardens, and a wide, straight drive leading to a single garage that houses an old and no longer very trustworthy Volvo.

Inside the bungalow there is a lounge, kitchen and two bedrooms, one of which he has designated as a study; but their uses are not rigidly demarcated. Sometimes he sleeps in the lounge, eats in the bedroom and, though he does all manner of things in the study, studying is not one of them.

It is not obviously an old man's house. It is not full of bric-à-brac, the smell of tobacco and big, brown immovable furniture. The style is faintly Bohemian, but not oppressively so. There is fitted carpet and a new, fitted kitchen, most unBohemian, but there are original oil paintings on the walls, and there are a couple of hundred feet of bookshelves in the lounge. The shelves are not quite full, and recently he has taken some steps to get rid of the less essential literature. The Sax Rohmers, the Warwick Deepings and the Arthur Mees have had to go, and he had to think twice about Dorothy Richardson. There is much else he might painlessly get rid of but, for now, the presence of books amassed over a lifetime and dragged behind him from one country to another is reassuring and comforting.

He still owns copies of all his published books, and of all the magazines and anthologies in which his short pieces appeared. He suspects he could live without those too. He is not a man who re-reads novels he wrote forty years ago. If he did, the pain and embarrassment of failure would overwhelm him. Yet there is still some pleasure to be had in the scuffed jackets and faded spines where his name appears. Now that so many passions have lost their urgency, seeing his name in print is one of the greatest pleasures he has left.

He looks slim and fit. He still has plenty of hair. His back and his shoulders sometimes give him problems, his digestion seems absurdly fragile, and his long-sightedness is getting worse. But he has most of his own teeth, brain and bowels function more or less efficiently, and his legs aren't bad considering. He spends a lot of time walking, not in any organised, joyless way; but as and when the spirit moves him he's able to take off into the Scottish countryside.

He has chosen Scotland for its comparative cheapness and for its light; but he might just as well have chosen a whitewashed house on a Greek island, a log cabin in Colorado, a depressing studio flat in Shepherds Bush, or an apartment in Manhattan bordering Harlem. He has no homesickness for America. It is another country, and one he doesn't actively dislike, but he no longer feels any attachment to it. It is just the place where he happened to be born. It is just another alien place.

He leads an ordered life. He can afford to pay his bills. He can still drive. He still reads. He has no difficulty occupying himself, and he finds it easier and easier to occupy himself by doing nothing. And he still writes.

The problem, as he sees it, for a man of seventy is not knowing whether death will arrive tomorrow morning, gently with the milk and post, or whether it still lies twenty-five or thirty years ahead.

He has written what he takes to be his major works, as major as he could manage, but that doesn't give him any kind of licence to stop trying. He doesn't want to start anything he can't finish, and yet he can't see any point in tinkering around for three decades with short, light, occasional pieces. So he is interested in open-ended structures, fragmented narratives that might begin (and more importantly, end) anywhere.

He has always been a fan of, for want of a better word, the media. The radio plays for most of the day, and he is addicted to television. The TV is good company, but company that can be turned off. He loves the way it teems with faces, voices and plots. He watches it all with studied inattention. He switches from channel to channel. He enters and leaves the room in mid-programme and mid-scene. He takes it in. It is a magic fund of people and stories.

He spends much of the day with a pen in his hand and a sheet of paper not far away. He jots things down. Perhaps that's all it is, not writing, merely jotting, keeping an ear open for an appealing

168

spurt of language or thought. He incorporates words heard on TV and radio, stories seen in the papers, and his own writing spins off on the associations these words evoke.

I'm not at liberty to reveal that at the present time. The Liberty Belle. I have work to do. And now this . . . We can't let this come between us. The sari: the name means simply a garment that wraps round the body. The body unpolitic. All part of the service. Nothing is kinder to your skin. Skin games. The skulls. More protection for your family. Tell us why you're here, Meredith. Two eastbound lanes are closed approaching Junction 5.

Of course, some parts of it seem a good deal more resonant and accomplished, more *important* than others, but that's fine by him. That's the nature of the beast.

This is perhaps not what Thornton McCain really wants to write. An autobiography beckons. He has had a long and interesting life. He has been to places and done things, and what he has to say about them he considers worth saying. He has met the famous, if only briefly. He remembers them. They, naturally, don't remember him. He has stood around at the cocktail parties of recent history, a drink in his hand, his cynicism at the ready.

The raw material of his life is still available. Little seems to have been forgotten. His mind is still inhabited by pictures of childhood and adolescence, scenes from his marriages, anecdotes, cabaret sketches where he played the doting father, the man of principle, the practised seducer. He has the urge to get this out and set it down before it dies. So why can't he?

Perhaps, he sometimes tells himself, like some schoolmaster of memory, it's simple lack of application. Experimental prose, for all its prolific agonies, slips easily from his pen. Dealing with a past, of bad marriages, limited successes, and children who turned out wrong, would be too difficult, however easily recollected.

Many things seem too difficult to him. Being bothered. Being polite. Making new acquaintances. He isn't a hermit exactly, though a week or two may pass without him talking to anyone. He doesn't find he has anything in common with his neighbours. He doesn't go to the pub. Old men in bars have always depressed him, no less so now that he's an old man himself. He certainly feels younger than he

169

imagines most men of his age feel. For that matter, he feels younger than most of the children, teenagers and adults he sees.

He is still in touch with his children, though not regularly, and they are no longer children, the eldest being nearly old men in their own right. Two sons are in the States and the third is in Madrid. They speak on the phone but only briefly because of the expense, and because Thornton McCain doesn't have a lot to say. Sometimes a letter arrives, sometimes a cheque. He has, to date, never been too proud to cash the cheques.

It is all different with the last of his children, his youngest daughter from his third marriage. She is only a little over twenty and she is in constant touch. She has the ability to make him feel simultaneously very young and very old. Old because it's fifty years since he was her age; young because she doesn't seem so very different from him. She is his favourite despite her prickliness and arrogance, her lack of humour and common sense, perhaps *because* of those things. She doesn't seem to have the things a person needs for survival, yet she survives. He loves her vulnerability.

She is strange. She is unstable. She is her father's daughter. She takes care of any financial or literary business that still comes his way. She does her best to promote him. She does it energetically and without complaint, though not necessarily the way he'd want it done. He doesn't know what he'd do without her. He knows he loves her far too well. This at least might indicate some kind of constancy in an art and life devoted to recording and imitating a world of peripherals, dislocations and provisional assessments.

As he gets older the world becomes, not stranger, but greyer. Food loses its flavour. The old enthusiasms fade. The stupidity and mendacity of others, while as wicked and as vile as ever, no longer move him to anger. The world seems worse than ever, but it doesn't bother him like it used to. He no longer takes it personally.

I never expected to be invited to Mike Gombrich's party. I didn't expect to be invited anywhere any more, but that was all right, since most of the time I never wanted to go anywhere. However, I did receive an invitation and I did go. I couldn't say exactly why I went. Partly it was a need to see people, partly it was the belief that I still held on to, that it was better to drink in company than

170

to drink alone, though that had never stopped me drinking alone in the past.

At some point in the last few months I had worked out that the sex maniac with the troilist tendencies in the Corvette had been Mike Gombrich. This didn't seem to have any particular consequences for me, and I didn't imagine he had any ulterior motives in inviting me so I accepted his invitation.

He lived in what might be called a penthouse on top of a select block of flats, cut in steps up a steep hillside. There were some impressive cars parked outside the block, belonging to guests at the party: Porsches, a Cadillac, an Aston Martin. A vandal with a good Stanley knife could have done thousands of pounds' worth of damage in a couple of minutes.

Inside, the flat was very new and glossy, with salmon pink carpet, tinted mirrors and recessed lighting. One whole wall seemed to be glass, with sliding doors that opened on to a balcony, which in turn looked from the top of the hill, across the valley, on to distant oak trees and a golf course. It was as expensive a flat as you could buy in Sheffield. It contained almost no furniture or personal belongings.

The party was crowded when I arrived. The main room was big, but it was already tightly packed. It was a very mixed crowd. It was no teenage party, yet there were quite a few teenagers, but there were also people in middle-age, and one or two who looked ancient. The hard core, though, were in their mid-thirties and looked professional and prosperous. I was aware that it was an oppressively good-looking, well dressed, stylish set of people. I was glad to see, if only across a crowded room, that Jim was present. I was sure that I wouldn't be the least prosperous or attractive person in the place so long as he was there.

Everyone was drinking hard, and that made me feel at home. Apart from Jim I couldn't see anyone I knew or wanted to speak to, so I headed for the kitchen where the drink was being kept.

I've always thought that some kind of time warp operates at parties. For the first hour you stand around, time drags, and you think you'll have one more drink then go home. Then suddenly it's four hours later, you're full of drink and you're talking animatedly to some woman who appears to be genuinely interested in what you're saying, and you think you may never go home again.

The music was loud. Spasmodic dancing kept breaking out. There was a lot of Springsteen, a lot of Talking Heads. It was that kind of party.

171

Mike Gombrich was in the kitchen. He forced a cup of punch on me and said, 'I'm glad you could come. I'm glad there are no hard feelings about that business.'

'No hard feelings,' I said.

'Simple case of mistaken identity.'

He put his hand out for me to shake. It was hot and dry and very businesslike, and it gave me the feeling that we were shaking on some unspecified deal, the kind of deal I'd be sure to regret.

'If you'll excuse me,' he said, 'this is quite an important party for me. I want to get round and talk to everybody. But I'll talk to you later, see if I can't get you to take a used car off my hands.'

I smiled. I tried to pretend I knew it was a joke, but I thought it might not be. Whatever the occasion, however many drinks he had inside him, I suspected that Mike Gombrich would always be looking to do a bit of business.

I hung around on the fringes of the party, and exchanged a few words about solicitors with a man in a safari suit. We agreed that solicitors were scum. His wife came to join us and we expressed views about chemical warfare and the lack of a good health club in the area. My brain was rapidly emptying of blood so I decided to find Jim.

He was easy to find. He'd been at the party long enough to take on an alcoholic glow. He looked very relaxed. He was chatty, good-natured, and had a big beam accross his face. It seemed obvious to me that something was wrong.

'Sorry I stood you up the other night,' I said.

'It doesn't matter. I'm sure you had your reasons.'

'You all right?'

'I'm fine,' he said, and he said it in a way that you were inclined to believe him. 'I've come to some conclusions about, well, about all sorts of things, but not least about women. I made a fool of myself over Elaine, but at least I now know what a fool I was.'

'Good,' I said.

'Women are a good thing,' he said, 'but you've got to rise above them. Of course you've got to treat them with respect, and not patronise them or treat them as objects, but you can't invest too much of yourself in pursuing them.'

'I'll drink to that,' I said.

'Look around the room at these women. They're wonderful, aren't they?'

'Some of them,' I admitted.

'No. They're all wonderful. They look wonderful. The way they move and talk and smell, their hair, their legs, their voices; it's all wonderful. I'm happy just to be around them.

'That one over there in pink, I tried to start a conversation with her. I asked her if she could name all of Shakespeare's plays. She couldn't. She looked at me as though I was out of my mind, like I was a piece of dirt. She turned her back on me.

'Now some men would be hurt, others would be angry. They'd call her . . . well, we know what they'd call her, something sexually gross. But not me. I've risen above all that. I'm not saying that I like having women turn their backs on me, but I can deal with it now.

'I look around at these women and I don't feel any need to possess them. I admire them from a distance and that makes me happy.'

'What are you on?' I asked.

I couldn't imagine Jim being any species of drug-user, but his detachment and spaciness suggested that there was more than alcohol in his bloodstream.

'Somebody gave me a cocktail,' he said. 'Gin, vermouth and campari. It's good stuff.'

'It's called a Negroni,' I said.

'I'll remember that. You know, I used to think it would all be different if I was famous. And it might be. Fame is sexy. Women might want me if I was famous, but how would you define that "me"? Would it be the real me they wanted? The real me isn't famous.

'And you know what else? I think I could probably cope with great wealth and great power, but I'm not sure I could cope with being famous. What do you make of that?'

'It sounds like you're finding out what you really want.'

'It does, doesn't it? I've learned a lot. Knowledge is power. Remember?'

'I remember,' I said.

'I've got to go and talk to Mike now.'

'Okay.'

'How *are* you by the way?' he suddenly enquired.

'Not so great, actually.'

'I'm sorry to hear that,' he said, and for a second he sounded genuinely concerned, but even as he said it he was walking away.

I wandered around the party. There was an argument about skiing going on in the hall, and a woman in a low-cut dress had had cheese

173

dip poured down her cleavage. It wasn't clear whether it was an accident or a courtship ritual. There was no shortage of offers to help her wipe it off.

The music was louder. I drank. Then Victoria and her husband arrived. I spotted them through a huddle of people, but the huddle divided and they swept towards me as though I was their very best friend.

'You're looking well,' Victoria said.

I knew she was lying but I said "Thanks".

'Long time, no see,' she said.

'That wasn't my doing.'

'Now now.'

She moved away and I was stuck with the husband. He was his vast, imposing self again. He asked me how my book was going and I was non-committal. He made a few mordant comments about what an unsteady profession the 'Arts' were. He felt happier with something more tangible: greed, punters who wanted to get rich quick; that was where the real money was, that was where he'd made his pile. He told me you had to speculate to accumulate, but he admitted that the world was a richer place spiritually thanks to people like me. He was glad there were people like me in the world.

'Money isn't everything,' he said.

'But then what is?' I asked.

'I'll tell you what is,' he said. 'The family.'

I nodded. I wasn't in a mood to argue, but I could have if I'd wanted to.

'That's right,' he said. 'We're having a baby.'

He began to extol the delights of fatherhood. I didn't drop my drink and I don't think I gawped too badly. In fact, apart from a slight reddening of the face, and the fact that I didn't take in much of what he was saying, I thought I reacted quite well. When he'd finished talking at me about it, or possibly before he'd finished, I walked away to get myself another drink.

I didn't catch up with Victoria for half an hour or more. When I did, she was flirting with some crew-cut athlete in a tracksuit. They were both drinking apple juice. I cut straight in. He looked put out. He probably thought he was doing very nicely with Victoria. Probably he was right.

'What's all this about the baby?' I demanded.

'I'm having a baby, that's all.'

'That's *all*?'

174

'It's a perfectly natural thing.'

'For some people maybe. I wouldn't have thought it was for you.'

'It's made my husband very happy.'

'Is it his?'

This was enough to make the athlete excuse himself and leave.

'I think so,' she said. 'I'm fairly sure. But it's definitely not yours.'

'Jesus,' I said.

'He's not been himself lately. He's been very down. I think it was having his cars vandalised, and he's had some big losses in his business. He's been very depressed. Having the baby will cheer him up no end. We might have rather a lot. I think he likes the idea of having a brood and being a bit of a patriarch.'

'Another kind of collection.'

'What?'

'You wouldn't understand.'

'I'm quite touched that you're upset. You're really very sweet.'

What else was there to do but shut up? There was no point in taking Victoria to task for having a baby. I tried to find something else to talk about. I told her about my postcard from Thornton McCain telling me to fuck off. She didn't see the joke.

I went to the toilet. It was some bathroom: a sunken bath, spotlights, stereo-speakers, mirrors, gold fittings. It was like being on stage. Actually, it was like being on a *revolving* stage. The drink and the noise and Victoria were making my head spin. All the same, my head was telling me that I needed more to drink, so when I'd finished in the bathroom I returned to the kitchen. I was looking in the fridge at a selection of foreign, bottled lagers when Jim tapped me on the shoulder.

'She's here,' he said. 'The girl of my dreams. Mike really wanted her here for some reason. Apparently she took a lot of persuading. Want to see her?'

'Why not?'

I followed him. We stopped on the edge of the dancing and Jim pointed out a thin, smart, young, ordinary blonde.

'That's Elaine,' he said. 'That's the former woman of my dreams.'

'Are you sure she's former?' I asked.

'Don't you ever listen to me? I told you. I'm over all that.'

'If you're sure.'

I looked at her again. She had a familiar sort of face, but it was

175

that phase of the party when a lot of people started to have familiar faces. She didn't look like a candidate to be anybody's dream girl, but dreams are funny things.

'But this could be your big chance,' I said. 'You're at a party. You've both had a few drinks. Talk to her. Dance with her. Go for it.'

'No,' he said. 'I know you don't believe me, but really, I'm beyond all that.'

He really looked and sounded as though he was.

'Well good for you, Jim. I wish I was beyond it all.'

'I'm well beyond it all,' a voice said behind us. It was Mike Gombrich. He was certainly beyond being able to stand without support. He leaned one hand on my shoulder and his other on Jim's in order to remain upright.

'They say you never enjoy your own parties,' he said. 'But I'm bloody well going to try.'

Then he lurched off and bounced into another group of people who kept him vertical a little longer.

'Good for you, Jim,' I said referring to many things, and nothing in particular.

I walked through some dancers, out on to the balcony. The air did me good, but the balcony was full of kissing couples and that did me no good at all. I went back inside, walked through the main room and found myself in the hall where there were doors leading off to a couple of bedrooms. One of the doors was open, so I peered into what looked like the spare room.

There was a pair of teenagers in there, a boy and a girl, aged about thirteen. They were sitting close together on the floor reading, and as they read they would from time to time burst into wild laughter. Although they were young, they looked and were dressed much older. She wore skilfully applied make-up, his hair was swept back with gel, and their voices and manners were extremely precocious.

'You two certainly know how to enjoy yourself at a party,' I said.

They looked at me, giggled, then held up the book they were reading. I should have known. Or perhaps I should have known better. They were reading volume one of *The Books of Power*.

'It's amazing,' the girl said. 'You should read it.'

'I have,' I said. 'Parts.'

'But did you see *this*?'

They closed the volume and the boy put it back on its melamine bookcase. I knew that each individual spine had one letter from the title on it, but even so I was still amazed at what they showed me. The boy kept re-arranging the order of the volumes, and therefore of the letters, while the girl did a sort of commentary.

'You start with *The Books of Power*, but with a little re-organisation you can come up with all sorts of other possibilities. For instance, a story about a ghost who lives in a garden.'

I saw that the boy had arranged the spines so that they read *Bower of the Spook*.

'Or,' the girl continued, 'a work about a man who decides to adopt a gay lifestyle but doesn't find it at all easy.'

The re-arranged spines now spelled out *He Works To Be Poof*.

'In the field of classical music,' she said, 'we come across the compositions of a woodwind player who was known only by his initial, namely *The Oboe Works of P.*'

And so it went on: a pro-carnivore plea, *O Sheep, Bow to Fork*; an exposé of philistinism among football fans, *We Boors of the Kop*; a story of popular dancing in Elizabethan England, *Bop Week Forsooth*; a science fiction piece about the sexual frustration of androids, *Oh, Few Robots Poke*; and my particular favourite, about postal workers who become obsessed with Chinese cooking, *Wok Bores of the P.O.* There were others, possibly dozens of others.

'How did you know about this?' I asked.

'What's to know?' the girl said. 'It was there. We happened to notice it, that's all.'

The letters were now arranged to read *Hot Pekes Woof, Rob*. I didn't understand.

'What's it all about?' I asked. 'What does this mean?'

They laughed at me. I knew I deserved to be laughed at. Then I was aware of somebody standing in the doorway beside me. It was Jim's ex-dream girl.

'What do you think you're doing?' she demanded.

'We're not doing anything,' the girl said.

'You leave those books alone,' Elaine snapped, 'Don't tamper with things you don't understand.'

'We weren't doing any harm.'

'It's true,' I said. 'It's not as if they were damaging the books.'

The kids left the room. The encyclopedia woman walked over to the bookcase and put *The Books of Power* back in their 'proper' order. I leaned on the door jamb and watched her. She definitely had something, a presence or an authority, but it wasn't something I liked very much.

'And you're old enough to know better,' she said to me.

'Better than what? What am I being accused of here?'

'Books, particularly these books, are fine and noble things. They shouldn't be toyed with and mocked.'

'I'm glad you believe in your product,' I said. 'It's a pity you don't have a better product.'

She kicked me in the shin. She was wearing red sandals. They didn't look particularly dangerous, but the kick felt like a blow from a sharp, deadly accurate chisel. I laughed. She went away. I sat down in agony. I rolled up my trouser leg and saw that she'd drawn blood. Fortunately I had a full glass with me. I settled down with it.

I looked around the room. It was full of junk. It didn't look like precious junk. I couldn't imagine a collector finding any desirable items among this lot. The junk consisted of old sports' equipment, camp-beds, broken lamps and furniture, tea chests the contents of which weren't visible, piles of old newspapers, a valve radio, much else besides. None of it fitted with the sleek image of Mike Gombrich and the rest of the flat, but perhaps we all, however sleek, have some spare bedroom of the soul where we keep the grubby, inelegant parts of our selves.

I know that writers are supposed to be irredeemably curious. Usually I'm not, and perhaps that explains everything. However, on this occasion there was a scrap-book on top of one of the tea chests that I couldn't resist opening.

It was full of newspaper cuttings, all of them book reviews, generally of critical and academic tomes, but occasionally of serious novels. Perhaps Mike Gombrich was a closet scholar. He didn't look the type, but I wasn't sure how closet scholars were supposed to look. For that matter he hadn't looked like the sort of man who'd own a set of encyclopedias.

I was flipping idly through the pages when a name leapt out at me. It was Mike Gombrich's own name, and it was to be found as a by-line on one of the book reviews. In fact, as I looked more closely, I saw that his was the name on all the reviews. It was hard to accept that a man who sold Alfa Romeo Spiders might also review Schiller, and I toyed with the idea that perhaps he had a namesake who reviewed books and he (Mike Gombrich the used-car salesman) had cut out and saved the reviews as some form of elaborate joke. But that seemed almost as hard to believe as that he might be both critic and seller of used cars.

I looked again at the books he'd reviewed and where the reviews had appeared. It was all very, very high-powered; biographies of Coleridge, social histories of Malaya, books on Smollett, Locke, and B. S. Johnson. Then I came across a cutting that would have knocked me to the floor if I hadn't been on the floor already.

THE JUNKMAN COMETH: AN APOCRYPHAL REVIEW

Those of us who have been watching the progress of Thornton McCain's writing (one would not be so naïve as to describe it as a literary career) began by assuming that he was employing a strategy of abandonment. In early works we witnessed him throwing out plot, character and structure. But if these were, so to speak, the bath water, where and what was the baby?

We might at one time, given the prevalence of first person usage in his writings, have been tempted to think the 'baby' was some notion of the individual, creative consciousness, of a fictitious but essential 'I'; but of late this first person has become increasingly elusive and allusive, inconsistent, multiple; giving us not a unitary and uniting voice, but rather a shifting babble of 'I's.

More persuasive then, might be to suggest that McCain is championing the primacy of the word, that his language stands by itself and for itself, independent of the novel in which it happens to find itself, unfettered by the vague worlds to which it appears to refer. This, however, would seem to pitch us straight into the semiotic shallows that McCain is so often at such pains to ridicule and revile.

However, the problem may to an extent be solved and resolved with *The Bullet Leaves the Gun*, in which we begin to suspect that McCain hasn't been abandoning anything at all.

One could never call his writings discursive, and yet they have always, in some sense, had wide boundaries. They have been repositories for arcane information, teeming invention, and jokes and anecdotes of varying quality. We can now see that rather than jettisoning the stuff of fiction, McCain may turn out to have been carrying out a process of ingathering. He has been beachcombing, picking up all manner of literary and verbal flotsam.

The Bullet Leaves the Gun is a short book, difficult, terse, yet somehow rambling. True, there is as ever no sign of plot, human psychology or formal design, yet there is within it a powerful accumulation of detail, cliché, description, dialogue, wit, that seems to amount to something very important indeed.

It is constructed from short, apparently discreet, often complex and poetic fragments, which seem unrelated to each other. I open the book at random to find, in very rapid succession, a description of diamond-cutting, a conversation between two Aboriginal children, a snatch of interior monologue apparently belonging to a woman giving birth to a monstrously deformed child, and a scurrilous parody of P. G. Wodehouse.

It might be tempting to believe that McCain is here finally abandoning all continuity and all sense; but towards the end of this dense and diamond-cut work, it begins to dawn on the reader that there is continuity amid the discontinuity and sense amid the nonsense.

McCain, it seems to us now, is a hunter/gatherer of ill-considered trifles in a world where ill-considered trifles are all that is to be gathered. His eyes and ears are wide open. They receive messages, millions of them, all of equal value and of equal banality.

Death-bed scenes, true romance, medieval sagas, literary pastiche, war stories, pornography and kitchen-sink dramas all jostle for dominance.

To have an open mind in the face of this might be to invite cerebral débris, but McCain welcomes the débris. He accepts and collects all this diversity of signal and sets it down, and in that setting down transforms it and makes it his own. He is a poet of the post-modernist wasteland. He is our most distinguished literary junk collector. It is important that we cherish him.

At last, some clue as to what *The Bullet Leaves the Gun* might be all about. I needed to talk to Mike Gombrich about this. I got up. I limped into the kitchen and got myself a beer. Mike Gombrich was visible at the very centre of the party, drenched in sweat, his shirt open to the waist, dancing with manic energy. The constant motion seemed to be the only thing preventing him falling over. The record ended and he stopped dancing. He staggered alone out on to the balcony. I pushed through the crowd and followed him out. The kissing couples had gone. There was only him and me. He supported himself on his elbows on the edge of the parapet. He was breathing hard and looked as though he might soon be sick.

'Hello Mike,' I said.

He turned round, startled. He hadn't realised I was there. He stared at me, his eyes trying to focus, trying to make out who I was.

'Steve,' he said at last, 'good party, isn't it? What kind of car do you drive at the moment?'

He didn't give me time to answer, not that I wanted to answer his questions. I had all sorts of questions of my own that I wanted to ask.

'Let me give you a tip about motor cars,' he said. 'This is straight from the horse's mouth. This is the best advice you're ever going to get. Cars are shit! Doesn't matter if it's a Daf, a Datsun or a Rolls-Royce. They're all shit. I mean it's all shit, Steve, you know that. Money, property, love, suburbia, art, it's all shit, but cars are the worst shit.'

'What about books?' I asked.

'Books are nearly as bad as cars. What are we talking about books for?'

'How about Thornton McCain? How about *The Bullet Leaves the Gun*?'

Mike Gombrich straightened up, turned to me, then grabbed me by the throat and tried to throw me off the balcony. He was very drunk and very uncoordinated, and perhaps his heart wasn't really in it, nevertheless he had a good grip on me and it wasn't a fall I was very keen to make. I shouted as loud and struggled as fiercely as I could. The shouting was loud enough to bring some party-goers out on to the balcony to pull Mike Gombrich off me.

'He gets like this sometimes,' I was told by one of his friends. 'He'll have forgotten all about it in half an hour.'

'But will I?'

'It doesn't mean anything. Have another drink.'

'What did I say wrong?' I asked.

Nobody told me. Probably they didn't know. They led him inside. I remained on the balcony, feeling groggy yet sobered. By the time I went inside a number of people had left. The party was noticeably thinner. There was room to move. The music seemed louder still, bouncing around the walls of the emptying flat. There was no sign of the host.

I went to the kitchen for another drink. Jim was talking animatedly to his Elaine. At first I thought he might have taken my advice and was trying to chat her up, but then I overheard what he was saying.

'So you see,' he said, 'although I've loved you passionately and from afar, I realise now that it was not to be.'

She moved nervously, baffled and overwhelmed, yet somehow

181

fascinated by the intense wave of feeling with which he was bombarding her.

'And one of the things I'm really trying to say', he went on, 'is that it's not what you do, it's the way that you do it. And it's not what you know, it's the way that you know it. I think you know what I'm talking about.'

Her face said that she didn't know but might not be entirely averse to finding out. Jim saw me standing by the fridge and waved for me to come over.

He said, 'I promised I'd remember the name of that cocktail, but I've gone and forgotten.'

'Negroni,' I said.

'That's it.'

I was aware that Elaine was staring at me disapprovingly. It didn't bother me too much. I thought there must be a lot of people she disapproved of. But her stare was so intense that before long I felt I had to stare back. So we stared at each other for a while, and then it clicked.

'Shit!' we said, more or less simultaneously. 'You!'

That's all we said, 'shit' and 'you', but it was enough. Hers was a scream of recognition. Mine was more a gasp of disbelief. It was her: the woman from my cocktail-bar days, to whose companion I'd served the piss cocktail, with whom I'd very briefly wrestled in the wet behind the bar, the woman who, in some sense, had cost me my job.

I can't say that I held much of a grudge, but she obviously did. The incident seemed to have lived and fermented with her. I'm sure that if there'd been a gun to hand I would have been a dead man. As it was, she moved as though to kick me in the shin again, but she hesitated a moment, as though unsure whether to kick me in the other leg and give me two sources of pain, or whether to kick me in the same one as before and make it worse. While she hesitated I fled from the kitchen and left the party altogether. Fortunately she had too much dignity to chase me.

I stood outside the block of flats feeling tired, ill, already assembling a hangover. I leaned against my car. There was no way I could drive home. I opened the rear door and climbed on to the back seat. I planned to lie low until the coast was clear and Jim's mad woman was out of the way; which in a sense I did.

I fell asleep and woke some time, possibly quite a lot of time, later. I sat up and looked out of the car window. All the guests' cars

182

had gone. Mike Gombrich's Corvette was still there, of course, and I could see a light on in his flat. I went in again.

The flat was now empty except for Jim and Mike Gombrich. Jim was asleep on the floor, by the glass doors to the balcony. He was comatose and very tranquil. Mike Gombrich was awake, shuffling through a pile of records. I wasn't sure if he would still feel murderous towards me, and if so why, but he asked me if there was anything special I wanted to hear, so I supposed he didn't. We settled on a record that claimed to be the best of Eric Clapton.

'This is the second time in one night that I have to apologise to you,' he said. 'I'm sorry.'

'It's all right,' I said, though I didn't particularly feel that it was.

'You mentioned a touchy subject.'

'Apparently. What did I say?'

'You mentioned that name. McCain. I don't ever want to hear that name again. But don't worry about it. You probably wouldn't understand.'

'I might.'

'I'd prefer it if you didn't.'

'Okay,' I said.

'Yes, it *is* okay. I'm forgiving everybody tonight, even that little cow with the encyclopedias. Come on, sit down.'

We sat down by one of the speakers. There was wine spilled on the carpet, a confetti of broken potato crisps, and a stubbed-out cigarette on the patch where I sat, but I wasn't in a fussy mood.

'People are disgusting,' he said, and I didn't disagree. 'Are you a card player?'

I wasn't sure if there was a connection to be made between card playing and the disgusting nature of people. In any case I wasn't a card player so I shook my head. That didn't seem to matter to Mike Gombrich. He produced a pack of cards. He did some fancy shuffles. He did a trick that involved palming a card and making it disappear. It was late to be doing card tricks, but I couldn't have thought of anything better to do.

'Are you a gambler?' he asked.

'Not with cards.'

'Then what with?'

'Life,' I said.

'Yeah, life's a gamble.'

I could see that if we weren't careful here we could slide into a maudlin, late-night, half-witted session of philosophy. I preferred the card tricks.

'Do you want to play a hand of something?' he asked. 'Poker or something? Have a little bet to make it more interesting?'

'I'm drunk,' I said. 'I'm not a card player and you've shown me that you can make cards disappear. What do *you* think? Besides, I've nothing to gamble with.'

'Of course you do. Everybody's got something to gamble with. Your car, for instance.'

'I want to keep my car.'

'I'll bet my car against yours. My Corvette. You've seen it. You know what it's worth. Let's gamble.'

'That's crazy.'

'If you don't want to play a hand of poker we'll do it on a cut of the cards.'

'I don't think so.'

'Why not?'

'Because I'd lose,' I said.

'But you might win.'

'I don't think so. And I'd hate losing more than I could possibly enjoy winning.'

'Okay, let's change the stakes. That shirt you're wearing, it's an all-right shirt, but you could afford to lose it. Your shirt against my Corvette. What do you say? What have you got to lose?'

'My shirt.'

'That's nothing. Go on.'

I knew I was going to lose my shirt, but he was right, I could afford to lose it. If it was so important to him to win the shirt off my back, then why not let him do it? I agreed to cut the cards. He did a few more fancy shuffles, then slapped the cards down on a damp patch of carpet.

'Ace high. High stakes,' he said.

I nodded. I cut the deck. I looked at the card. It was an ace of hearts. I smiled. So that was the idea. He would draw an ace as well and then the game would be over and we'd be equal. Or perhaps after he'd drawn the ace he'd want to make it the best out of three. Probably he'd set up the deck so that I was bound to cut the ace. Maybe he just wanted to show how skilled he was at controlling the cards.

He made his own cut of the deck. He showed the card to me with some satisfaction. It was the two of clubs.

184

'Want to make it best out of three?' I asked.

'No,' he said. 'That wasn't the deal. You've won. Don't insult me by trying to change the arrangement.'

'This is silly,' I said.

He handed me a set of car keys. I didn't for a moment think they were the actual keys to his car. Then he gave me the registration document already filled in for a change of ownership with my name and address on it. I smiled, no doubt a little nervously. I supposed I was going to be on the receiving end of some sort of practical joke. There had to be a sting, a punchline.

We went down to the carpark and I was amazed when the keys he'd given me fitted. I sat on the soft grey leather seat. It was a little cramped and very alien, but no doubt you'd have got used to it given a chance. I knew I wasn't going to be given the chance. Mike explained the controls, told me about gear ratios, the rev limits, the servicing schedule. He apologised that the radio and cassette player were broken. I thought the joke was getting a little weary. He showed me how to start the engine. It made a very satisfying snarl.

'It's nice,' I said.

'I'll drive it to your house for you,' he said. 'You're in no condition.'

We swapped seats and Mike Gombrich drove me home. It was some measure of how drunk I was that I let him do it. He was right, I was in no condition to drive, but I was in a considerably better state than he was.

I still assumed that we were playing an increasingly complex charade, at the end of which he would drop me at my door, laugh at me for thinking that I'd really won his car (not that I did), and he would then leave a trail of rubber as he accelerated away. But that didn't happen. When we got to my house he parked neatly, turned off the engine, and handed me the keys again.

'You ought to get a garage,' he said. 'A car like this is too great a temptation for vandals and car thieves.'

'Okay Mike,' I said. 'I'm home now. The joke's over. It was a good joke. You had me believing it for a while there. Now take your keys back, and thanks for the lift.'

He didn't say anything. He turned his back and walked off into the night. What did it matter? Nothing had happened that couldn't be sorted out in the morning. It was too late and I was too tired to go chasing after him. I searched my pockets for the house keys.

Even before I got the door unlocked the telephone started to ring.

185

I was going to ignore it, but the fact that the phone call was coming at three or four in the morning, or whatever time it was, suggested it might be too important to ignore. It took me a long time to get the door open and let myself into the house, but the phone kept ringing. I got to it and answered.

'Hello Steve. It's Rachel.'

'Rachel?'

'Your estranged wife. Remember?'

'I know who you are. I don't know why you're ringing at this time in the morning, that's all.'

'Well you weren't in earlier. I've been ringing all night. I thought you might be staying out with one of your lovers.'

'Are you drunk?'

'A little.'

'Me too,' I said. 'It suits me.'

'That's something we have in common, at least.'

'Is something wrong?'

'No. Nothing at all. Everything's better than it's been for a long time.'

'You must be drunker than I am.'

'I've been celebrating. I've come to a decision that's going to make me very happy. You'll probably like it too.'

'Don't tell me you're having a baby.'

'Sod off Steve. This is important.'

'So's having a baby.'

'I've resigned.'

The phone line wasn't very clear, and I thought she said '*I'm* resigned,' so naturally I asked 'to what?', and she, probably not hearing me very clearly either, and not realising that I hadn't understood, said, 'My job.'

'So you're resigned to your job,' I said. 'So what? Is that really worth celebrating?'

'I've resigned. I handed in my resignation. Quit. Finished.'

'Jesus. Really?'

'I thought you'd want to congratulate me. I thought you'd be pleased.'

'I am. I'm pleased for you. It's about time.'

'I realised you were right.'

'I usually am.'

'Usually Steve, you're a complete pain in the arse, but on this occasion you were right. Advertising is so much crap. It's all

186

pretty and colourful and well designed and researched, the words are well chosen and very persuasive, but what does it amount to? Manipulation. Coercion. But I don't need to tell you this.'

'What happened to the campaign for *The Books of Power*?'

'Huh? Why do you want to know?'

'No reason.'

'It got shelved. They didn't have the money for a campaign. Big ideas, small pockets. The agency will be lucky to get paid for the preliminary work we did. Tough titty, eh?'

'What are you going to do next?'

'I don't know. Something. Have some time to myself. Think about things. Travel. Maybe sell the flat. There are options. We could have lunch.'

'That'd be nice,' I said, and I sort of meant it.

'I'll let you get to bed,' Rachel said. 'Nice to talk to you. I'll ring you soon, or you could ring me.'

'I will,' I said, and I sort of meant that too.

I put the phone down. I sat on the settee and stretched out. I wasn't going to make it up the stairs tonight. I closed my eyes. I felt the room moving slowly but relentlessly. I could feel the wooden frame of the settee pushing painfully up through the cushions and into my back. There would be a lot to think about tomorrow, not least how to get this car back to Mike Gombrich.

Mike Gombrich walks away from the house and away from his Corvette, but he is also walking away from something more. He has reached a conclusion. Something has ended; an era, and much else. He walks briskly to his flat. He is in no hurry, yet there's something he's eager to get done.

When he enters his flat all is quiet and still, especially Jim. Mike Gombrich admires his serenity, but knows that it is about to come to an end. He goes into his kitchen, ignoring the mess and spillages, and makes a pot of strong, black coffee. He takes the pot and two cups through to the living-room. He puts them down on the carpet. He shakes Jim awake.

'Sorry,' says Jim. 'Time I was going. I must have dozed off.'

'You don't have to go,' Mike Gombrich says, 'but you do have to wake up and talk to me. Here's some coffee.'

187

Jim drinks some coffee.

'Good party,' he says.

'I enjoyed it,' says Mike. 'There were a lot of people here I hadn't seen in a long time. It'll be even longer before I see them again.'

'I've been thinking about parties,' Jim says.

'Not now, Jim. I want to talk about work.'

'I know I've not been at my best.'

'That's not what I want to talk about. I want to talk about me.'

Jim relaxes. He thinks that will be an easier thing to talk about.

'What can I tell you?' Mike Gombrich says. 'I've been running Killer Kars for the best part of ten years now. I'm not quite forty, so that's over a quarter of my life. And mostly it's been great, the best ten years anybody could have had. I've enjoyed it. I was good at it. I liked cars. I liked selling. For most of those ten years it was the ideal existence; but now it isn't any more. The thrill has gone.'

'It'll probably come back,' Jim says.

'No it won't. I know myself well enough to know that it's gone for good.'

'You sure?'

'Yes.'

'Well, you know best, but . . .'

'You know what I did before I ran Killer Kars?'

'Of course not. You'll never tell anybody.'

'Now's the time for the big revelation. It's not that big. I was a teacher, a university lecturer, in English Lit. I was a bright lad. I got published in the right places. I reviewed for the right magazines. I went to the right conferences. I was as good at that as I was at selling cars; but one day the thrill went out of that too, so I walked away from it all and went into business, dealing in flash secondhand cars. It was a change from dealing in flash secondhand opinions. So you see, I'm used to changing horses.'

'Right,' says Jim, unsurely.

'You know why the thrill went out of the academic life?'

Jim shakes his head.

'All the time I was lecturing, I was working on a book. It had a great title, *Fragmentation and the Fictive Wish: a Re-valuation of the novels of Thornton McCain*. It took me years. I worked on it for seven years. I thought it was pretty good. I was close to finishing it when out of the blue I got a letter from Thornton McCain saying he'd heard I was writing about him and would I do him the honour of letting him read it?

'I made a copy of what I'd written so far and sent it to him. A couple of weeks later I got another letter saying he'd read it, and would I like to be a guest at his home in Scotland when we might discuss my work in detail?

'Of course I was flattered. I was knocked out. I thought this was it. I thought I'd written a masterpiece that was going to get its subject's approval. I thought I was going to become *the* Thornton McCain scholar.

'I got the train to Scotland. He met me at the station. He took me to his home. We had lunch. He was very free with his drink. Throughout he was very polite and hospitable. Then we started talking about my book.

'It was the worst three hours of my life. He talked very calmly and rationally and in those three hours he completely destroyed seven years' work. He pointed out omissions, inconsistencies, stupidities, contradictions, illogicalities, a lot of simple untruths. He said, essentially, that I didn't know what I was talking and writing about.

'Now, most critics would say that an author is the last person to know what's true and untrue about his work. But Thornton McCain was different. I listened to him crucifying my own work and it became absolutely clear to me that he was right and I was completely and utterly wrong. I was a fool, a cretin, an intellectual spastic.

'After that I couldn't ever take my own critical credentials seriously, not ever again. I managed to write one more piece on Thornton McCain. It was an apocryphal review of a book I hadn't read, that nobody had read, and that McCain hadn't finished writing. Very smart. And then I walked away from it all. I changed, and that's when I started Killer Kars.'

Jim blinks, tries hard to follow the story, wonders what the punch line is, tries hard to think how he should be responding.

'A man changes,' Mike Gombrich says. 'You get to the point where you don't need the things you used to need. Everybody knows you can't take it with you, but I wouldn't want to take it with me even if I could.

'A lot of people like to measure a man by what he's got. I've decided to measure myself by what I can give up.'

'Are you giving up Killer Kars?' Jim asks. 'Is that it?'

'That's it. I'm giving it up. I'm giving it away.'

'Eh?'

'Giving it away. I wouldn't want to sell the business. I don't need what it would give me, so I'm giving it away.'

'But what are you going to do with no job and no money?'

Mike says earnestly, 'There are plenty of people in this world with no job and no money. Poor naked wretches. I won't be alone. It'll be interesting to have nothing.'

'Interesting?' says Jim.

Jim hopes that Mike is just drunk. We can all get disillusioned and anti-materialistic in those long, grey, hungover hours before dawn. But Jim knows that it's more than that. He knows, too, that if Killer Kars goes down the tubes he'll be out of a job. It isn't a job he likes much any more but it's all he's got. He knows that fate has something in store for him. He hopes it isn't unemployment.

'So I'm giving you Killer Kars,' Mike Gombrich says.

Jim doesn't take it in.

'You're the most deserving person I can think of. I know you'll do a good job.'

'How drunk are you?' Jim asks.

'Being drunk has nothing to do with it. You know that.'

Jim does.

'I've got all the paperwork here.'

He takes a large brown package from behind one of the speakers. It has Jim's name on it.

'There's everything you need in here: contracts, deeds, loan and credit details, bank references, some important names and addresses. It's all yours. Don't open it until tomorrow.'

Jim isn't sure if he really means tomorrow or later today, it being five in the morning. Either way the contents won't mean much to him. As he takes the envelope he knows for certain that Mike really does mean it and that this isn't some temporary, drunken, self-destructive impulse. He is giving away his business, giving it to him. Jim doesn't know how he feels about that.

'But I don't know anything about cars,' Jim says.

'You'll learn.'

'And I don't know anything about selling or about business or about anything really.'

'You'll learn all that. Anybody can learn to run a secondhand car business.'

'I'll try,' says Jim, 'if that's what you want.'

'That's what I want.'

'If you ever want the business back . . .'

'I'll never want it back.'

Jim realises there's no point in saying much more. He is horribly sober now, and he realises that this is the impending destiny that he somehow knew was just around the corner. It is not what he imagined or hoped for, but he supposes that's how it is with impending destinies. He decides to walk home. He says goodbye to Mike. Mike Gombrich is left alone in his flat. Jim has an urge to tell him not to do anything silly but resists it. In a few hours Mike Gombrich will be gone and nobody in this story will ever see or hear of him again.

It was early afternoon before I found the inner strength that enabled me to get out of bed. I dressed hurriedly and incompletely, and summoned up my memories of the previous night. They were muddled, like some garish dream sequence, yet I didn't think I'd got up to anything that I needed to be ashamed of.

I padded into what had been my study. I looked at the bare shelves and the bare desk. I remembered the brief period when this emptiness had brought me a kind of relief. Not today. I opened the curtains and saw that Mike Gombrich's Corvette was still in front of my house. I hadn't dreamed it. Perhaps it would have been better if I had. At least it hadn't been stolen in the night and, as far as I could see, it hadn't been vandalised.

After a little breakfast, I tried to return the Corvette. I had some vague idea that my own motor insurance allowed me to drive any car. I only had to drive it a mile and a half to Mike Gombrich's flat. How much could go wrong between here and there?

I was glad that Mike had explained some of the controls to me last night. I was surprised that I'd retained a certain amount of what I'd been told, enough to get the car started, into gear and moving. Things like windscreen wipers, the horn; the lights would have been harder to work out.

I drove to the block of flats. I kept the number of gear changes down to a minimum. The place where all the cars had been parked last night was now occupied by two removal vans. I noticed, too, that my own car which ought to have been there had gone. I parked the Corvette as best I could, then climbed the stairs to Mike Gombrich's door. On the way up I found myself in convoy with a team of removal men who were putting furniture into the flat. Well, it *had* seemed a little empty last night.

The door was open, so I entered. There was a man and a woman there, obviously not removal men. In fact, they looked more like new owners of the property.

'Is Mike around?' I asked, regardless.

'No he bloody isn't,' said the woman. 'I wish he bloody well was.'

I gave my uncomprehending look.

'A bloke sells you his flat,' said the man. 'You sign all the papers. It all seems to be going well, then you move in to discover he's left a roomful of stuff behind. And he obviously had a farewell party last night and couldn't be bothered to clean up after it.'

'What are we supposed to do with all this crap?' the woman asked.

The crap she was referring to was the contents of the spare bedroom, including *The Books of Power* and Mike's cuttings album.

'When you find him,' she said. 'Tell him we've got a bone to pick with him.'

'I'll tell him if I see him,' I said.

There were a number of things I might have done then. I could have gone to Jim and asked him when he last saw his employer. I could have phoned Rachel or Victoria, or even Mrs Edwin Rivers. Perhaps the most sensible thing would have been to return to bed and wait for everything to wear off. But as you know, I was going gently out of my head at this time, so I loaded my cassette recorder into the Corvette and set off to see Thornton McCain. I knew his address from the abusive postcard he'd sent me. If only I could see him *everything would be all right.*

I had plenty of things to occupy my mind on the way there, lots of things to think about. Why had Mike Gombrich given me his Corvette, sold his flat and disappeared? Why had he tried to throw me off his balcony? Why would he have a set of *The Books of Power*? Why would anyone? Why was the saleswoman for *The Books of Power* at the party? Why were Victoria and her husband? Why were they suddenly having a baby? And why did that piss me off so much? Why wasn't I serene and beyond it all like Jim? Why *was* Jim so serene and beyond it all? Why had Rachel suddenly decided to abandon advertising? Why had she found it so necessary

192

to tell me? Why was I going to see Thornton McCain? What the hell was I going to say to him? What did I think I was doing?

No doubt there was a lot else I ought to have been thinking about. It might have been nice to think there was some single answer that would have dealt neatly and conclusively with all my questions, but I didn't think there was and, even if there had been, I wasn't really silly enough to think I'd discover it while driving up the A1(M) with a hangover.

I was also much concerned with how to drive this car I was in. I suspected that a Corvette that looked like this one wasn't a natural candidate for the slow lane, but that was where I remained initially. Sometimes I'd get ambitious and overtake a lorry or a Morris Minor, and after a couple of hours getting acclimatised I pushed up to a steady seventy and almost began to enjoy myself.

It was getting dark when I reached Scotch Corner and stopped for petrol and a sandwich, and it was starting to rain before I'd got past Newcastle. I got lost in the centre of Edinburgh and it was the late evening when I arrived in the village where Thornton McCain lived. I asked directions. I was treated with suspicion, but that was probably the car. I eventually found the characterless bungalow that corresponded to the address on McCain's postcard to me, though I found it hard to believe that this was where the great cult writer lived. This was by no stretch of the imagination a wild, ruined place. It failed to live up to my preconceptions.

There were lights on in the bungalow but the curtains were open and I could see, through the big picture windows, that a colour television was on, though I couldn't see anybody watching it. There was no doorbell so I knocked hard with my fist. Sprightly footsteps immediately came to the door. The door opened and a man who might very well, but just as easily might not, have been Thornton McCain was revealed.

'Yes?' he said.

'Thornton McCain?'

'Yes.'

And then we both said, 'You!'

The man who had opened the door did indeed prove to be Thornton McCain, but more immediately I knew him as the man to whom I'd once served a piss cocktail.

'Oh my God,' I said. 'I'm sorry. Oh my God.'

I found Thornton McCain staring at me with some fascination and then with some amusement.

'You'd better come in,' he said. 'Have you come far?'

He said it very calmly and with great acceptance, as if he regularly had malicious characters from his past knocking on his door.

'You do remember who I am?' I said, thinking we might as well get that clear from the start. I didn't want him suddenly to realise.

'Of course I do. Got any new recipes?'

'I'm sorry about that,' I said. 'You can't believe how sorry I am.'

'Fine,' he said. 'Did you really come all this way after all these years in order to say you're sorry? I'm impressed.'

I wanted him to keep any good impression he might have of me so I said, 'Well, in a way, yes.'

'I was being monstrously disagreeable that night, as I recall,' he said. 'My working life was going through a bad patch.'

'Mine too,' I said.

'Actually, with a little embellishment it's become one of my favourite anecdotes,' he said. 'I tell it quite often. The best stories are always told against yourself.'

We had walked through into the living-room by now. It was small and very hot. The sound from the television was loud but he made no move to turn it down.

'I didn't realise who you were,' I said.

'Would it have made a difference?'

In one way, of course, it wouldn't have. At the time I was working in the cocktail bar I'd never heard of Thornton McCain, and therefore wasn't a fan. Even so, I probably had more respect for writers than I had for most other classes of humanity. I might have been prepared to make allowances, but then again I might not.

'You'd better have a drink,' he said. 'No Dry Martinis in this climate.'

He poured me a generous malt whisky, taking a not quite so generous one for himself.

'Are you still a barman?' he asked.

'Not any more.'

'What do you do now?'

'I suppose I'm a writer of sorts.'

'What sort?'

'I don't really know at the moment.'

'You're not a journalist are you?'

'No.'

'And not a literary critic?'

194

'Definitely not.'

'Then I suppose you'll do. Once we've ruled out those two possibilities, I think I can cope with most other types of writer.'

'I wrote you a letter,' I said.

'What about?'

'It was a fan letter.'

'Did I write back telling you to fuck off?'

'Yes.'

'I always do that, not that I get many fan letters. It's not meant as an insult. It seems to me that anyone who really appreciates my work would enjoy the joke. I think if I have one message to give to the world at this time of my life, "fuck off" is as good as any.

'And I typed it, of course, and didn't sign it. I won't sign things these days. I used to, then I'd find that items I'd signed for supposed fans were turning up in auctions and booksellers' catalogues. They weren't exactly fetching a king's ransom, but they were making somebody a lot more money than they'd ever made me.'

'Weren't you flattered that collectors were prepared to pay money for your name?'

'I don't have a lot of time for collectors.'

'Good for you,' I said.

'Not that sort of collector, anyway.'

'That's what I was supposed to be writing about,' I said.

'Collectors?'

'Yes. What they collect. Why they collect. That sort of thing.'

'Why *do* they?'

'I don't know.'

'I understand there are a couple of serious Thornton McCain collectors in the States. They own all the published works, some manuscripts, a few letters; not vast collections exactly. They must be out of their minds.'

For a second I thought I ought to find their addresses and rush over there and interview them. Then I remembered that I wasn't doing that sort of thing any more.

'Still,' he went on, 'if people want to collect something I'd rather it was the books of Thornton McCain than of anyone else. Rather me than Norman Mailer. Of course, there are complications with living authors. You may think you have a complete collection, then the old poop goes and writes something else. Maybe that's the joy of it. Like I said, they must be out of their minds.'

'Are you still writing much these days?' I asked.

He looked at me wearily as though he had been asked that question too many times in the past but had yet to devise a satisfactory answer.

'I'm afraid so,' he said. 'Every day. That is, I try every day, so that if I fail, at least it isn't for want of trying.'

'What are you working on?'

'I don't regard myself as working on anything in particular. I'm just a receiver, an antenna. I pull messages out of the air. I don't know where they come from. I accept them gratefully, and write them down. Naturally, it doesn't come out like Jane Austen. It comes out a bit of a mess sometimes, frankly. Random signals, something like that.'

'So you collect random signals?'

'I wouldn't put it like that.'

But he wasn't prepared to tell me exactly how he *would* put it. His manner said that I wouldn't understand. Maybe he thought I was an idiot. Perhaps my *faux naïf* pose, that I'd considered so useful for interviewing collectors, had become a permanent trait.

'Have you ever had writer's block?' I asked, hardly improving my style.

'Hasn't everyone?'

'How do you get round it?'

He shrugged. 'How do you get round anything? You ignore it and hope it goes away.'

'And if it doesn't?'

'It doesn't. Writer's block isn't the worst thing in the world.'

'For a writer I'd have thought it was.'

'Not being a writer isn't the worst thing in the world, either.'

Was that the advice I needed? At the time it sounded like a very wise remark. Perhaps my meeting with Thornton McCain really would make everything all right. Why did I need him to tell me that being a writer wasn't the most important thing in the world? Shouldn't I have known that already? Couldn't I have worked that out for myself?

'The writing that you're doing now,' I said, 'is it going to be published?'

'I don't know,' he said. 'I don't know that I can be bothered. It needs a lot of editing. I'm not much of an editor. Someone else can do it after my death. My posthumous works will make quite a chunky volume.'

'So you care about posterity?'

'Are you sure you're not a journalist? You keep asking very journalistic questions.'

'It's habit,' I said.

'All right,' he said, not entirely convinced but prepared to give me the benefit of the doubt. 'No, I don't care much about posterity, but I don't care much about the here and now, either. I've got nothing to prove. I've written my major work.'

'Is that *The World Seen Through Plexiglass?*'

He grimaced slightly. This too was well trodden ground for him, and ground that was swampy and unwelcoming.

'That book's all right, but it isn't what I call my major work.'

'What then?'

'You probably haven't heard of it. It's a little-known work of mine: *The Books of Power.*'

I suspect I looked like a cartoon that you could have labelled 'astonishment'; the eyebrows arching to heaven, the dropped jaw, the gaping mouth.

'What?' I said.

'I told you you wouldn't have heard of it. *The Books of Power.*'

Since I obviously hadn't mis-heard, I could only think there must be two works with the same title. It happened often enough.

'Not *The Books of Power?*' I said. 'Not the one in eighteen volumes with multicoloured bindings and the melamine bookcase?'

'You've done your research,' he said.

'You mean we're talking about the same book?'

'Yes.'

'It wasn't research,' I said. 'I don't know what it was. Coincidence?'

'Have you read it?'

'Some of it.'

'And you sound as though you didn't like it very much.'

'Well . . . I didn't know it was written by you.'

'Just like you didn't know it was me in the cocktail bar. Would it have made a difference?'

'It shouldn't, but I suppose it would have.'

I tried to remember what I'd read of *The Books of Power.* Did any of it have the great man's stamp? The authentic McCain style and tone? Frankly, no.

'But hold on,' I said. '*The Books of Power* say terrible things about Thornton McCain.'

'Of course. I could hardly be vain enough to praise myself in my own book. So I went for the throat. It was a joke. I still like jokes. And it helped perpetuate the myth of *The Bullet Leaves the Gun.*'

We both fell silent, though of course the television set still blared. I don't know what Thornton McCain was thinking about, but I was thinking about conspiracy theories.

'Look,' I said, 'I don't really know why I've come to see you. At least I might have when I set out but I don't seem to any more. I love your writing, I really do, and things haven't been going very well for me lately; my writing, my relationships, my marriage. I know it sounds crass, but nobody understands me. I thought you might.'

He looked at me with all the suspicion I deserved, as though he'd taken a harmless-looking stray dog into his house and only now was he considering that it might be rabid.

'I'm not an agony aunt,' he said.

'Of course you're not. But look, one of my best friends in Sheffield bought a set of *The Books of Power* and memorised every word. And he fell in love with the saleswoman. I now know that she was the woman who was with you in the cocktail bar. Then it turns out that my friend's boss also has a set of your encyclopedias, and he's written a review of *The Bullet Leaves the Gun*, a book I've never seen. And now he's disappeared. And I tracked down a copy of *The Stiletto and I* but had it stolen. Meanwhile I started an affair with a woman who's a fan of your work, and we overcame our sexual problems using *The Bottle Blonde*. And my wife, who works in advertising, was going to do a campaign for you. Well, doesn't it all sound a little *strange* to you?'

'A little,' he admitted.

'And you know what's strangest of all; some of the collectors I visited had some kind of disaster happen to their collections. And some of the places I went, your saleswoman went too. And I don't pretend to have a clue what this is all about, but a lot of roads lead to you, and somewhere in all this I think you've got something to answer for.'

Thornton McCain got up. He turned down the sound on his TV set. The silence was welcome. He poured two more whiskies, both bigger than before. His big, old, white hands were perfectly steady but his calm, easy manner had become frayed. He picked up a small colour photograph that was lying curled and glossy on his mantelpiece, and handed it to me.

'Yes,' I said, 'that's her. Elaine, I think her name is.'

'Elaine McCain,' he said. 'She isn't only a saleswoman, she's also my daughter from my third marriage. My youngest. She's very good to me. She takes care of my business affairs, sometimes too zealously.'

'I see,' I said, not that I did. I could see that her passion for and belief in her product might be explained by daughterly enthusiasm, but it didn't explain much else. She hadn't seemed like a dutiful daughter that night in the cocktail bar.

'She's a little odd sometimes,' he said.

I gave my 'Tell me more but only if you feel you really want to' look. He seemed to want to.

'Well yes, she gets into fights in cocktail bars, that's one of the things she does; and that might seem strange enough, but she also has certain destructive tendencies. She likes to see herself as a force of nature. She likes disorganising things. What you were saying about these collections, I'm afraid it fits. A fine collection of almost anything might be more than she could tolerate.'

'I don't think I'm following this.'

'She destroys things. She tried to mutilate a Peter Blake assemblage in the Tate on one occasion. I was hoping she'd grown out of it.'

'You mean she's mentally disturbed?' I asked.

'That's as good a euphemism as any. Generally she's harmless to people, but she's rather hard on property. I tend to blame myself.'

I swallowed my drink. There was obviously a lot more that could be said, but I wasn't sure that he was going to say it. And I wasn't sure if what he'd already said was designed to make things clearer or more obscure.

'The writer's job,' Thornton McCain began, 'is one of pattern-making, putting things together. That's what I've been doing obsessively for the last fifty years. As a result of that obsession I'm sure I've neglected my wives and children. They've naturally tended to resent that. The wives have left. The children have become unhappy and confused, Elaine particularly. Creating chaos is a way of asserting her existence and taking revenge. Does that make sense?'

'But why does she go around selling *The Books of Power* if she feels that way?' I asked.

'I don't know,' he replied. 'I expect she's a very confused young woman.'

'And surely *The Books of Power* are precisely the kind of thing she'd hate. Doesn't an encyclopedia by its very nature organise and pattern facts?'

'Do you think so? No wonder she's so confused.'

All right, it hadn't been a very bright remark. I knew I was being toyed with, but I wasn't sure at what point the toying had started. I was well aware that Thornton McCain had no reason to be honest with me.

He said, 'You'd better take a look at this.'

He crossed the room and went out. I followed him from the living-room into the hall and from there into the room he used as a study. He opened the door for me to look in.

The room reminded me of a lot of other rooms I'd been shown recently. It was perhaps fifteen feet square and was lined with tall, unmatching bookcases of various widths and heights. Some were glass-fronted, some made of dark wood, some of metal. There was a filing cabinet and a small desk with a typewriter, and a noticeboard above it.

One glass-fronted bookcase contained three or four copies of each Thornton McCain book, though I noticed there weren't any copies of the mythical *The Bullet Leaves the Gun*. There were bound volumes of the *Philistine Review* and *Inner Spaces*. There was also a set of *The Books of Power*. The rest of the shelves in the room contained piles of manuscripts and typescripts, some of them looking tattered and dog-eared, others looking pristine. Some of the piles consisted of pages torn from notebooks, others were loose sheets of different sizes, postcards, envelopes, memo pads, many bearing the same tight, black handwriting, like barbed wire across the paper.

Of the typed pages, some looked like final clean copies, others were heavily annotated. Some pages would contain dense, single-spaced prose, others might have only a paragraph or a solitary sentence. Some of it was set out as dialogue with stage directions, some was in diary form. Some of it looked like poetry.

The mass of writing stacked up on every shelf, in mounds of greater or lesser organisation, some looking like skyscrapers, some looking like ruins.

Certain groups of pages were held together by staples or bulldog clips. Some had holes punched in them and were laced together with pieces of coloured string. On the noticeboard above the desk were pinned what I took to be the most recently typed sheets. There was even a piece of paper in the typewriter, a page that ended halfway through a sentence.

'You've been busy,' I said. 'What is all this? Are they novels? Or short stories? Early drafts?'

'Forget that use of the plural. You're only looking at one work here.'

'But it's . . .'

'Yes, it's a big mother. A few million words the last time I counted. I call it *The Bullet Leaves the Gun*. Like I said, it'll need some editing. Do you know any good editors?'

I told him I didn't.

'But I don't understand,' I said. 'I thought *The Bullet Leaves the Gun* had been published.'

'How did you get that idea?'

'It said so in . . .'

'In *The Books of Power*.'

'An unreliable source, eh?'

'I'd say so,' he said.

'But I also read a review.'

'An apocryphal review?'

'Well yes,' I admitted. 'Whatever *that* is.'

'An apocryphal review of a non-existent book by a disillusioned reviewer. There was a time when that sort of thing was considered fashionable.'

'But the book exists now.'

'Oh yes, it exists now all right. You're looking at it.'

He gestured magnanimously round the room, urging me to pick up a sheaf of papers, any sheaf, and read some of his work. I picked up a few of the smaller, less densely packed pages and started to read them. This was the first one:

Useless dead memories of an unhappy childhood, a desire to be friends, lust for a girl in a supermarket, a belief in some higher order, the need to scream, the urge to run. It is all collage.

Yes, that had the authentic Thornton McCain flavour about it. Perhaps it was a little loose and disorganised, but organisation had never been his strong suit. The next piece of paper I looked at read:

It is all discarded, all wasted time, shedding hair, ejaculations off the cuff, perverts who'll pay good money for your secretions. Escaping laughter, bad breath, ideologies abandoned years ago. Want to make something of it?

The next sheet of paper I picked up was an old department store receipt for a pair of trousers. On the back were these disconnected sentences:

Do-it-yourself may be far from your mind as the festive season approaches. I enclose a cheque for £9.95. There's a whole new look to communications coming your way. Finally he is destroyed.

The last was a photocopied page from some previous work. The typing had been scored through and he had written over it in thick, blue pencil, possibly a laundry marker.

He waits under eaves, in alleys, under manhole covers. He longs for a casually dropped confidence, a secret, toe-nail clippings, phlegm. It is an unclean job. The scrapyard of experience, obsolescence built into us. A necessary design fault. We try to be blameless, but we are the product of insufficient testing and low safety standards.

'Is this finished?' I asked, pointing round the room.
'No. It's a work in progress. It'll only be finished when I die.'
'It's great,' I said. 'This is it. This is exactly what I wanted to say.'
'*What* did you want to say?'
'About collecting.'
He looked at me dubiously. 'Tell me about it,' he said.
'Well, it's hard to know where to start. I began by thinking that collecting was just rather a naff hobby. Then I met a few collectors and I thought it was some kind of neurosis. And now I think it's *metaphor*.'
I said that with a certain amount of triumph, as though I'd solved the riddle and now had access to the giant's treasure.
'Ah,' said Thornton McCain.
'Collecting', I said, 'is an act of appropriation. The world is arbitrary and disconnected. By starting a collection you start to make connections. You decide what matters and what's valuable. You make a neat world. You make a collection in your own image.
'And (and I don't want to sound too absurd here) that's what life's like. We gather to us what seems urgent and necessary. It might be objects or it might be money or it might be people. That's our

202

personal collection. That's what we have to show. When you die the collection gets broken up.

'Life is the accumulation of experience. Everybody says it's good to have "lived". This "living", this accumulation, is somehow supposed to enrich our lives. Dying won't seem so bad if you can point to some collection of experience that proves how much and how well you've lived.

'We're all collectors, and most of us collect ephemera because we don't have access to anything else. It's all residue. It's all beside the point. The thing itself is elsewhere and we're condemned to pick up the trashy souvenirs.

'So then I suppose you have to ask yourself whether value isn't as likely to be found in trashy souvenirs as in anything else.'

I petered out. I wasn't quite sure what I'd said. I knew it wasn't one of the great speeches. Thornton McCain didn't respond for a long time. I thought I must have embarrassed him into silence.

At last he said, 'There was some young man who once tried to write a book about me. He called me a junk man. That seems about right. I couldn't let him know that he was right, of course. I told him it was nonsense. I scared him off. But in fact I think he was right. And I think you're right. I take away the rubbish. I pick up the whispers that everybody else discards. I collect the junk but I make it my own.'

'Yes,' I said. 'I think that's what I meant to say.'

'You're quite smart for a cocktail waiter,' he said. 'Frankly, I didn't think that I was going to like you, but you'll do. Have another drink.'

The rest, I suppose, is history. Thornton McCain liked me enough to let me stay in his house for a while. He was very accommodating. I slept on the living-room sofa. I tried to be a good house guest. I bought food and whisky. I kept the bath clean. I tried to be unobtrusive.

We woke most days with slight, dull, whisky hangovers, and stayed out of each other's way. In the afternoons Thornton would watch television. He was totally undiscriminating. Jessie Matthews musicals, programmes on how to cope with retirement, wildlife documentaries, low-budget soaps, all were equally acceptable. He

203

would occasionally jot down a few notes on a sheet of paper, but I never saw him do any of what I would call writing.

While he watched TV, I selected and read chunks from his magnum opus in the study. I felt honoured. I had the time of my life. In the evenings we settled down with a bottle of whisky and we talked, or rather, Thornton did.

He had been on his own a long time. It had been a long time since he'd had much conversation with others and somehow he'd lost the art. All he wanted to do was talk, at length and relentlessly. And all he wanted from me was the capacity to listen. Sometimes I would ask him to clarify something he'd said, or I'd suggest some topic that would set him off on a new torrent of reminiscence; but essentially the long, long monologues about his life and times and work might have progressed in much the same way had I not been there.

I like to think it was respect and affection, rather than an eye to the main chance, that made me record our 'Talks'. In the course of the next week we filled thirty tapes, and even then there was much that I missed, things said late in the evening when the tape had run out and I was too drunk to notice or change it. Thornton gave me his oral autobiography; discursive, wide-ranging and encyclopedic, yet never becoming just an old man's ramblings.

I heard about his parents, his unhappy schooldays, brief success as a college long-jumper, his chaotic ill-advised marriages, shit jobs, brushes with education and academia, his wanderings around Guatemala, Cyprus, Tasmania, Afghanistan, his sexual encounters, long-lasting love affairs, visits to dangerously unhygienic brothels. Occasionally there were scathing and cynical comments on public events, politicians and social change. He mentioned his war, though it was interesting that that was one of the few things he didn't want to talk about at any length, referring only to a spell in England and the absurdities of military intelligence.

He spoke of his poverty, the years of neglect, the years when he didn't and couldn't write, the rejections and the failures, the scattered small scale successes. He discussed his children, his pastimes, interests, obsessions, Berkeley in the 'sixties, the harmful effects of the media. I heard his opinions on Jack and Robert Kennedy, Harold Wilson, Pol Pot, Orson Welles, Braque, Billy Graham, Guy and Anthony Burgess. He recalled meetings with the good and the great, or at least the famous; Peggy Guggenheim, Max Miller, Veronica Lake, P. G. Wodehouse, Marshall McLuhan. There were

204

his flirtations with Hollywood, socialism and primal therapy. He talked about his essential rootlessness, his days as a barman, his liking for Britain, finally his flight to Scotland.

Of course, it would have been out of character for him to have told me all this neatly and sequentially. Instead, he proceeded by a form of free association, sometimes bordering on Surrealism; leaping decades and continents, as interested in apparently trivial detail as in great events and movements. He linked together memory, memoirs, personal history, character sketches and jokes; a fermenting pool of recollection.

There were also, of course, the anecdotes. These came thick and fast, at irregular intervals, usually sounding apocryphal, often seeming to have no point. Yet they had the considerable virtue that I'd never heard any of them before.

'It was 1970 and I was in William Burroughs' apartment off Piccadilly. There was some kind of party going on, a few media people, a few rent boys (not always easy to tell them apart), a lot of vodka. There were probably drugs too if you wanted them, but there was absolutely no food. Well I hunted around the kitchen, found a few old potatoes and put them in the oven to bake. And when they were cooked I said to William Burroughs, "Do you have any butter?" And he said, "Butter is a virus." '

'I ran into Ernest Hemingway in Idaho in 1960. I was in my forties. I'd had three novels published, had two marriages behind me, and I thought I was quite the grand old man of letters. But Hemingway kept treating me as though I was some teenage upstart, and I didn't like that at all. In the end I couldn't take any more so I said, "Ernest, you're all bull." '

'There were three cars pulled in at the petrol station. The driver of each car was a man in his sixties. They all had white hair. One had glasses, one had a moustache, one had a moustache *and* glasses. They looked alike; but one was driving a Bentley, one was driving a brand new Lada, and one was driving a beaten up Ford Escort. And I thought to myself, "It would be wrong to read too much into this." '

'It was 1952 and I was at the private view for Dorothy Miller's "Fifteen Americans" at the Museum of Modern Art. I got stuck in a corner with Jackson Pollock, a man I'd never liked much. He was drunk as a skunk, barely coherent, but he was saying that he wanted to get in his car and drive to Florida. Did I want to come with him? I tried to tell him he should go home and sleep it off, but he wouldn't listen. "Hey Jackson," I said. "Why are you such a drip?" He tried to hit me.'

'I was at a small house party at Sissinghurst in the summer of 1950 and Harold Nicolson and I were talking about this and that, mostly about sexual inversion actually, and Harold said he thought women were fine, noble, exquisite creatures but he'd never really been very keen on going to bed with them.

'I tried to offer a little worldly advice. "Ah but, Harold," I said, "perhaps you've never met a *real* woman."

'Speaking of which, I met David Hockney at his degree show at the Royal College of Art. I thought his paintings were terrific. I certainly wish I'd bought one. Hockney seemed a pleasant enough young man, but he was rather shy, quiet, softly spoken, diffident.

'"You know, David," I said, "you might have a lot more fun if you dyed your hair blonde."

'And I met Marilyn Monroe at a dinner party in Pasadena in 1956. She was looking radiant. Her conversation wasn't especially witty or sparkling but at one point she leaned over to me and whispered confidentially in my ear, "Frankly Thornton, it's nymphomaniacs who have the *most* fun."

'It was a March day. The sun was shining but the pavements were wet. Two men were walking down the street, one on each side of the road. They both had big, orange, plastic satchels and they were delivering free newspapers, one doing each side of the street. As I passed between them, one shouted to the other, "I must be psychic."

'I ran into Thomas Pynchon watching the greyhound racing at Catford Stadium, in 1978. He was looking good. He'd lost weight, he had a good suntan, and he'd won a small fortune on the dogs. "You know Tom," I said. "No publicity is bad publicity."'

I enjoyed listening, being an audience. It was gripping stuff. He wasn't a great storyteller exactly, but he was clever, funny, and above all interesting. I had no idea what I would do with the recordings I was making. For that matter, I had no idea what I'd do with the rest of my life. I couldn't see further than the end of my stay with Thornton McCain. I thought the recordings would be good to have as a souvenir. They seemed more worthwhile and personal than the autograph I'd once wanted.

It never occurred to me that the recordings themselves could form the basis of a book. The Thornton McCain revival seemed a long way off then. Public and literary interest in Thornton McCain was almost nil. It would take his death to change that.

It was the middle of November by then. Each morning I would look out of the window and see Mike Gombrich's Corvette (I still thought of it as his) sitting in front of the bungalow, salted with frost.

It was on such a morning that Thornton needed to make one of his routine trips to the doctor to get something for his bad digestion. We had stayed up late and I was still asleep when he left the house. He didn't wake me. There was no reason why he should have.

I don't know whether he couldn't get his own car started or whether he liked the idea of turning up at the surgery in a wicked black Corvette. Whatever the reason, I woke up to find that Thornton and the car had gone. It didn't give me any great cause for alarm. The surgery couldn't be that far away. Thornton was an experienced driver, and if I could manage to handle the car anybody could.

It was the middle of the afternoon when the police arrived to tell me the story. Thornton had got to the doctor's all right, picked up his prescription, and then, perhaps pleased with his achievement, enjoying the car, had gone for a joy-ride. He must have been having a good time. He picked up a German female hitch-hiker. The news photographs show her to be buxom, big-eyed, and with white, spikey hair.

They must have driven for an hour or so before the car ploughed off a clear, straight, innocent stretch of road, into a line of pine trees, two hundred yards from a Little Chef. Neither Thornton nor the girl survived.

At first I couldn't believe it. I somehow thought and hoped it was somebody's tasteless, unfunny joke; possibly Thornton's. But the police weren't joking. I knew I had to start believing it.

I sat down and reached for a drink. Thornton's whisky. I felt sick and empty and dizzy. I felt infinitely let down and betrayed. I didn't know by whom or what.

The police, of course, thought the circumstances, and I, were suspicious and disreputable as hell. They didn't know what was going on, or what I might actually be guilty of, but they knew they didn't like it.

The newspapers, by contrast, loved it. It made a great story. A grand, if obscure, old man of letters dies in a wild American car in the company of a Euronymphet. I could see the appeal. It was news. If he had died sedately in his bed, he would, at most, have merited a few lines here and there; but now it was all over every paper. The tabloids thought it was weird and mildly scandalous. The broadsheets thought that too, but they also ran obituaries and assessments. Some said he was a brilliant maverick. Some said his experimentalism was barren and old-fashioned looking; but they all agreed it was a scandal and a disgrace that every one of his books was out of print. They didn't, naturally, know about the availability of *The Books of Power*.

I spent a day in Thornton's bungalow, surrounded by and looking at his possessions; not only his books and manuscripts, but his plates and cups, his comb, his spare spectacles. They were pathetic, yet overloaded with meaning and loss. Staring at some of his old suits hanging in the wardrobe I began to sob uncontrollably.

I went home. There was nothing for me in Thornton's sad, full yet lifeless, bungalow. The holiday was over. My real life, for which I had no time, and in which I took no interest, was elsewhere.

I caught the train to Sheffield. I travelled very lightly apart from thirty tape cassettes. My house smelled as rank and musty as ever. There was a silt of bills, free newspapers and soap powder coupons behind the front door. There was also a letter from Alastair, my former editor. He'd seen my name in the reports of Thornton's death. This proved that he read the *Daily Mail*, the only paper to mention me by name. He wanted to have lunch. He'd pay my train fare to London. I couldn't think of any reason not to go.

It was a very good lunch. Throughout, Alastair made no reference to my unwritten and unwritable book about collecting. That seemed to be behind us. Much could be forgiven me now that I was the man who had almost been with Thornton McCain when he died.

There had been further re-organisation at Alastair's firm and he had been moved away from health, sideways into fiction. I thought that sounded like a step up. In this process he had magically become a lifelong fan of Thornton McCain. What a damn shame it was that the books were out of print. He, personally, was going to make sure they became available again, at least two or three of them, at least the more commercial ones. He'd as good as signed a deal with Thornton's daughter.

I told him the story of my time at the bungalow. I told him about the recordings I'd made. He dropped his fork. A crescent of calf's liver fell on to the tablecloth. I told him that Thornton McCain's study contained an unpublished manuscript, several million words long, and he very nearly became delirious.

And that is how Thornton McCain and I became bestsellers. The several million words were savagely edited by Alastair to make a huge slab of a book, called, naturally, *The Bullet Leaves the Gun*. On publication it was universally agreed to be an important, daring, indispensable, if largely baffling, book. It spent six months on the bestseller lists in this country, and about half that time in the States. It was much bought and, I suspect, little read, but when did that ever have anything to do with anything? Personally I thought it was the best book I'd ever read.

Of course, Thornton wasn't available for author tours, interviews, chat-show appearances and signing sessions, but that didn't mean he wasn't promotable. And I certainly did my best to promote him. My own book, *Conversations with Thornton McCain* (the title was meant to contain a good measure of irony) didn't sell nearly as well as 'The Bullet', but that was only as it should have been. And I like to think that my book helped the sales of Thornton's, even if not nearly as much as *his* book helped the sales of mine.

Dealing with the McCain estate, two surviving but divorced wives, four children in two continents, and no will, hasn't been easy I understand. Fortunately, there are people at Alastair's firm who are supposed to be good at this sort of thing, and I'm pleased to say I didn't have to become involved.

All the family agreed that the important thing was that Thornton's writings find their public. Everyone, even Elaine, thinks it's good that I became and remain involved, though Elaine couldn't resist trying to sell me a set of *The Books of Power*. Actually, she succeeded. Why not? I could afford them, and, of course, I regard *The Books of Power* in a very different light now I know that Thornton McCain was their author. I might have been able to pick up a cheap secondhand set from Jim, but that's another story.

The family, unlike the Scottish police, didn't consider me in any way culpable for the old man's death. I think it would have been unfair of them if they had, but I'm sure there are some families who would have. In this case, the family seems to know what sort of man Thornton was. They aren't your average bunch of grief-stricken relatives. Nevertheless, I suspect they may be fighting for years to decide who gets what share of royalties from *The Bullet Leaves the Gun*.

Of course, I feel a certain amount of guilt about the whole business. I worry sometimes that I'm exploiting a man's death, but I pacify myself by saying, first, that I was a fan of Thornton McCain and did what little I could to spread his fame, long before he died. Secondly, if it wasn't me exploiting him it would be somebody far worse. And thirdly, whatever I do or don't do, Thornton McCain will still be dead. I wish he was around to enjoy his success, but that was never going to be one of the options. I only knew him for a very short time, but I miss him. I wish he was still alive and writing. I wish I could have a drink with him and listen to him talk.

Thornton will be hard pressed to write a follow up to *The Bullet Leaves the Gun*, but we think we may have solved that problem. His next publication will be *A Shorter Book of Power*, and I'm the one doing the shortening. Condensing eighteen volumes into one isn't easy, especially since every word of it now seems so savagely ironic and vital. Everyone trusts me to do a good job. They know I care about Thornton's work, and my integrity is thought to be unimpeachable. Alastair and I are 'very excited' about the project.

There's a certain kind of writer who doesn't need a chapter at the end of a book where he collects together all the loose ends of his story, and clumsily ties them together. I admire that kind of writer, but I am not one of them.

There are a number of questions I'd like to try answering, for my own benefit as much as for the benefit of the story and the benefit of any imagined reader. Questions like: who scratched Mike Gombrich's car? Who stole his collection of ladies' knickers? Who, if anyone, stole Edwin Rivers' beer cans, if they existed? Who wiped Eve Leviticus's tapes? Who wrecked Victoria's husband's cars? Was it an accident that destroyed Ted Langley's house? Who, for that matter, took my research material?

I can answer some of these questions with some degree of certainty. For instance, yes, I think it *was* an accident that destroyed Ted Langley's house and his collection of jokes. Others I'm not so sure about.

To begin with the certainties, then. I know exactly who took and destroyed my research material: it was me. I wasn't robbed. I was lying to you in the interests of a good story. I loaded the stuff into several large bin sacks and took it with me that day I visited the dump. There I enabled it to become one with all the rest of the useless, discarded rubbish. It was, I suppose, a silly thing to do. I thought, foolishly, that if all the data disappeared, then somehow I

210

might be let off the hook. I thought my editrix might take pity on me and tell me it didn't matter and that I could forget the whole thing. This is what we call a crass miscalculation.

It could have worked another way. I was weighed down by a great load of raw material, and destroying it could have been a release, the sort of liberation I needed to enable me to write the book. I don't completely buy this. I don't think Ted Langley would either. He wasn't liberated by the destruction of his jokes. He has been forced to abandon his career as a stand-up comedian and he's trying to make it as a 'straight' actor. Last Christmas he was in *Mother Goose* at the Alhambra, Bradford. I'm not sure that this could be described as a release.

As for who scratched Mike Gombrich's car and stole his collection of knickers, who knows – and, to some extent, who cares? I imagine it was nobody special: vandals, burglars, perverts. The world is full of them. It might be interesting to think they had some programme and theory behind them, but they don't. The world is jammed with pinheads who like to go around messing up things that other people take pride in. It can be expensive cars, but it can just as easily be a new bus shelter. It doesn't signify very much.

Somewhere along the line I thought that Jim might have scratched the Corvette. Why not? Sabotage by the workers is a fine old English tradition. And it wouldn't have been impossible for him to know about and steal the collection of knickers. Jim was not a happy man, not least sexually, and his frustrations might have manifested themselves in this weird and unlikely way. These days I think I was crazy to think that.

And for a time I suspected the skinny kid who won quizzes. He looked as though he was carrying any number of chips on his shoulder, and (what can I say?) he looked the type. But looking the type and wearing anarchy badges isn't enough to build a conspiracy theory out of and, in any case, a conspiracy theory isn't required here. We don't need to posit any organised force of destruction. Small, individual, localised, disorganised forces will get the job done too.

That's why I'm not sure that Thornton was right about his daughter. Sure, being the daughter of a writer, especially one like Thornton McCain, might make you a little strange, and no doubt he knew her better than most people and had reasons for his suspicions. She may have been crazy, but that doesn't mean she was some elemental destroyer of systems. Perhaps that's what he wanted her to be. I wonder why he wanted that.

211

I admit it's not impossible that Elaine just might have decided to wreck the car collection belonging to Victoria's husband. He hadn't bought a set of encyclopedias and he'd made an unwelcome sexual advance. But crazy or not, I don't think that's sufficient motivation. *And*, there are other explanations.

A man like Victoria's husband, wealthy, a bookmaker, might make plenty of enemies in his daily life, and one of them, a disgruntled punter or some rival bookie, might have decided to take revenge by breaking some of his prized possessions. It worked, too. He was immune to the regular loss of his wife, but the loss of his cars got through all the defences.

And could Elaine really have been responsible for wiping Eve Leviticus's tapes? Would she have known how? And why would she even have been aware of the existence of Eve and the tapes? Besides, Eve too must have mingled with some suspect types, the ones who sold her drugs. I don't know a damn thing about the drugs underworld, but it wouldn't surprise me if somebody somewhere within it had a grudge against a weird little rich kid who went around taping conversations.

I can't see that Elaine could have had anything to do with Edwin Rivers, either. His collection of beer cans may or may not have existed and may or may not have been stolen. There are days when I think Edwin really had a collection, and days when I don't. There are days when I think his wife and son stole it, days when I don't. To be honest, though, I don't spend very much of my time thinking about it.

There are two collections in this story that I still do spend time thinking about. The first is Jim's collection of knowledge from *The Books of Power*, and the other is Victoria's collection of lovers.

Jim's collection of diverse facts, gleaned from a single source, looks, at first, to be impregnable. It is in his head, and the inside of Jim's head seems more secure from vandals than most places. But even there the process of destruction will already have started: the process of forgetting. Memory fades with the dying of cells, and the way Jim drinks the cells are dying fast.

Victoria's collection is different. It is scattered in time and space; men and events connected only by Victoria's presence and participation. The collection's very existence relies on a kind of dispersal. Further dispersal is not a threat. If Victoria were to settle into being a dull little housewife and dutiful mother (not that I think she will) she might be inclined to regret and renounce her collection, but that still

212

wouldn't destroy it. Her collection is untouched and untouchable. I think this gives Victoria some kind of last laugh. I think she'd appreciate that.

Other questions: where are they now and what are they doing?

Jim runs Killer Kars, not supremely efficiently or profitably as far as I can see, but he's taken some management courses and he's still in business. He was, for instance, quite successful in organising the restoration and sale of Victoria's husband's cars. He now offers a car valeting service which does quite well, but he doesn't get his hands dirty or personally get the cars clean any more. He talks sometimes about selling up and opening a driving school.

Mike Gombrich is gone, apparently for good. No doubt he is alive and well somewhere and presumably he's neither selling cars nor writing book reviews. Wherever he is, he's probably having a great sex life.

Edwin Rivers also remains absent. Wherever *he* is I assume he's still having a fairly miserable time of it. He never seemed to be designed or constructed for happiness, but he's probably happier where he is now than he would be at home with his wife. Let's hope so. It would be nice, though far too glib and unlikely, to imagine him sitting comfortably and happily, surrounded by beer cans of all nations.

Elsewhere, Victoria has had a baby daughter which she's called Stephanie, Eve Leviticus is retaking her GCSEs at a technical college, and Elaine McCain now runs seminars on the art of selling.

As for Rachel, she seems content, and I like to think that I made and continue to make some small contribution to that contentedness. She hasn't, despite what she said on the phone that night, given up advertising completely; the money's far too good for that. She works two or three days a week as a freelance copywriter, and on the other days she does 'good works': for the Samaritans, a Well Woman Clinic, and a housing association. This isn't exactly what I'd had in mind, but it must be better than working full time in advertising. Sometimes we meet for lunch, sometimes for dinner. Sometimes we sleep together and sometimes we don't. It's a better arrangement than our marriage ever was.

I took the money from my literary successes and was able to afford a not-very-large flat in an unfashionable area of London. It felt like coming home.

I know that a rolling stone proverbially gathers no moss. It's never seemed to me that a stationary stone is a great gatherer of moss, either, but I have to admit that since I stopped rolling quite so frantically and aimlessly as I once did, the moss, lichen and fungus, the worldly goods and the consumer durables, have begun to gather around me.

I haven't gone crazy buying products. I'm not surrounded by mountains of hardware and 'beautiful things'. I have what I believe are known as 'one or two nice pieces': a Charles Eames chair, a Le Corbusier *chaise-longue basculante*. Nice condition. Well insured. I have no shame.

I'm pleased to say that so far I haven't experienced a recurrence either of secondary impotence or writer's block, but I'm not complacent and I'm keeping my fingers crossed.

And how do I feel today about anecdotes? Discovering that Thornton McCain had a penchant for anecdote, and considering that my book 'Conversations With' is stuffed full of them, I'd be a fool to despise them.

The anecdote is a way of telling, but also a way of being. Any event, any story can be reduced to anecdote. 'So then the old bugger leaps in the Corvette, drives off and picks up this blonde German hitch-hiker.' We are all aware of people whose lives, at least as they describe them to us, are made up wholly of funny things that happened to them on the way to or from somewhere. I don't think Thornton McCain quite fell into this category, and at least the anecdotes he told were his own. These days, then, I'm more tolerant of anecdotes than I used to be, but I still don't really approve.

As I mentioned a long time ago, if you look up 'Collecting' in the eighteen volume *The Books of Power* you will find no entry. However, in the forthcoming one-volume edition you'll find the following:

COLLECTING
Dust collects. It falls on old moquette, on walnut veneer, on corduroy and melamine. It settles on picture rails, in the curves of porcelain shepherdesses, in the corners of junk-rooms; ground-in dirt . . .

Well, you know the rest. I'm afraid I wrote that. It's my little joke. I don't think Thornton would have objected. He liked jokes. I think it's a reasonable pastiche of one of the ways he sometimes wrote, and it sums up, in however oblique and ironic a way, the whole collection of events and experiences that led me to Thornton McCain and (if we're being poignant) led me to myself. It reduces a lot of agony to a few columns of prose. It belongs in *The Books of Power*.

No doubt some future generation of McCain scholars will discover my little textual bastardisation and I will be exposed. I like to think that I won't be judged too harshly. After all, even editors need to have fun. Perhaps there will be a second McCain revival, and demands for a scholarly edition of Thornton McCain; a new, authoritative collected works.